SOUTH

SOUTH

A Novel

RICHARD PLOETZ

Arcade Publishing • New York

Arcade Publishing books may be purchased in bulk at special discounts for sales promotion, corporate gifts, fund-raising, or educational purposes. Special editions can also be created to specifications. For details, contact the Special Sales Department, Arcade Publishing, 307 Fifth Avenue, 4th Floor, New York, NY 10016 or arcade@skyhorsepublishing.com.

Arcade Publishing® is a registered trademark of Skyhorse Publishing, Inc.®, a Delaware corporation.

Visit our website at www.arcadepub.com.

10 9 8 7 6 5 4 3 2 1

Although inspired in part by real life, *South: A Novel* is a work of fiction, and the usual rules apply. All characters, events, and incidents have been fictionalized and reflect the author's imagination, and none should be understood as a literal depiction of any person, event, or incident.

Library of Congress Cataloging-in-Publication Data is available on file.

Cover design by Erin Seaward-Hiatt and Kai Texel
Cover image credit: John Duffield

Print ISBN: 978-1-64821-199-7
Ebook ISBN: 978-1-64821-200-0

Printed in the United States of America

Stories in *South* previously published in the following literary magazines:

"Flowers For Antonia": *Portrait of New England*
"Live With Me": *The Bookends Review*
"Choices" and "Snowstorm": *Adelaide Literacy Magazine*
"Wind Harp": *Roi Fainéant Press*
"Chez Jules": *Ravens Perch*
"Home": *Front Range Review*
"The Battery": *Oracle*
"Bounty": *Nonbinary Review*
"A Small History": *Crazy Quilt*
"Montana Fix": *American Literary Review*
"Jeanette": *Outerbridge*

For Carol Dudgeon

However intense my experience, I am conscious of the presence and criticism of a part of me, which, as it were, is not a part of me, but spectator, sharing no experience, but taking note of it; and that is no more I than it is you. When the play, it may be the tragedy, of life is over, the spectator goes his way. It was a kind of fiction, a work of the imagination only, so far as he was concerned.

—Henry David Thoreau, *Journal*

The difficult thing is inventing when you are encumbered with memory.

—André Gide, 3 November 1923

CONTENTS

NEW YORK

EPILOGUE

TROY

GERMAN DAY

Bert Staub leaned against the fender of his old Plymouth coupe, glad for the shade. He wore plaid Bermudas, scuffed tennis shoes, and a new white T-shirt. Noticing a movement at the blinds in the second-story window, he looked away. The brown shingled house was identical to the houses that flanked it except for the two big maples in the front yard. They appeared potted in the small grassless plots, roots heaving the concrete walk that went between them up to the stoop.

Trudy Steiner came around the corner of the house. Tall and slim with broad shoulders, she wore a two-piece blue bathing suit. Her sun-blonde ponytail bobbed as she walked toward him.

"Hello."

Bert took her hand, bent exaggeratedly, and kissed it, slapping the heels of his sneakers together.

"Can we swim at this shindig?" he asked. "I threw my suit in the car."

"If you like swimming in the Hudson."

Behind the house in the shade of the garage sat several stamped metal chairs; Bert pulled one out onto the lawn beside Trudy's chaise longue. He liked how she looked, lean and full-breasted, long honey-tanned legs. Vanilla suntan oil. He had formed no strong opinion of her body during their Philosophy course but had liked her soft voice and brown, faintly skeptical eyes.

"We can leave if you don't like it," said Trudy. "It's mostly kids and old folks." She picked a pack of Salems out of the grass beside the chair, took a cigarette and lit it.

Across the chain-link fence at the end of the Steiners' backyard rose the green corrugated frame of their neighbor's swimming pool. It appeared to fill the entire yard, and one dove straight in from the back porch.

"I've never been to a German Day," said Bert. "I'm three-quarters German, you know, one-quarter French. *Voulez-vous coucher avec moi*?"

Trudy exhaled smoke in two faint blue jets.

"Why don't you come to New York with me?" Bert said. "My grandparents are in California. We could stay at their apartment in Astoria, take in a show—"

Trudy raised her left hand, the engagement diamond blazing.

"Strictly friends—Scout's honor!" Bert laughed. "Maybe Leo and me'll go down. He's got a week of furlough left."

Trudy's father stood in the kitchen listening to news on the radio. A short, blocky man, he put Bert in mind of an unabridged dictionary with arms and legs. His white hair was squared in a butch cut and his ears stood out like knots. Thick glasses magnified blue watery eyes; he had cataracts that were "ripening," and when ripe, would be harvested.

Mr. Steiner stared blankly at Bert.

"You met Bert a couple of months ago," Trudy reminded her father. "When you picked me up after class?"

"Staub!" Mr. Steiner abruptly remembered. "Your old man is a big wheel over to . . ." He began rifling a pile of *Troy Records* on the end of the counter.

Trudy offered Bert a lemonade.

"Give the man a beer, for God's sake," said Mr. Steiner without looking up.

He found a paper, folded it open, handed it to Bert. His father, tall, wearing a three-piece suit, smiled up from a crowd of young women in tank suits and bathing caps. "Walter Staub, Dean of Students at Troy Community College, greets the Swim Team," read the caption. There was no story.

"I invited Dad to the German Day—I hope you don't mind," Bert said. "But I'd be surprised if he came."

"It's nothing to cross the street for," said Mr. Steiner.

"Dad can speak German, and I thought . . . He doesn't get out much since Mom died."

Bert drank from the can of Carling Black Label.

"I used to know Kraut," said Mr. Steiner. "Only thing I spoke till I was six. Now . . ." He appeared to think. "*Bis mo key*? That's 'kiss my ass' in Canuck."

Mrs. Steiner arrived abruptly, crowding the kitchen. A large-breasted woman in a pink-flowered jersey dress, she appeared top-heavy on spindly legs. She didn't look at Bert. Her daughter was engaged to marry James Farrell of Watertown, Massachusetts, and Mrs. Steiner hadn't liked the kiss she'd witnessed from the upstairs window, however much "in fun" it had been.

Trudy introduced Bert.

Mrs. Steiner nodded curtly. "Too bad James couldn't get over for the day. Last year he enjoyed himself."

"Good riddance," said Mr. Steiner.

"Ed, you shouldn't talk about your future son-in-law that way."

"Three beers and the monkey's under a tree. Wouldn't even try the blutwurst, for Chrissake."

"James Farrell is going to be an engineer," Mrs. Steiner informed Bert. "He's studying at MIT."

"Oh, Ma," Trudy sighed. "He's taking a few courses this summer."

"He is going to have a very good job when he graduates. You may be grateful for that."

"Bert's going to be a writer," Trudy said.

"Ready to hit the road?" Mr. Steiner opened the trash can and dropped Bert's empty in.

"Change your shirt before we go," Mrs. Steiner ordered him. "You got grease on the front already."

As they descended Spring Street in the Plymouth, Bert said, "Your mom's afraid I'll steal you away from James Farrell."

He liked the serious, almost mournful way her brown eyes regarded him.

"Are you in love with the guy?"

"I've known Jimmy since kindergarten. The Farrells used to live the next street over."

"Childhood sweethearts."

"When he moved away, we started to write. We've gotten to know one another. Jimmy's a very decent person."

Bert bobbed his head. "Sounds romantic."

They passed the Spring Street spring, a pipe coming out of a wooded bank. A station wagon was parked in the turnout, and a man was filling plastic milk jugs.

"Harry Vole," said Trudy, waving.

"Do you sleep together?"

She turned to him. "Are you ever serious?"

"Absolutely."

They had stopped for the red light at River Street when the Steiners' metallic gold Oldsmobile pulled up behind. In the rearview, Mr. and Mrs. Steiner looked like two squat white dolls perched on the bench seat.

"It's amazing your father drives with those cataracts," Bert said.

"They were nearly hit a couple of weeks ago. Pop asked Ma if it was clear to the right; she looked left and said yes."

They passed over an iron bridge onto an island in the river, then followed the dirt road to Conroy's Picnic Grove at the southern tip.

The air over the parking field sparkled with dust, sun beat down on the cars. A tall teenager in lederhosen and elf hat waved Bert into a spot beside the Oldsmobile.

The entrance to the German Day Picnic was marked by a banner hung between two poles. Mr. Steiner paid the entry fees and bought coupon books for everyone. Beer, food, games—everything was paid for with coupons. Bert had taken his wallet out but was ignored.

Ancient pines dominated the grove; the picnic benches scattered under them looked like dollhouse furniture. Along one side of an open playing field, food tables had been set up under awnings. Aproned women tended gas grills, frying bratwursts, weinwursts, bauerwursts. Pans were heaped with sauerkraut, warm and cold potato salads, coleslaw, fresh pickles. A man in a bow tie was slicing rye breads that look like footballs. Behind the last table, a woman cut cakes, pies, strudels, and dipped ice cream. Clams on the half shell and draft beer could be had farther on under an open tent.

Across the field, facing the food tables, stretched the midway of games; mostly roulette wheels, but also a Ping-Pong toss for live goldfish, handed to you in a plastic bag of water if you won. An ancient ring-the-bell test of strength concluded the midway. At the far end of the field, where a home run might reach, stood a rickety wooden dance pavilion, the river glinting through it.

"Don't be dainty, Helen!" cried Mr. Steiner. The big woman forked sauerkraut onto two plates (which she held in one hand), already heaped with wursts and salads. She completed one plate with rye bread, the other with white rolls.

They bought pitchers of beer and found the table Mrs. Steiner had staked out. Mr. Steiner's older brother, Zak, and his wife, Marie, had joined the party.

Looking over the picnic grove as he ate, Bert said to Trudy, "This is right out of Brueghel."

"Who's that?" Zak was pointing at Bert with a chunk of rye.

Trudy introduced him, for the second time, as her classmate from school.

"Boyfriend?"

Mrs. Steiner leaned forward: "James Farrell couldn't come today, Zak. He is studying all weekend for an examination."

Zak chewed noisily, sweat standing out on his forehead.

Bert called down to him, "Great food, huh?"

Zak's small eyes fixed on Bert suspiciously.

"He says you've got the ugliest mug he's ever seen!" Mr. Steiner shouted at his brother.

Marie turned away from Mrs. Steiner and said, "Don't pay Ed no attention."

"He wants to fight you!" called Mr. Steiner.

Just then a voice boomed from a loudspeaker: "The parade is about to begin. All marchers to the bandstand."

Marie pointed toward the dance pavilion where an old man in a red shirt and lederhosen was standing on the steps, speaking into a microphone: "Will Mike Klein come to the bandstand? Mike, your parents are looking for you. Come to the bandstand, Mike."

The marchers were gathering in front of the pavilion; younger children holding small American flags.

"Isn't that Charlie Miller?" asked Mr. Steiner.

"He's Father Germany again," said Mrs. Steiner.

"How much he get paid?"

She looked at him. "He's the Master of Ceremony."

Marie took Zak's plate back for a refill.

Bert and Trudy sat on the grass a little way off with their beers.

"Your father and Zak are a couple of characters," said Bert with a laugh.

"I'm sure they're fascinating studies for one of your stories. I wonder what you'll write about me."

"But you haven't happened to me yet!"

Trudy regarded him gravely for a moment then shrugged. She told him how her father and Zak had made beer during Prohibition, Zak brewing at the farmhouse up in Poestenkill, Pop delivering to Troy speakeasies.

Charlie Miller was marching, lifting his thin legs and bringing them down, raising puffs of dust. A trumpet player in seersucker suit and bow tie followed Charlie, playing "Cherry Pink and Apple Blossom White." Then the children came shuffling, flags at their sides. The parade crept around the perimeter of the field.

"In my day," Mrs. Steiner attempted to speak in an undertone to Marie, "a young lady who was engaged did not cavort with a young man other than her fiancé."

"Cavort?" Mr. Steiner practically barked. "What's that, *cavorrrrt?*"

"So, there you are, down in the cave, tied up, facing the wall." Bert gestured with a clamshell at the blank wall of the tent. "Behind you, a fire, and behind the fire, your mother holding up a cardboard cutout of James Farrell, causing the silhouette to fall on the wall."

They were in the beer tent sharing a dozen raw clams.

"Since this is the only way you've ever seen things, you take the shadow of the cardboard man for the real Jimmy—the pipe dream of married life, the flickering illusion of happiness—"

"And who is it, I wonder," said Trudy, squeezing lemon juice onto a clam, "coming down to save me and lead me up to the real world?"

Before Bert could reply, he saw his father across the field, standing under the German Day banner.

Tall, slender, strikingly handsome with a strong, balding forehead, Walter Staub wore a short-sleeved lavender shirt, dark blue slacks and butter-colored loafers. Deeply tanned, he resembled an older Rudolph Valentino.

He took Trudy's hand, covering it with his: "Bert has spoken of you in glowing terms—he didn't begin to do you justice."

Trudy smiled. "He said you're acting in a play?"

"A minor role. I told Dimitri I didn't feel up to anything major this summer. Pete, the husband in *The Birthday Party*. A small part, but I'm doing something with it." He turned to Bert: "You must bring Miss Steiner to a performance."

"Dad's a terrific actor," said Bert. "I still remember his Willy Loman in *Death of a Salesman* when I was in high school."

"Yes," said Walter, taking out a pack of Chesterfields, "Emma—Bert's mother—got so taken up in it . . . She was upset I had to die every night. Emma hated that play, though I have to admit it was a high point, artistically, for me."

He offered cigarettes, but neither Trudy nor Bert wanted one, so he put the pack away.

"Ironical, isn't it, that I should have to die in a play—every night—and Emma . . . Emma couldn't act if her life depended on it."

"C'mon," said Bert, "I'll introduce you to Trudy's folks. I'm afraid we've already eaten."

"I wouldn't mind a pilsner," said Walter.

As they walked toward the beer tent, Trudy said, "I understand you speak German?"

"It's been a while," said Walter.

Bert gave coupons for three large paper cups of beer.

"When I was a boy in Corona," said Walter, "my folks went to German Days, two or three a year. The adults all spoke German, while the kids spoke English. Oh, we knew German, but . . ."

"I haven't heard much of it spoken here today," Trudy said.

"No," said Walter, his voice going suddenly flat. "Things should be chucked that aren't used."

However, when Bert introduced his father to the Steiners, Walter addressed them in German with a little bow.

Bert noticed Mrs. Steiner stiffening, taking his father's performance for showing off. Mr. Steiner looked stupefied—as though this larger-than-life man had walked right off the page of the *Troy Record*. His head was thrust forward, bobbing, trying to comprehend the forgotten language of his childhood.

"We're gonna throw horseshoes," he said abruptly. "You wanna join us, Mister—Mister—"

"Walter," Walter Staub graciously provided. "Indeed, a game of ringers." He looked inquiringly at Bert.

"You go ahead," said Bert. "We're meeting Leo."

They emerged from the pine grove onto a narrow meadow edging the river. The afternoon sun was blinding, reflecting off the wide slow-moving water.

"I'm a battery, charging—" Bert had his palms out to the shining, mouth open, tongue sticking out.

Trudy was laughing when suddenly he kissed her. She shoved him and he collapsed in the long grass, lay squinting up at her, the sun glowing through her light cotton dress, revealing long legs straight up to the crotch.

"That's not fair," she said.

Two boys on the pebble beach below them were skipping stones. Bert counted four skips, then three. He thought of Leo who had met Karen a week ago and was already sleeping with her. Leo had said her pubic hair was so thick it stuck out the edges of her panties. Bert had seen them earlier on the midway—Leo clowning at the test of strength machine, and, from behind, Karen's small, ripe body in a tight pink dress set on high heels. She was like a flamingo at a blackbird party.

Trudy was great, Trudy was a trouper you could go through war with. He never seemed to meet the helpless, voluptuous, utterly exotic female.

He rested his hand on Trudy's waist; she took it off.

"What's fair?" he said. "I should leave you alone?"

She studied his face in the dancing light, didn't say anything.

"I'm a little high," he said. "However, for the good of your soul you should send Mr. James Farrell—"

She was gone down the bank and walking out on the beach, practically dissolving in the doubled sun. She bent and selected a stone, sidearmed it like a boy: three spreading dimples before it sank into the fourth.

Bert followed her out. "Tell you what: whoever gets the most skips in three tries, wins."

"Wins?"

They were walking toward the sounds of a waltz. He could smell frying wursts, feel the hot sun on the backs of his bare legs. There was his father sitting at the picnic table with Mrs. Steiner. She held herself half-turned away while he sat at ease, one leg draped over the other, talking, gesturing with his long hands. Maybe he was saying what a swell couple her daughter and his son made? Mrs. Steiner looked like a cartoon character about to explode. She didn't like his father—or him. Trust. She would never accept him, even if there were no James Farrell.

As he and Trudy reached the top of the wooden steps, the waltz stopped. Inside the pavilion, a woman in a tight pink dress was speaking to a man on the bandstand who held a clarinet. The drummer occasionally ticked his cymbals with the foot pedal. There was an electric guitarist and the trumpeter who'd been in the parade. All wore seersucker suits and bow ties. A burly man, prematurely balding, stood grinning behind the woman.

"Leo!"

Leo's grin widened until he looked positively oriental: "At length, at last!" He gave Trudy a sidewise glance: "The Teutonic Goddess incarnate!"

Trudy offered a hand, "Sorry to disappoint you."

"Au contrary!" Leo lidded his eyes at her, speaking to Bert: "Shame on you keeping such splendor all to yourself!"

"Unfortunately, Miss Steiner is unavailable. Going to be married. To someone else."

"Oh! The gods are unkind!"

"Something that swings?" Karen was trying to explain to the clarinet player who didn't speak English—none of them did. She swiveled her hips: "Swings!"

The clarinetist held up three fingers, and the quartet launched into a polka.

"Oh, for Christ's sake!" She turned to Leo. "Do we have to stay here?"

"Groove it!" Leo made fists and began to gyrate.

Bert tried to polka with Trudy, but she was tense in his arms and he stopped.

"Don't be mad at me. I care about you."

The music changed to a waltz and he held Trudy in an exaggeratedly formal way until she relented, relaxed a little against him.

Leo whirled Karen by. He dipped her, lower and lower, until she lay on the floor, scowling up.

Bert laughed: "When Leo gets out of the Air Force next spring, and I've graduated, we're hitting the road. He knows some construction people in Denver—we'll get a stake together there, and head out. Up into the Rockies—South America—who knows—Malaysia?"

"Do you even know where *Malaysia* is?"

Bert turned her hand so her palm lay against his chest: "When we get situated, why not join us?"

"Just send the address," said Trudy.

Leo cut in and Bert found himself with Karen's short, packed, perfumed, and clinging form.

"That hairy, bald-headed son of a bitch!" She had her face flat against Bert's chest. "I think I love him."

Bert told her how Leo and he had been friends since fifth grade. "We were in Boy Scouts together."

"*Boy Scouts*?"

Her body, another animal's, moved easily with his to the music. It felt marvelous, like he'd become Leo.

At one a.m. they were sitting at a booth in the Kenmore drinking Piels with shots of Fleishmans. After leaving the picnic they had spent the night at Albany clubs, and then Bert suggested the old hotel for a night-cap. The Kenmore, Albany's pleasure dome of the thirties, was near the end of its slide into oblivion. The ballroom where Frank Sinatra once sang now grew mushrooms watered by leaking pipes. The fancy guest rooms upstairs had become the last resorts of the down and out.

"Longest bar in Albany in its day—maybe still is." Bert gestured toward the darkened end. "Goes on another hundred feet."

"Must be four hundred spiders crowding those three bums," grumbled Leo, who had been for staying at the Embassy Club.

Three shabby drinkers were spaced along the bar. They communicated only with the bartender, a skeletal seventy-year-old with a three-day growth of white stubble on a long Irish face remodeled by fists long ago. He stood behind the bar in a dirty half apron, sleeves clamped up with garters, eating a late meal of porterhouse and fries.

"Murphy," said Bert with awe. "That man presided over the glory days." He nodded at a boarded-up archway. "If this was 1930, Legs Diamond would be sitting through there in the Rain Bo Room with his bodyguards and mistress, Kiki Roberts."

Leo stared at the archway dubiously.

"Legs was murdered just a few blocks north of here—"

"Well, Jesus Christ on a crutch," Karen said, downed her whiskey, and coughed. She was drunk and angry at Leo for flirting with the waitress at the Embassy.

The bartender came to their table with a tray of fresh shots and beers.

"When are you going to reopen the Rain Bo Room, Mr. Murphy?" Bert asked.

Murphy gathered up the empties. "Well, sir," he rasped, "whenever you put up the money."

"Think we could get Cab Calloway to come back and do a benefit?"

But Murphy was already on his way back behind the bar.

"I hear you and Bert are going to Denver when you get out of the Air Force?" Trudy spoke to Leo.

He stared at her for a moment. "We've made some plans."

"Denver?" Karen opened her eyes.

Leo leaned across the table toward Trudy and Bert: "You're coming across the flatness of Kansas, and—suddenly—there they are—like the Walls of China, piled one on top of the other. You want to get up into them, lose yourself—those wondrous lumps of terra firma that don't quit until the sea in South America. A mule instead of a car; a tent instead of a dingy room; and fresh air instead of smog, dust, gas fumes and all the rest." Moved by his vision, Leo slumped back in his seat.

"I didn't realize you were a mountain climber," said Trudy.

Leo finished half his shot, set the glass down deliberately: "We're all trying to find who we are—Bert by going back and writing about the past; me by constantly running from what is now. So, as an answer, or at least a start, I'm going to head up into those beckoning mountains—"

"What about me?" said Karen, trying to follow. "What am I supposed to do?"

Leo ignored her, his eyes fixed on Trudy: "To depart the world as it is and return to the place it was. My only wish is that Bert, maybe the only one who can understand me even a little, will join me on this one venture of life. You wouldn't deny him that?"

Trudy laughed a little incredulously: "Who am I to deny Bert anything?"

Leo just gave her a knowing look.

"Whoa, now—" Bert laughed.

"And when you do it," Leo's glance swung to him, "do it right. Do it on the long, long road—"

"I have to go to the far, far ladies' room," said Trudy, getting up.

"Me too," said Karen. "The shit's getting deep around here."

"Don't do anything I wouldn't!" Leo called after them. Then he said to Bert, "Better watch yourself with that one."

Bert laughed. "Trudy and I are pals."

When she returned, Trudy played Tony Bennett's "San Francisco" on the juke, and she and Bert danced.

A small, wizened man at the bar in a worn suit had turned to watch. When the song ended, he hailed them and bought them drinks.

"Steve's the name an' I'm drunk as a skunk!" he said.

Steve shook Bert's hand and told them he'd been a typesetter at the *Times Union* for fifty years. Retired. Last year fell and broke his hip while drunk. He hoisted the aluminum cane that hung on the bar beside him and shook it.

"Fuck 'em all, that's my motto!"

"Keep it down," called the bartender.

"Nuts to you!" answered Steve, then put a finger to his lips and shhhhed.

Leo was talking to a woman who had come in and sat at the bar. She was blonde, around fifty with a decent, slightly plump figure encased in a white pants uniform.

"He wouldn't throw me out," Steve confided to Bert and Trudy. "I'm the sombitch's meal ticket—up yours, Murphy!" He shook his cane again, immediately becoming contrite. "He's seen it all."

Leo went to the juke, plugged Ray Charles's "Born to Lose," his favorite, and danced with the woman from the bar. Bert cut Karen off as she staggered out from the booth. He danced with her and felt her fists lightly strike his back.

"There's beaucoup of her and it's toothsome and lonesome—and, oh my, does Leo feel the call of the wild . . ."

Leo was talking to Bert as they stood peeing into urinals that looked like marble sarcophagi tipped on end.

"She practically propositioned me, babes! I mean, could you dig those legs wrapped around you?"

"Yeah, yeah . . ." Bert mumbled.

"I bet I can get a room in this dump for twenty bucks. Listen—" Leo hit the flush valve and nothing happened. "Drop Karen on your way home—she's zombieville. I'll leave her in your back seat. Eighty-eight Lark, second floor, girlfriend's name is Jane."

The two women faced one another across the booth, Karen snoring and Trudy blowing smoke rings. Leo lifted Karen and carried her out.

"Just us mice," Bert said.

He took her hand: "Look at old Steve, he thinks we're lovers; lived his whole life typesetting and he thinks we ought to be happy. It's like we're inside a crystal ball; Steve is watching us."

Trudy was sitting across from him, framed by the booth's dark wood. She no longer seemed to be studying him; her eyes had grown unguarded, the hint of a smile played around her mouth. At some point she must have loosened her hair, blonde waves now draped over her shoulders.

Bert lifted his beer: "To where past meets future."

They were dancing to Sinatra when Leo returned. He sat beside the woman with his back against the bar, talking to her and watching Bert and Trudy. The woman stayed facing in, sipping her drink, buttocks spread like a plum on the barstool.

Trudy laid her head on Bert's shoulder. The juke threw its colors like a peacock. Sinatra crooned. The old barkeep stood motionless; the back of his skull reflected in the mirror.

"I got the most skips . . ." Bert said.

Trudy closed her eyes; she could see the lights off the afternoon river shimmering.

"What do you want?"

NOVEMBER

Walter Staub sat at the breakfast table reading last night's paper. Smoke from his cigarette on the Firestone tire ashtray rose straight up a foot before ruffling like ribbon candy.

Bert punctured his poached egg with a fork; it oozed over the toast.

"I dreamed of Mom last night. Standing in her bedroom, hair kind of lit from behind by the sun. She didn't say anything, just stood there looking at me. She was younger. She was wearing an apron. It was Mom, but not quite. She was different—"

"She wouldn't be the same." Walter took off his reading glasses.

"I can't help what I dream."

"Your mother's gone over two years. She is part of us, there's no reason to . . . I don't even keep pictures around. Furthermore, I'm going to sell this house after you leave." He put his glasses back on and took up the paper. "Sometimes it feels like my life ended when hers did."

Bert ate some of the egg-soaked toast. There was a frown on Walter's face as he read.

"How about a squirrel stew for supper?" Bert said. "I was thinking of going hunting with Timmy."

"What about classes?"

"I'm done at one thirty."

"Well, be careful. You're thinking for two people." Walter stood, brushing crumbs from his vest. "Squirrel hasenpfeffer. Your mother made it a few times." He slipped on the dark gray matching jacket that hung on the back of the chair. "Seeing the Steiner girl today?"

"Uh huh."

"You ought to invite her over sometime."

"Yeah, we might get a decent meal."

"I'll bet she can cook. That German peasant stock—like Emma."

Walter went to the hall closet, put on his overcoat, a scarf, and his dark homburg. He looked like an ambassador.

Nancy sat on the love seat in the window alcove wearing a pink terry-cloth robe. Her feet were up, and she was painting her toenails dark red. It smelled like an autobody shop.

Bert crossed the empty room and sat on the edge of the love seat. Nancy's soles were dirty. The parquet floor had a layer of dust and litter—canceled checks, textbooks on hair-coloring, styling, one high-heeled shoe, socks pulled inside out. No furniture except the love seat, which had left drag lines to the alcove.

"You looked like a Botticelli: 'Madonna Painting Her Nails'—"

"Don't touch," said Nancy.

Bert undid the tie of her robe.

"You promised you'd help me study for the test."

He slid his hands up the outsides of her thighs, over the swell of her boyish hips.

"Goddamn it, Bert."

He gazed into her sallow face, pinched nostrils going in and out like a sensitive animal's, brown protuberant eyes regarding him intently. They had met at Ole's two months ago; he'd sat on the stool next to hers and bought her a beer. At one point as he was quoting something from Descartes, she had leaned over and kissed him on the mouth to shut him up. They'd gone back to her place, the top floor of a brownstone across from the park. *Clothes flew, buttons*, he wrote later to Leo, *dust pumped out like the old love seat was on fire—she is one hot little creature, amigo! It was like we were on a ship at sea at night shoveling in the coal—Faster! Faster! I was thinking of that part in MOBY DICK where the Pequod is driving along at night, all her blubber pots fired! And then, when it was over, drifting rudderless on our little love seat on the vast, dusty parquet sea. Ah, sweet oblivion. To screw and to die. I see why the male black widow almost gratefully lets himself be eaten afterward. Everything else is going to be anticlimax. Have you experienced anything like this after the primordial act?*

Nancy drew away from him, leaned into the arm of the love seat, but didn't close the robe. Her eyes looked huge and black, the nostrils going in and out.

"If we stopped fucking, would you love me?"

Trudy sat reading at one of the Boulevard's green Formica-topped tables. Her oval face was tilted as though gazing into a mirror; one hand cupped a white coffee mug.

Bert had walked over from Nancy's.

Trudy smiled as he slid into the other chair. "Someone overslept today."

"Actually not. I decided to prove my freedom and cut Existentialism. I sat in the park."

"You didn't miss much—I can give you the notes."

"I'd like to take those notes from your lips."

Trudy briefly widened her eyes at him.

He recited, mock-seductively:

Had we but world enough and time,
This coyness, lady, were no crime.
We would sit down and think which way
To walk: and pass our long love's day—

"You're in fine form," said Trudy.

He tipped back in the chair, opening his arms to take in the room: "This old place, coffee and a muffin—you. It could never be better." He almost teared up, at the truth of it.

She was looking at him, bemused.

He tipped his chair back down. "You like me, don't you? It's just this: I wouldn't do anything deliberately to hurt you. We're friends. We have to want what's best for each other."

Her face was threatening to turn into his mother's, though they really didn't look all that alike.

"Hear from your ex-fiancé lately?"

Trudy fished a cigarette from her purse. "I keep having the thought I've thrown away a perfectly good life."

Bert lit her cigarette. His gaze came to rest on the grime-darkened fresco of Albany's Union Station on the wall opposite.

"I've been seeing someone," he said. "A girl I met at—"

They walked in silence to the parking lot across from school.

"Marriage has gotta be like canoeing a river," Bert said. "It looks good on television: two people rounding a bend, autumn leaves, snow-capped mountains. You imagine great camps, fish frying over the fire, stars—"

Trudy shut the door and started her father's Oldsmobile; it rolled out of the parking lot, crackling cinders under its tires.

Timmy's round glasses were fogged with perspiration.

"Good day for h-h-huntin'," he grinned.

Timmy was thirty-two. He and his mother lived next door, and Timmy had once babysat Bert. He wore a red and black wool cap, matching coat, and denim overalls tucked into rubber lace-up boots. He held an old single-shot twenty-two with a homemade stock.

"G-got ammo?"

Bert tapped his pants pocket. "Show."

Timmy held his rifle out at "present arms" and opened the bolt so Bert could see that the chamber was empty.

The pipeline road, two ribbons of cinder, followed the buried conduit from the Clarksville reservoir into Albany. Closed to cars, it cut through old farming country: fields growing up to brush, abandoned woodlots.

"We goin' D-D-Dufrenses?"

"I thought we'd try the beech woods back of the Leonard place."

Timmy nodded vigorously, then thumbed his glasses back up his nose.

They walked without talking. Timmy leaned as though into a head wind. Bert had spent half his time growing up it seemed trying to avoid Timmy. He had lingered through school until Bert caught up in twelfth grade, and they graduated together.

High and far ahead five black crows slowly crossed the gray sky. Bert switched hands on his rifle. It was as though the two of them walked under a huge bell jar, warmish and still and clear, the darkness and gloom held outside.

The flat "pang" of Bert's shot was gulped by the damp air. He bolted a fresh shell and rested the rifle across his outstretched legs. He was sitting on a bed of leaves, back against a beech. Timmy popped out from behind a tree a hundred yards away.

"Missed—" Bert waved. "Go back."

Timmy had yet to fire. Bert was trying to teach him to shoot on his own judgment, which is why they weren't sitting together as usual. It was making Timmy nervous.

Bert opened the pack of Chesterfields he'd taken from the carton in his father's closet and lit a cigarette.

After lovemaking, Nancy had lain curled against his back. He was just drifting off when she said she loved him. Nancy and he had amazing sex, spent time in Ole's, never had a real date. An occasional supper at the Chinese joint near the beauty academy. He didn't see her all that often. Trudy—sometimes he felt almost physically revulsed, as though she was his sister.

Bert stubbed the cigarette out in the damp ground. His saliva was bitter. He imagined Timmy sitting propped against his tree. What was going through that head?

"Hey!" Bert yelled, getting up.

"D-d-didn't see nothin.'" Timmy was relieved to be back.

"We'll bird-dog," said Bert. "Maybe we'll scare up something. When I move, you stand still—you're the shooter."

Timmy's glasses gave back the light of twin mirrors. His chin, a lumpy potato, sprouted four or five red whiskers.

On his fifth move, Bert flushed a squirrel from the hollow base of a maple. Timmy didn't see it, so Bert broke the rule and snapped a shot as the gray body scrambled upward.

"Get 'im? Get 'im?" cried Timmy, running toward Bert.

"*Point that gun the other way*!"

The squirrel, unscathed, had gained the upper branches and was running out to transfer to the next tree. Bert steadied, got the small shape into the gold bead of his front sight and squeezed.

The squirrel fell ten feet before catching a branch and running back in. It disappeared around the back of the tree.

Bert ordered Timmy around that side. As he circled, the squirrel, a hundred feet up, backed around from the other side. Bert fired.

"Got him!"

Instead of falling, the squirrel dragged itself up into the high crotch of the tree.

"Stay there." Bert waved Timmy back. "Can you see him to take a shot?"

"Uh—yeah—think so."

"Shoot."

"Me?"

"Take a shot!"

There was the "wang" of Timmy's twenty-two.

"Got 'im!"

"Bullshit . . ." Bert climbed onto a large glacial boulder, high enough so he could just see the squirrel's back. He fired and watched the animal lift with the impact. But it remained in the crotch. He fired eight more times before the squirrel was dislodged.

Timmy had it laid out in the leaves: a big male with testicles like gray furred marbles. Its body had been mangled by the hollow-point bullets, one eye exploded from its socket.

"Make a hole," said Bert.

"D-d-don't want him? You said—uh—eat what we—"

"Dig a goddamn hole!"

"Superb spaghetti." Walter laid his fork beside his plate. "Aside from being a trifle al-dente."

"Dad, I've been seeing this girl. Nancy."

"I thought—"

"Trudy and I are—friends. I've been, well, sleeping with Nancy."

Walter said nothing.

"I don't want to marry her. I don't want to marry anyone. I have lots of . . . It's just things are getting . . . Nan's a decent person, it can be great between us, but . . ."

Walter lit a cigarette. "You don't want to marry her."

"Yeah. Actually, it hasn't come up."

His father regarded him through the cigarette smoke.

Bert had no idea what else to say.

"Remember Joan Furness?" Walter said at last. "The Van Rensselaer Players—deep voice, looks a little like Faye Dunaway?"

Bert nodded.

"The only time in thirty-seven years I was unfaithful to your mother."

"*Joan Furness*?"

"She played my mistress in *Death of a Salesman*."

"I know who she is."

Walter put out his cigarette in the spaghetti sauce on his plate. "Your mother had unqualified trust in me. Her innocence was her shield. What I want to say, my boy, is it's your life in the end. I needed Joan Furness, or someone like Joan Furness, and I suppose she—Joan and I—*screwed.* Screwed our brains out. On the piano—" Walter's eyes lit up and he laughed—"Boom, boom, boom! In the prop room, in the car after rehearsals—Willy's mistress was Walter's mistress—life imitating art!" Walter blinked, looking at Bert. "I could almost have confided in Emma—like she was my mother—we were that close. And in the infinite wisdom of a woman, she would have understood. And of course been devastated. We—she and I—had settled down. I was almost sixty and felt—like I was old. Worse, a coward—attracted to women and never acting on it. Never feeling I had the right. And then Joan . . . Sex is a kind of reproductive madness. What's it got to do with love which is patient, tender, puts up with crap and keeps its eye on the ball. I love your mother this minute and she's not even alive."

Nancy was smiling at something the bartender said when Bert came in.

"Why, hello," she said, sliding her hand up the inside of his jeans, fingertips lightly brushing across the crotch, "lover."

Bert ordered a beer.

"You said you loved me."

He remembered all too well. They had been walking in the park, and *I love you* had popped out of him. What he'd meant by it was he loved her spirit, her decency—her generosity in loving him. He loved the light on the leaves, the air—

She hugged his arm. "So, what shall we do?"

Bert took a sip of beer, set the glass back on the coaster.

"Go back to my place? You know?"

He could see her in the bar mirror looking right at the side of his head.

"Tell me you don't want to climb all over me—"

"Nan—"

"Nan—" she mimicked. "I wanna have a baby with you, Professor. I want you to fuck me and a baby come out and us live and die in good old Gloversville." She finished her Tom Collins. "Fuck us, right? Who the hell are we?"

As she went up the stairs ahead of him, he put his hands under her skirt, cupped her belly, slipped down her panties. As he drew up her skirt, she murmured, "I love you . . ."

"I love you," she cried as he entered her, biting his mouth, raking her nails down his back.

"I'll be heading out to Denver at the end of the month," said Bert. "See Leo. Do some hiking. He says those mountains are something."

"Uh huh," said Trudy. "'A mule instead of a car, fresh air instead of smog, dust, gas fumes and so on—'"

Bert laughed, hearing Leo's words from that night at the Kenmore.

"Is it into the 'Great Beyond' you'll be heading?"

"I know, it sounds . . ."

They were quiet for a while, then Trudy told him she'd taken a job teaching high school English in a town north of Boston.

"Robert Frost, right?" said Bert. Which sat kind of hollowly. "We'll get together when I'm back - before the end of summer . . . I mean, school won't start before Labor Day."

"I'm moving to Boston," said Trudy. "An old girlfriend—needs a roommate."

"Well," said Bert, "sounds good. Maybe I can . . . crash—or something?" And he laughed, feeling suddenly oddly embarrassed.

"Mmm," said Trudy, enjoying the moment. "Conceivably."

JOURNAL 1966

27 AUGUST

Trudy rushed to Albany Medical Center this morning. Convulsions stabilized. They give her twenty-four hours to deliver the child, artificially induced, or will do a cesarean. She and it poisoning each other—conflicting blood types—acute toxemia. In intensive care. They won't let me see her but talk to me often. Compassionate, intelligent young doctors. She is in good hands. Never felt so useless. Pitocin dripping into her veins, starting her womb contracting three months early.

In the emergency room, curtained off, Dad and I on either side of the gurney talking to her when suddenly her eyes roll up and she is convulsing. I pin her to keep her from flipping off the gurney—Dad batting through the curtains yelling for a nurse. With the needle the spasms stop; she drifts into unconsciousness.

Young, healthy, athletic, we hadn't gotten around to seeing a doctor since Trudy became pregnant. Six months. We joked that when the moment came, she would squat behind a bush and have the baby.

This morning Dad and I were eating breakfast while Trudy slept in. We hear the toilet flush and a body hit the floor—then a sound like someone hammering with their fists. Trudy lay rigid on her back in front of the toilet, eyes rolled up and jaw clenched. Her body vibrating so her heels pounded the tiles. I recalled in a panic that a person could swallow their tongue during convulsions, and yelled to Dad for a spoon. It was like trying to pry open a clam—I popped out a front tooth but got the spoon in and could see her tongue.

Sunset deepens over the distant Helderbergs. A band of river below holds light like a mirror in a darkening room. The moon is just risen, full and heavy, yellow as cheese. Bats flitter after insects.

Seven miles upriver Albany glows. She is there alone in a hospital bed, unconscious, her body laboring to save her.

I walk in the cemetery across from Dad's; moonlight falls through the maples, lighting gravestones. At the new section there are no large trees, and the moon, freed, hangs up there now brilliant white. I can feel its power pulling like a tide: may it be drawing her back to life.

The living room lamp is on; as I cross the lawn, Dad appears in the picture window and sits in his easy chair. He looks like a miniature man in a cigar box diorama. He looks old, the light stealing color from his skin. I won't forget his walking beside you as they rolled you into the ER. I didn't hear what he said, only saw your answering squeeze of his hand.

29 AUGUST

Baby girl delivered around one this morning. I saw Trudy for the first time, for five minutes, her face swollen like a punched-up boxer's; fingers, ten fat sausages. She recognized my voice in the darkened room, smiled weakly. The worst is over: she is separated from what was killing her.

Through the window the child was in an oxygen tent with a warming light on her. A tiny doll. White and perfect, a shock of black hair. She lay on her back taking ragged gulps of air. Stabs of air. Pain must be all there is—everything harsh, unbearable—air, light, sound, the touch of cotton. No mother's warm wet cave; in nature such life would vanish at once.

30 AUGUST

Watched through the nursery window. Began counting her breaths and couldn't stop.

31 AUGUST

Died early this morning. Trudy knew before I said anything. She didn't cry, there was a kind of numbness. I named the child Cassiopeia on her death certificate. If she had lived, there may have been retardation, or worse.

Walking with dog on the river island. Michaelmas asters in bloom, goldenrod, mullein, and in open swampy places, masses of purple loosestrife. Tea made from its leaves is said to help you lose strife. Still and hazy-hot; the bridges insubstantial as crepe thrown across the river.

A numb sense of relief it's over.

The dog trots alongside, her pink tongue lolling, saliva stippling the dust.

Fall asleep on a grassy bank by the river, fishy smell of mudflats in my nose. When I wake, a tug is passing between the giant rusted legs of the railroad bridge. Shadows have grown longer.

This life, this life to be lived. Cassiopeia existed for three days and has sunk back. Mom traveled fifty-seven years around the sun, is gone. What should one do in this brief time?

I pick a bouquet of wild asters for Trudy which I'll bring this evening. Something to combat her mother's formal gladiolas.

2 SEPTEMBER

Trudy recovering in leaps, the swelling of her body gone. I read her Emily Dickinson, Winnie-the-Pooh. She listens raptly; she has been away a long time.

The moon has begun to grow lopsided, waning, its job done.

6 SEPTEMBER

Trudy home. A Japanese robe from Dad, breakfasts in bed from me. She teases about the tooth which I've kept in a baggie in the freezer. I thought they might be able to reattach it the way severed fingers are sewn back on. I hadn't needed to get the spoon between her jaws. An old wives' tale, people swallowing their tongues.

12 SEPTEMBER

Fog came up the hill and drowned the upper town. With morning sun it retreats riverward. The cemetery is an empty battlefield, clouds of drifting cannon smoke, shafts of sunlight. Hint of blood in the maples. I can feel the season turning this morning and am restless and excited.

Trudy lies on the lawn sun-bathing, nearly her old self—even a new tooth. She is scared when she thinks how close to death she came—but in a remote, haunted way—the mind trying to construct a reality which the body alone passed through. Does not remember labor or delivery. Wishes she had held the child. An absence she doesn't know what to do with. Her full breasts ache. Something was taken from me while I slept, she says.

19 SEPTEMBER

Morning. Trudy sketches Dad sitting in a lawn chair beside the flagpole. There is no flag, but she puts one in, hanging languidly over him. I sit behind on the grass, watching her work. The sun feels good on my shoulders. Smoke drifts from the cigarette between my father's fingers. Trudy makes charcoal lines as if each were final and miraculous.

VERMONT

JOURNAL 1968–1969

7 AUGUST

We put down $8000 for a cabin on Camel's Hump Mountain, North Duxbury, Vermont. The owner generously loaned us the additional $1500, interest-free, to be paid back over two years. She liked it that we were young and "artists."

19 AUGUST

Yesterday, we climbed Camel's Hump Mountain, named Le Lion Couchant, "Couching Lion," by Samuel de Champlain. From the top we surveyed our valley. This is where we live.

Jewelweed crowds the edge of the lawn, hummingbirds hover amid the bright orange horns.

The brook's constant murmur. In the pool below the cabin, three trout in the crystalline water.

Our cellar is the old vat of the sawmill that occupied this site. Logs were rolled down into it from the upper hill, washed and peeled, and transferred to the saw house, now our sunken patio. John L, our neighbor, told us that the mill had ceased operating thirty years ago.

I walk up the road above the cabin. Across first bridge a side road rises steeply, leading to an upper valley. A hundred years ago a small community had subsisted here. Now cellar holes, structures half fallen, a few deer camps. A teardrop-shaped graveyard surrounds an old sugar maple. The grass has been mowed, and some names are legible on the weathered marble stones. Across from here the valley rises to Camel's Hump Mountain. As though their final resting place was chosen for the view.

1 SEPTEMBER

What does it mean we *own* the cabin, the half acre of land? What will it take to belong here?

3 SEPTEMBER

I started chopping down a dead elm beside the pool, but the ax was dull and I had no energy. Lunchtime we see it's favored by a woodpecker, tearing at the bark for insects, then a kingfisher perches on a branch on his way down stream.

4 SEPTEMBER

Married three years today. Trudy baked bread, a turkey roasts, and we shall toast with a wine called Rubicon.

I felled a very straight dead elm and sawed a section for a post. Dug a hole up next to the road and set it. Painted our name in forest green on the big rural mailbox: B & T STAUB.

9 SEPTEMBER

We live in the bottom of a gulch, wooded hillsides rise steeply up both sides. The only distant view is north across the river to the Green Mountains. When the brook is low and quiet you can hear trucks on the interstate.

Next spring, in the parcel above the cabin, we'll make a garden. Now it's weeds and asters, goldenrod and sumac—then it will be tomatoes, peppers and peas, squash, cabbages, beans. From this garden we'll can and freeze vegetables for winter. Potatoes stored in the root cellar. Dried herbs hanging from the rafters. There's wild berries and apples from the abandoned farms above. Maybe I'll get back into hunting.

10 SEPTEMBER

Tonight we drove to Wayne Martin's, one of the remaining dairy farmers on the river road. John says he sells fresh milk, fifteen cents a quart. Bring your own container.

We met Mr. Martin as he came into the tank room to empty a pail of milk. A thin, lean-faced man, middle aged, amiable and obliging. Yankee—or Vermont—accent. A slight limp. With his instruction I drew milk from the tank into the gallon jar we'd brought. Mr. Martin went back to his milking in the barn. There were rows of stanchioned black-and-white Holsteins. He told us his father, born on this farm, lived in a new house down the road. He still helps with haying and woodcutting.

11 SEPTEMBER

Up early, rain hammering the roof. Gradually the brook rises, the water roiling, mustard-colored. By noon it is roaring past the cabin. A bit nerve-racking.

13 SEPTEMBER

How substantial the abandoned farmsteads above. As though the people meant to stay a while, even more than a lifetime—are buried there. After working on the railroad in the river valley, they went up and settled this land—piled up stone walls to mark their property, keep in the one cow, planted apple trees, set out a maple grove for sugaring. Along this stretch we call Old Farm Road I get such a sense of human habitation even though they're all gone.

14 SEPTEMBER

Hummingbirds still here though jewelweed flowers are scarce. Many of the seedpods are dead ripe—lay one in your palm and it explodes from the heat, scattering seeds. Another name: touch-me-not.

Across the brook, a milkweed parachute floats in the still air. On my red shirt cling tiny burr-stickers shaped like khans' hats. Whoever invented Velcro must have gotten the idea from these. I pick them off and toss them into the brook where they float off.

A hot day. At Turtlehead Pool, I strip and dive in — COLD!!! Scramble out to recover on a boulder in the sun.

16 SEPTEMBER

On Old Farm Road this morning I dig out two young spruce and two white pine. Transplant them around cabin, much watered with Ridley Brook.

Wash clothes in the machine former owner left us—hang them on a line strung outside.

Trudy boils elderberry juice into three pints of thick, spicy, slightly bitter jam. To relish midwinter.

20 SEPTEMBER

Dad visits bringing our new border, Cindy. He and Mom had gotten her as a puppy from the Albany pound. A golden mutt with a lot of collie.

22 SEPTEMBER

Cool mornings.

Farmer Martin says we shouldn't have frost until the next full moon, around the first of the month. He is usually saved from it an additional two weeks by cloaks of river fog.

24 SEPTEMBER

Dad brought my old wooden toy box up, where I'll keep my journals. The inside of the lid is scribbled with crayon—perhaps the earliest journal. There's a copy of *Walden*, and Mom's old blackberrying stick.

Last evening to Old Farm Road with T and Cindy. Such fragrances in the damp evening air: rotting apples, fern, wet leaves, pine, mushrooms.

The Hump and Ledges soft in purple light, heaped against the sky. Trudy thinks we should hike up some afternoon and spend the night, be there for sunrise over in New Hampshire.

28 SEPTEMBER

While getting milk I learn that Farmer Martin sugars, or did up until two years ago when the man who helped collect sap for him moved away. He has about two hundred trees and 1,200 buckets, a sugarhouse, and a season of wood cut and stacked. I said I'd be glad to help out—I'd read a book on maple sugaring. To which he replied, "Well, I guess you might learn by doing." Nothing was agreed upon, just some hints and who-knows.

A Sunday morning—set a fire in the fireplace. Trudy jots in her journal, Cindy drowses on the couch. A month we've been here. Still, little writing. Looking forward to the focus of winter.

2 OCTOBER

Went fishing and caught six trout, only one large enough to consider eating, which I did, but then put back.

10 OCTOBER

Viola C. White's *Not Faster than a Walk* faded halfway through, suffering as journals do from fragmentation. It's like a collection of poems, to be read and appreciated in bursts. I come out of the library having lived through five years of Thoreau's life in two hours, my head spinning!

The journal is source material. Rilke's *Notebooks Of Malte Laurids Brigge*, which he labored over nearly ten years, sweating his journals into fiction. Thoreau's which evolved into *Walden*.

12 NOVEMBER

First snow. Fat white feathers in the still air.

15 NOVEMBER

Trudy, in her journal: "Reading Bert's mom's letters is like sitting across the kitchen table from her."

17 NOVEMBER

Today two years ago Mom died. There is no returning from a morning's tramp to a warm kitchen smelling her yeast cakes baking, Mom over the stove in her apron—no Dad and Poppy at Scrabble, no Gram on the porch, smoking. No coming back, because who would be coming back?

20 NOVEMBER

Snow last night and cold. This morning flakes spiral and dash erratically; the wind rushes into the hemlocks across the brook—they release a snow cloud drifting toward the cabin.

30 NOVEMBER

Back to the cabin after a week home. Saw Dad as The Statue in *Don Juan in Hell.* Dropped by the old Kenmore. Murphy not there: an affable man named Floyd tending bar. I asked about Steve, who stays up in his room now. May have to go into a home. A woman in a tight pantsuit—could almost be the woman Leo picked up!

I felt a little sad, missing the folks Trudy and I used to see here—Murphy, Steve, Alice. But then maybe it wasn't so different. A little different from the old days of the Rain Bo Room and Sinatra . . . But there were still Trudy and me; we played the juke and danced, talked with our heads close together. It was like it had been not so long ago.

3 DECEMBER

Heavy wet snow. Cindy chased a deer behind Silver Farm. Hump in clouds while the Ledges clear and stark. This is new country to Mom. Virgin country for memories. We've been out of touch for two years and all this is unknown to her.

6 DECEMBER

Trudy and I bake five Christmas stollen, block-print eleven cards, saw seven logs. Walk. Crystalline day—two inches of powder in the night. Ice collars, beaded and ruffed, around boulders in the brook. Ice daggers hang from the eaves.

Powder on frozen snow crust that holds my weight—if I had skis, I'd slip along quiet as night. Bobcat or fox tracks? The elderberry bush we'd picked in September is bare bones. I hadn't noticed then, but it stands beside a cellar hole.

Yesterday we ate a roast of John's pig.

As I lifted the lid of the kindling box a little buff and brown mouse looked up at me: his house, his house.

7 DECEMBER

Toward evening John and Janice came by on his snowmobile—a red, bright-faced man and a red-cheeked little girl. "Isn't it great!" he exclaimed. I had chopped a dead tree down, and Trudy and I were sawing at it rather ineffectually. John went and got his chain saw and cut it right up into fireplace logs.

9 DECEMBER

Two below this morning. The brook has been strangled down to a two-foot channel. John pushed our car last night to get it started. He loaned me a long extension cord to reach a hot plate up underneath if it won't turn over. We gave him a warm apple pie from Silver Farm apples stored in the cellar.

The cabin is a cave where we hug the new iron stove from Sears.

15 DECEMBER

The temperature hovers around zero. I walk after breakfast. Wind whipping. My beard and mustache freezing into a mask. Trees creaking and cracking in their sheaths of ice.

The snowplow goes through on the hill road and I wave at the high window where two mackinawed Vermonters sit like grizzled gods.

"Didja see that kid? Up to his chestnuts in it. Christ of a storm. Better take the bridge a mite inside."

"Ayeh."

18 DECEMBER

Such purity in bare trees, snow, sky. Things could not be reduced or made more essential.

Hump clear, looking oddly small and remote today, like you could hold it in your hand, or put it into a snow globe.

1969

2 JANUARY

Back from ten days "down below"—Christmas with Dad and Trudy's folks. T off to Boston visiting friends. I returned to the cabin with Cindy for the New Year. It felt like home. It is home, peaceful under a great Russian hat of snow. The brook is a soft image of itself, completely covered over—a snow stream.

Read Trudy's *Cabin Poems* this morning—another view on our world. I see her so clearly, especially as she's not here—a woman, separate, different from me—almost a stranger in her words.

Climb halfway up Old Farm Road to see the Hump in moonlight: white, remote, unearthly. Shadows cross the road, trees cracking and clashing in wind, snow winnowing over a drift in the moonlight, bearing a few leaves. Venus in the south, bright over the head of our valley. I walk to Third Bridge and turn to come back. Orion, belt sword and bow.

4 JANUARY

Snow this morning, light and dry. I clear a path up to the car, lifting blades of feathers. The great steel snowplow goes rumbling past blowing this stuff to the side.

12 JANUARY

Snowflakes individual and exquisite, holding their minted shapes. Like Thoreau's wreck of chariot wheels. The sun falling on the snow reflects here and there a single perfect hexagon. A mitten full is an airy interlocked mobile of these shapes, melting along the surface of leather. With a single sustained breath I bore a hole into the snowbank. To clear the road the snowplow might swap its steel blades for two lusty-lunged giants.

13 JANUARY

A Monday, gray and cold. Read T some poems; she reads me some of hers. It feels brittle between us. Do the poems work as a cycle? Do they belong together? Do either of us have any perspective? I go for a walk. She stays in.

21 JANUARY

In the high crotch of a maple, a jumble of sticks wedged. Hawk's nest? Must check in spring. Now one of Trudy's snow Buddhas sitting in it thinking.

Beauteous day. Near First Bridge startled by melting snow hissing off a hemlock. The sun giving such warmth, but when it settles behind the Hump, cold comes on little frost feet. Where the road opens downhill, I stand gazing at North Mountain in evening lavender. I could almost spread my arms and float down to the cabin.

22 JANUARY

Three p.m. walking frozen snowmobile trail over deep snow. Sun is gilding the valley while already slipping behind the Hump. Calm and peaceful, winter mountains. Not a sign of man. Deer tracks.

Stop at the old sapsucker-bored tree where we gathered apples in the fall.

Beech leaves go "walking" across the snow, urged by wind.

Tonight we are invited to a meeting of the Waterbury Historical Society to learn what's going on with Camel Hump's proposed park.

23 JANUARY

Met Lionel ("Lye'nl") at the Historical meeting. An old-timer with a true accent. He held forth about how Sam de

Champ Plain was no hero of his what with marrying a ten-year-old and letting the Injuns torture one another—must have been full of Canuck wine when he came a' sailin' down the lake 'n saw the Hump with snow on it—in *July*—humpf! He calls it Lee Couchin. when clear enough it's a hump. Probably never seen a camel. An' I'll argue I don't care to the last straw to keep it the Hump.

26 JANUARY

Met an old inhabitant of these parts yesterday on Other Farm Road, Grant Howell. Owned the camp at Elderberry Corner (now a cellar hole). He has built the new camp in a field just above. Plans to plant potatoes. "New ground, they ought to thrive."

There's an overturned car a little farther downhill, an old Nash Metropolitan. Driving to town one morning, Grant went over the bank. He was not harmed, but it would cost too much to get the car out and fixed, so he left it.

He must be seventy-five or eighty, born and lived all his life here (the last thirty-three years in Waterbury). Stays up here summers, generally rising at four in the morning. This summer he plans to climb up the Ledges and take a picture of a bear. Hears them hootin' to one another.

28 JANUARY

Fifteen degrees below zero, brilliant and clear. Put a letter up in the mailbox, cock the flag, and walk a short way up the hill. But hurry back to the cabin's warmth. Truly our burrow where we live—not just exist like hibernating bears—but live—write, think—as though it were summer.

Read Emerson's *American Scholar* this evening. A beautiful mind, sharp and clear. How much more contemporary than most of my contemporaries. I feel I could meet him on a walk up the hill road.

8 FEBRUARY

Waning moon in the early morning sky. Sun beginning to vault more vertically over our gully. Spring on the way.

10 FEBRUARY

Snowstorm. Begin Upanishads. Aware of self wandering through everyday life.

13 FEBRUARY

Trudy says the brook snores all winter long. She makes displays of colored leaves she pressed last autumn, fixing them on white paper with a coat of varnish. The varnish makes the paper translucent. Held up to a window, they're like stained glass.

A short walk lengthened is better than a long walk shortened. Aiming at First Bridge and back for a nap, I go on to Third Bridge and return too refreshed to sleep.

16 FEBRUARY

Water is leaking in above the front door, so for two and a half hours this morning I am on the roof shoveling and hoeing, chipping and salting the little glacier that has formed along the edge.

18 FEBRUARY

"More snow 'n I kin remember," says Norbert Martin.

23 FEBRUARY

February's great winter blanket slowly subsiding crystal on crystal. A dog barks down in the valley. Together in the dark we make love.

25 FEBRUARY

Beautiful snow, still falling.

Trudy uneasy with the coming changes in our life. She writes poems, keeps her journal, paints, bakes, reads, takes long walks. "What am I going to do with my life," she asks. "This is glorious, but we have four months of savings left. Go back for my master's? UVM? Full-time job?"

The cabin is an experiment. Is this our life?

27 FEBRUARY

I built a fire and we drank the good Emerald Dry with Cabot cheese, black olives, and wheat bread. We talked. Maybe rendezvous with Leo, head down to Mexico? "One life determines the next," says Trudy. We *are* free. We don't have to be *anywhere*. We promise not to leave until we have drunk this cabin to the dregs.

1 MARCH

When writing's going well I feel like a medieval monk illuminating a Bible.

This afternoon on Old Farm Road, "maple sugar icicles." Deer had nibbled low-hanging branches of a maple tree, the sap had run out, drip by drip, and frozen in icicles off the branch tips. Three- or four-inch brownish icicles sweet tasting. Do deer return to lick them? Maybe from observing this, Indians tapped maple trees and boiled the sap into sugar, which could be stored.

6 MARCH

. . . he doubted he had wisdom of any serious sort to offer. He was wiser in his work—one would be who revised often enough. He wished Gary would go to some of his books for answers . . .

From "An Exorcism" by Bernard Malamud

My life has been the poem I would have writ
But I could not both live and utter it.

Thoreau

10 MARCH

Dad came up Friday afternoon (the 7th) and left today. Saturday we skied Sugarbush and Mad River, crowded; Sunday all day at Stowe. Sunday was especially good—fresh powder, no crowds.

Strange relationship with Dad—the triangle of we three. My wanting to talk and examine—*understand*—confounds everything. We murder to understand.

Riding back from Burlington after dropping Dad off, T and I talk and talk—about him and us—and the sudden release from pent-up days in a one-room cabin. We talk trying to get at the awkwardness and unease—*inarticulateness*—of when we're together. Who is my father? Who am I who thought I knew him? What does Mom's death mean to him, to him and me?

11 MARCH

Down below in town they say it has been a hard winter. But what is that to us? An abundance of snow and below zero temperatures creates no hardship up here, and such beauty. In town they tire of winter—the cold, slush, more snow . . . Up here time is suspended in winter.

13 MARCH

Drive in to town returning books to the library. A Victorian shell smelling of attic, radiators purr, a little "museum" in an alcove displays vintage photos from the town's early days. Trudy renews *An American Tragedy*.

THE IDES OF MARCH

On Old Farm Road it's so warm I take off my winter coat. At a swampy place, pussy willows to bring back to T.

Little Janice, all out of breath, comes ringing the cabin bell. "Don't go aout back!" She gasps over Cindy's barking.

"What!" I shout. "Don't go aout back—we think we saw a BEAR!" And right then her mother yells from their backyard, "Janice you get back here and stop bothering!" And the little girl trudges away home. Come to save our lives and her mother is afraid she's bothering.

18 MARCH

As I left with a gallon of milk, I said to farmer Martin, "I am amazed to see—to *smell*—such evidence of spring. It seems we hardly had winter!" He smiled, giving nothing away.

I come out of the warm winter barn (thirty-five steaming milkers heating the place) smelling—hair, beard, coat, pants—of cow manure. And bear it home for Trudy!

Fifty degrees in the afternoon. The brook begins to snore more loudly.

21 MARCH

First Day of Spring! Rain and wet snow; sound of the brook. Days grow longer!

Start Fireball tomato seeds in pots.

22 MARCH

Eighteen degrees this morning—a little restraint in the Dionysian thaw. The snow cover, roughly three feet deep, over which we have been traveling like snowshoe rabbits, no longer supports us, we slump through at every step. But what a vast amount of snow there is—what a Great Melting must occur—what waters must funnel past our cabin before the land is free.

24 MARCH

Last night aurora borealis in the sky over the cabin. There was hardly any color, just a milky white. Trudy and

I leaned against the car and watched it wavering and flickering. She said it looked like a silk veil being gently shaken.

29 MARCH

Tomato seeds sprouting!

8 APRIL

Yesterday to Waitsfield shopping; poked into the bookstore. Trudy began a conversation with one of the young hip proprietors. I just stood there awkwardly. Riding home I could feel her annoyance: "What could have been an interesting encounter, goes nowhere. It's not like we know anyone."

At the Waterbury library, picked up *New England Vegetable Garden*, *Sand County Almanac*, *Ring of Bright Water*, *A Little Land and a Living*, and *Waiting for Godot*.

Alice Post quite talkative, we mulled over the sad lack of sugaring this spring. She said not one farmer in Waterbury had hung out pails—mainly lack of help, and old people getting older. When she and her husband first came here there were ten or twelve sugaring. Her husband would help out. Their first year, Alice tapped a few big maples above their place. She boiled on the kitchen range which unglued the wallpaper—which was fine as they were planning to repaper.

Maybe next spring we'll advertise in the local paper: "Young couple interested to help out sugaring. Inexperienced but willing. Will take pay in maple syrup." I told Alice I bet we'd get some takers.

She volunteered that the Camel's Hump park proposal passed through the State House of Reps, and should soon make it through the Senate, and the governor's signature.

I'm not sure how this will affect us. At least the idea of a ski slope and resort up our valley is dead.

10 APRIL

In Montpelier, while the car was being serviced, Trudy stopped in the employment office. She spoke with a man with a "worn-out tie" who gave her a listing: salesclerk at a shoe store in Burlington, dishwasher in Stowe, janitorial work at the Waterbury hospital.

After paying off the cabin and selling the car, we might be able to live, economically, on about $1200 a year. And we should be able to figure out part-time ways to make that . . .

11 APRIL

Phoebe starting to build a nest under back porch roof.

20 APRIL

A wren sings from a cedar beside the road—bursts of sharp bright notes. I hear another over the sound of the brook. The wren is our dipper or ouzel—she loves flowing water.

Deer carcass under a tamarack on Old Farm Road melting snow uncovered a month ago. Now bones and skin—probably eaten by raccoons, foxes.

22 APRIL

Yesterday I began to turn over the garden. The soil dark and loamy. It smells so good—almost edible!

John came over as I worked. He had just returned from a sale at the Montpelier supermarket. Along with big jars of jam and peanut butter, he stocked up on frozen vegetables: ten cents a pack. You can't beat that, growing stuff yourself, he said. But allowed that some folks liked growing a garden.

He said he planned on another pig this year—it would be easy enough raising two. If we were interested. Last year, spring through fall, it cost him, purchase price and grain, about 60 dollars and yielded over a hundred pounds of meat. Seeing as we had a freezer, he said, we could put up a winter supply.

28 APRIL

Crocuses planted in the yard last fall are flowering—gold and white, lavender. I don't think I will be much of a flower gardener. It's almost superfluous with the woods and fields, the mountain's alpine meadows. Nature's garden surrounds us, and is finer than mine of fat irises and flocculent phlox. Growing vegetables—that's another story.

Two days ago little Janice thrust in the door a plastic bag of wilted dandelion greens. "To eat or something," she said. I picked them over, rinsed them, and we had an excellent salad—slightly bitter—healthy. So yesterday I gathered a crop of the greens from along the road. Thank you, Janice!

1 MAY

Before breakfast I brought Trudy up to a patch of wake-robins in bloom—her May basket.

4 MAY

First planting: Lincoln peas! I had carted pig shit from John's pen up to the garden and dug it in. Rich stuff. He has another pig, six weeks old. 'Blossom' Janice named him.

6 MAY

Third glorious morning in a row! Planted oakleaf lettuce, carrots, onion sets, yellow and red, spinach.

Trudy at Turtlehead Pool painting.

Dandelion greens for lunch.

10 MAY

Trudy makes the season's first pie—rhubarb—from a forgotten patch beside Silver Farm.

12 MAY

Drove with John to one of the Long Trail camps he looks after. And so I discovered my neighbor is a socialist! He treats the shelter as though it were his own, cutting wood, digging out a spring, repairing the stove—while fully acknowledging it belongs to everyone. He tsk-tsks over people who don't treat it well (garbage over the floor when we came, windows shot out.) There used to be a handsaw, but someone took it. "I guess they wanted the saw more than they wanted the camp," he said. He likes to putter around here on his days off. Thought T and I might like to camp here. I didn't say, but the cabin is our camp and can hardly be improved on. Ironical that John who lives a couple hundred feet from us drives to his "camp" ten miles away. It would not occur to him to shoulder a tent and sleeping bag and hike up into the woods across the brook and camp. There would be little puttering around to do.

16 MAY

First dip in the brook!

2 JUNE

Dad is planning a trip to Europe. A "grand adventure." May drop in on German relatives he's never met!

He took it on himself to mow the grass in the sunken patio. Including all the flowering dandelions we'd planned to pick for wine.

10 JUNE

Phoebe has finished her nest under the eaves. "Fee-bees" as I write.

21 JUNE

Summer solstice: longest day. Now they start growing shorter.

Trudy asks me if I'll look for work. I don't know. Dad has offered to loan us enough to get through fall and winter.

Should I try working the earlier journal into a novel?

> *All novelists must indulge in long passages of dreary pseudo description and "literary lying" to arrive at the physical proportions of the novel in the first place.*
>
> LeRoi Jones

23 JUNE

John catches trout from our brook. Last night he gave me four; we fried them with spinach from the garden. He recommends carpentry work for the summer, thinking there would be jobs around. The problem: I'm no carpenter.

24 JUNE

Rain all yesterday, drizzle this morning—excellent for the garden. I go up and look three or four times a day. It grows—in the night—in my absence—its independence, its *life*, is its own. Yet I planted it, weed it, and by and by shall eat it. We have a relationship.

3 JULY

Working now transcribing my old Concord Journal. Dead spots and blindingly alive spots. Tedious stretches. Don't be impatient, start editing this early. Let it be. As LeRoi Jones says, the importance of the "physical proportions" of a book—it's not all climaxes, a lot is context. Shut up and keep typing.

12 JULY

Phoebe's nest knocked down—a squirrel? Three of the young birds dead in the wet grass, the fourth alive. I make a nest of a shoebox and tack it up where the old nest was. Put the bird in it. Wait by the back window as it calls and the parents flutter and flutter. They find it and are feeding it. Will it live?

17 JULY

Phoebe gone from the shoebox. Not in the grass, so hopefully it made it. The two old birds around.

26 JULY

Rainy day for which the garden gives thanks in squash the size of my thumb, pinky-long cucumbers, long green beans.

27 JULY

Celebrated birthday at an old-time fiddlers' contest at Craftsbury Common.

2 AUGUST

Standing in my garden. Monarch butterflies and small white moths. Cornstalks chest high. Ball Head cabbages. Peas finished.

The dog has fleas.

The little bird made it! He follows his mother around, big as she, begging food.

4 AUGUST

Property tax due: $191.25.

Three phoebes dead in the grass.

One made it.

7 AUGUST

We climbed the Hump.

17 AUGUST

Blackberries ripening along Other Farm Road.

Grant sitting on the porch at his camp; stopped to chat. In his younger days he lived off the land—hunted deer and snared rabbits. He did a lot of canning and preserving—kept about fifteen crocks with items salted down—fish, greens, cabbage, beets, etc. Knows a spot for horseradish along Kneeland Flats. Would pick in the spring and grind. "Good on everything." And fiddleheads—the kind to eat (no fuzz)—below the falls. Only wild edible he hasn't tried is mushrooms. Doesn't care to get poisoned. Calls poplar trees "popples."

20 AUGUST

Forty-four degrees—first hint of autumn.

Applied to drive school bus for the regional high school. Contingent on my passing the driving test tomorrow. Substitute teaching available too—for both of us.

21 AUGUST

Letter from Dad, on his Grand Tour, in Copenhagen visiting shops, a castle, museums. He saw an American kid on a street corner with guitar singing "I wanna go home." Met someone in Paris. Hamburg next and the unsuspecting relatives!

22 AUGUST

Yesterday to Montpelier for bus test. Old-timer driver of everything from farm tractor to tractor trailer, Clarence, failed the written test. Didn't even get to wheel that mother of a bus around for the man and show how it's done.

Clarence laughed, smoked his pipe, said he didn't care, more time to fish and hunt.

Mrs. Williams who sailed through the written test couldn't drive the bus well enough. That left Louise and a guy from Waterbury Center and me to pass the driving part. I am now a licensed school bus driver!

Trudy touchingly proud.

30 AUGUST

Got bus yesterday. It fits in the top of the driveway like a great yellow plug.

1 SEPTEMBER

Hazy warm morning. The brook clear as glass—leaves occasionally fall into it and are carried away. The boulders sit, stolid in the sun. Asters and goldenrod, bees. Jewelweeds hanging out their orange horns.

A year ago we came here.

CHOICES

The school bus fit the driveway like a big yellow plug. Bert pulled the door closed after him, squeezed by and went down to the cabin. It was almost balmy for mid-September; across the brook a moosewood was beginning to turn, pale leaves reflecting in the water.

He poured coffee. Trudy was on the deck out back, sketching. She hadn't heard him come in; the brook, low and soft though it was, muffled sounds. He watched her for a moment through the back window, perched on the rocker. Hair in a single loose braid.

"I'm back," he called.

She was sketching the dead elm, its branches hung with silver-dewed spider webs.

"There was a fight on the bus," he said, leaning against the railing. "Brewster Morris and—"

Trudy was pointing with her charcoal. Curled in the sun on one of the stone deck steps was the milk snake. They had seen it often but never gotten used to it—thicker and longer than a garter snake—nearly four feet, and banded coral, black, white, coral and black . . .

"He won't be around much longer," said Trudy. "The hummingbirds have already left."

"Anyhow, I had to pull over to break it up. Those redneck McCalleys can't leave Brewster alone."

Trudy was cross-hatching the shaded side of the trunk. "Well," she said, "he does ask for it. That black armband—"

"*I'm* tempted to wear one. He wouldn't defend himself—just sat down in the aisle."

Bert went inside and sat at his desk, stared at the scene he'd been working on before the morning bus run. His hands still trembled from yanking Artie McCalley off and slamming him into a seat. The armband cost Brewster a lot of grief. Gordon King had stopped Solid Geometry to ask didn't he think it a little unpatriotic what he was doing? Brewster's reply landed him in Bonacker's office.

Bert had watched the war down at Granny's, her black-and-white Zenith framing burning jungles against the Vermont night. He would sit on the moldy-smelling couch in the farmhouse parlor, munch a sour milk donut and watch Nixon talking earnestly. Bert would see small, skinny, half-clad Vietnamese standing in front of burning huts. He would watch napalm splash, thinking if the set were in color it would be amazing.

Then, six weeks ago, he'd read the clipping his father had sent him: Danny Morgan, killed on his patrol boat. Rounding a bend in the river he'd taken a machine gun burst in the chest from the near bank. In seventh grade Danny used to get on the school bus two stops ahead of Bert. The bus then took the long run through the country—over an hour—to get to the junior high school. He didn't know Danny. Painfully shy, each sat alone. Bert could recall the tension in his gut always wondering if someone would sit with him. One day he got on, greeted Paul the driver—and sat right beside Danny. Danny put his lunch pail on the floor. A friendship that only existed on the bus that one year, though they were in the same class and graduated together. Danny received the Purple Heart and burial in the cemetery next to the athletic field. From his grave, Danny could watch himself practicing the shot put for the record he would break in high school.

The late bus ground up the mountain, reaching the saddle where Kirk's sawmill sat, and began the three-mile descent into Winooski Valley. The Green Mountains stretched north in a great heather-hued wedge burnished by the setting sun. Hill farms, their meadows marked by stone fences, extended down into the main valley.

Bert caught the sudden pungency of a tangerine: someone peeling leftover lunch fruit.

He lightly gripped the great steering wheel, holding the bus in the long-banked curve that sank and sank into beauty.

"So, how goes the writing?" came a mildly ironic voice from behind.

Bert glanced up into the big rearview: with his dour expression and straight shoulder-length black hair clamped to his skull with a beaded headband, Brewster Morris looked like a pasty-faced Indian. His humorless self-assurance was easy to mistake for arrogance.

"*Comme ci, comme ça*," said Bert.

"There's a sit-in at school Saturday. Press. Could be interesting." Brewster smiled thinly. He had gray, wide-apart eyes and yellowing teeth.

"Maybe I'll drop by—*Don't throw those peels on the floor*!"

After dropping most of the kids in Waterbury Center, Bert headed out the river road. Brewster lived with his mother in a square white clapboard house backed by a paintless barn and ramshackle outbuildings. He told Bert the farm hadn't operated since his father had tipped a tractor over and crushed himself to death, eight years ago.

Walter Staub arrived with a bottle of champagne and a youthful expression. The champagne cork bounced off a boulder and dropped into the brook. Walter filled three glasses and, raising his, proposed a toast to his marriage.

"What!" Trudy exclaimed. "When?"

"Someone you met in Europe?" Bert guessed.

"Jeanette!" Walter laughed happily. "French—a Parisian—forty-five years old, blonde, gorgeous—*earthy*—and sense of humor! If you could hear this woman laugh, you'd fall in love too!"

They toasted; Walter refilled the glasses: "I saw her at a little bistro near my hotel. She was sitting alone, reading a book—and crying. Actually weeping! I couldn't take my eyes off her. What—words—could such a woman be so caught up in—completely oblivious. No one paying any attention. It's Paris! I sat at a table and ordered *un verre de vin rouge*. It began to feel like I was in a play. Suddenly, I was standing over her table blurting out my name—like a kid—honestly, I don't even remember getting up—and then—what? Total blank!" Walter's incredulous laugh bounced off the hillside. "I thought, this is it: here is a woman I want more than pain—more than bread—and I've made an ass of myself! But she's looking up at me—blue eyes appraising! 'Well,' she says, with this charming accent, completely non-plussed, 'you might as well sit down, you've come this far.'"

Bert laughed—he could just see his father—"It does sound like a play!"

"I like this woman already," said Trudy.

Walter poured more champagne. "Jeanette's incredible—passionate! Lord! Sophisticated—she knows three languages, can play the piano—Schubert, Chopin—oh, man—goes caravanning in the South of France every year with her boys!" He looked at Bert. "Completely different from your mother."

"Sounds like it," said Bert.

"I mean *profoundly*. It's like a new chapter opening in my life—one that had always been there, but never—opened."

"You sound like a different person," said Trudy.

"I'm in love!" Walter opened his hands and looked mildly astonished at his declaration. "We've set the date for the first Saturday of the New Year. The minister that married the two of you is performing the ceremony in my living room. You'll come, of course. Jeanette's flying over Christmas week. I can't wait till you meet her!"

Trudy said, if they didn't have plans for Christmas, they were welcome at the cabin.

"That's a great idea!" Bert exclaimed. "An old-fashioned Christmas—we'll cut a tree up in the woods—carols—fires in the fireplace—"

"I expect we could almost guarantee snow," Trudy said with a smile.

"We'll roast a goose—with Mom's prune stuffing. I'll get out the old recipes—kale, a bund kuchen—"

"Don't forget the creamed onions," said Walter. "Christmas in Vermont."

They ate supper on the deck, the late sun lighting the entire hillside across the brook. Trudy had made a chicken potpie with vegetables from their garden.

"Next year," said Bert, "I'm going to grow wheat—so even the crust will come from the homestead."

"It's marvelous," said Walter. "You raise your own food, cut wood for fuel, pay cash." He held a carrot disk between his fingers. "Your lifestyle, generally applied, would run this country backward into the previous century."

"Not such a bad idea," said Trudy with a laugh.

Bert said nothing. He'd once tried to discuss Thoreau's philosophy of self-reliance with his father, only to have Walter say he'd laid *Walden* down after the first chapter, finding the author unbearably smug and self-righteous.

They finished and Trudy suggested the two men take a walk while she did dishes. They would have dessert and coffee when they returned.

"I saw that apple pie on the counter," said Walter. "You can bet we won't be long."

It was dark as they walked up the hill road, a few stars pricking through the thick canopy. The brook, low, was nearly silent, seeping from pool to pool.

Walter brought a cigarette to his lips and drew, briefly illuminating his features. The face of an Arab, Jew, Turk—cruel or, equally, kind. Bert didn't know.

"It's the good life you've found here. You have a wife, your own place, a perfectly viable, if subsistence, economy. I'm not your father anymore." He chuckled. "We're equals."

They walked until Walter asked if they were going to the top of the mountain.

"One thing—promise me," he said as they turned back, "don't go on at length about Emma."

Bert shrugged. "Sure."

"Don't 'sure' me. I was married for thirty-eight years. It's a touchy—*potentially treacherous*—subject with Jeanette."

"I'm not supposed to mention Mom?"

Walter sighed.

"I mean, no bund kuchen?"

"You have to understand," said Walter, "I love Jeanette—we're entering unknown waters. I just want, want it to have the best chance."

After a few minutes of silence, Bert said, "I think Mom would be glad you're getting married."

Trudy and Bert got down to Granny's for seven o'clock. Local news started off with the demonstration: a shot of the "Students Against the War" sitting in a formation that looked like an airplane, on the plaza before Harwood Union. Bert, larger than everyone else and seated in front, appeared to be the pilot. Fortunately, the reporter identified the formation as a peace sign.

Bert was interviewed by the pretty reporter while in the background the kids were singing "If I Had a Hammer." As he talked about getting to know Brewster on the bus, having his "consciousness raised" by the war, death of a "close friend," etc., Bert on Granny's couch groaned and squirmed.

When the reporter cut him short to interview the kids, Bert on the couch cried out: "What a boob! Could anyone make heads or tails of that!"

"It was fine," said Trudy. "You were sincere."

"I hadn't shaved—I look like an axe murderer!"

He was silent as Brewster's face filled the screen, talking unselfconsciously about the necessity for civil disobedience, etc. Bert found himself choking up. No petty ego getting in the kid's way—the issue was more important. Bert struck his knee:

"Why did I go over there? I couldn't even lip-synch the songs right."

"It was important," said Trudy. "More than just kids involved."

"A moronic bus driver? Goddamn it, Bonacker probably saw this. What a way to get canned."

Trudy patted his knee and went into Granny's bedroom. Bert heard the Scrabble letters spill into the box lid.

He went on watching. Coming up was a big anti-war protest, nationwide—people staying out of work—sit-ins, petitions, marches.

Granny sat against the headboard of the bed, wearing her quilted vest, yellow comforter over her legs, long gray hair in its customary evening braid. With high cheekbones and sharp gray eyes, she looked like an Indian. Trudy sat on the edge of the bed studying the Scrabble board that rested in the old woman's lap.

"You're a TV star," said Granny.

Bert grunted.

"He was there," said Trudy. "That was something."

"Maybe he's not as flat as he looks—" Granny put four letters down from the g of giant to make grant.

Bert could never bring himself to ask Granny what she thought about the war. Around her, everything seemed unimportant except the moment they were in.

Gordon King came out of the school's back entrance where Bert was hosing down his bus. After delivering the kids that morning, he'd spent the day substitute teaching. He still had the five o'clock run to make.

Bert nodded to the math teacher.

King continued toward the parking lot, but then, as if against his will, turned and came back.

"It really, all of it, makes me sick. Your friend, Brewster Morris, thinks you're living proof of something. A writer, I hear, some kind of—escapee from the city living up on the hill, telling everyone 'be yourself.' I can see what's going on in the kid's head. He thinks there's something called freedom. How much *freedom* do you pump into that Beetle you drive around?"

King stood as though rooted into the blacktop, worn leather briefcase hanging from one hand, black lunch pail from the other. He wore a tan golf jacket, and a breeze was lifting strands of hair that had been combed across his bald spot.

"I guess you caught the news on TV," said Bert.

"A job is a job. You drive bus, I teach math. It's no different than working for GE, for Chrissake! In ten years, I retire, the kids will be gone, and the wife and I will get in the van and go. A check coming in every month. In the meantime, I'm free in my mind. I think what I want and I keep my mouth shut. Do you know what I'm thinking?"

King set his lunch pail down to wipe his mouth with a handkerchief. Bert could feel the cold of the bus fender through his denim jacket.

"I don't know, Mr. King, we have different ideas about civic duty—"

"*Civic duty*!" dry spittle flew. "Stick to driving the goddamn bus and stop messing around in the heads of these kids!"

Bert was exhausted or he would have laughed. "I'm sorry to say, Mr. King, but it's the other way around."

King made two stammering attempts to retort. His lips came away from his teeth in a grimace—he picked up his lunch pail and slowly, as though heavily burdened, headed for his Chevy Malibu, which sat alone in the middle of the parking lot.

Bert got back to the cabin after seven. Trudy had left a note on the counter, weighted with a red maple leaf:

> *Such a beautiful morning, I can't resist—taking Cindy and heading for the Ledges. Granny says there might still be a few blueberries.*
>
> *Back before dark.*
>
> *Love, me*

He walked up the brook to the pool where they swam, squatted on a boulder above the clear, icy water. It was nearly dark. A green apple came over the little falls at the head of the pool and floated across, bobbing when a trout nosed it. The apple disappeared over the spillway and was lost in the riffles below.

Two hours later, the dog scratched at the door, Bert heard footsteps in the driveway gravel. Trudy had started back late and got caught by the dark. Stumbling downhill through the woods after the dog, she'd come out on the river road.

She was euphoric: "No blueberries—but *grasshoppers*! All over the Ledges, sunning themselves, flying up rattling as you climbed. I kept thinking *rattlesnakes* and jumping, even though I know there aren't any around here anymore. Sunset was unbelievable. I could see the White Mountains all the way in New Hampshire. A blue heron came flying up just below where I sat. It was a Chinese watercolor."

Trudy talked as she made herself a peanut butter sandwich—about swimming in the beaver pond, about the porcupine the dog treed, about an old sugar camp she'd stumbled on, metal taps half swallowed in maple trunks.

"Why didn't they take them?" Trudy wondered. "Metal taps must have been valuable."

The fire was flickering through the seams of the iron stove. Bert could barely follow Trudy's talk, he was so tired; she seemed a visitor from another planet. An old sugar camp in the mountains . . . He was thinking about King's anguished face, about a war in a jungle that he somehow felt responsible for.

"I found a pile of sap pails almost completely rusted away," Trudy was saying. "I wonder if they left the arch up there. On the last day of sugaring, just . . . walked away." She nibbled her sandwich. "Where did they go? California? Maybe just to Burlington. They must all be dead now. What's funny is how alive they are up there—like it's yesterday, sap steam rising through the red-budded branches, horses knee-deep in snow, the men in woolen coats and beards, faces red in the arch fire . . ."

Bert invited the Students Against the War to the cabin to hold their pre-protest meeting. Trudy baked a sheet pan of carrot cake, went down to Granny's for the evening.

The eleven kids in SAW decided they would stay out of school and go to the sit-in at the Capitol in Montpelier. Brewster warned that they could be arrested and demonstrated passive resistance: he and Jackson Bell dragged Brewster's girlfriend, April, limply across the cabin floor.

Someone asked Bert if he would be joining them in Montpelier.

"I thought I'd come over after the morning run."

"You're driving bus that day?" exclaimed Jackson Bell.

Bert smiled. "The mailman and the bus driver, you know. Bonacker insinuated, anyone taking off other than for an emergency could be facing consequences."

"Bull!" cried Jackson Bell. "He can't hold your job over your head."

"The war *is* an emergency," said April, flushing.

"Hey, people do what they can," said Brewster. "Let's figure out how we're getting there."

On Protest Day, Bert made his morning bus run wearing a black armband. In Montpelier he sat with a group of Bread and Puppet people, not trying to get through to where SAW had camped near the top of the Capitol steps. None of the kids got arrested; Bonacker suspended them for a week.

It was snowing pretty thickly. Bert and Trudy stood in a meadow half grown up with young spruce; the short, fat tree he had cut stayed nearly upright, propped on its stiff branches. Resiny, white chips were fast being covered by the snow.

"I like Jeanette—from her letters," Bert said, lashing the ax to the toboggan. "She's been through a hell of a lot." Trudy helped him settle the tree onto the toboggan, and they began pulling it side by side across the meadow.

"Nazi soldiers quartered in your house for nine months." Trudy shook her head. "Can you imagine? We have no idea what it's like to live through a war."

Bert looked at the snow-filling woods, SS troopers on skis in their white parkas were slipping through.

"Yeah, we just have wars in other people's backyards." He winced, hearing himself repeating something Brewster had said.

The dog stayed close, running ahead and coming back for them, running out and coming back. They followed an old logging road into hemlock woods.

"This is going to be the first real Christmas since Mom died," said Bert.

"It might be easier if you didn't try to resurrect all the old things," said Trudy. "You have to wonder how Jeanette's going to feel."

"It'll be okay. It's a celebration—we're welcoming her into the family, and Mom's part of that."

They rested for a moment, backs turned to the slanting snow, the tree on the toboggan sticking out on both sides.

Bert already felt a little bad cutting it down. Sacrificed for an occasion that was really a memory of another time.

The logging trail crossed a frozen stream then descended steeply. Bert had to walk behind, holding the toboggan back by the rope. After a while they emerged onto the hill road. The tracks they'd made coming up were already almost entirely covered. Trudy kneeled on the back of the toboggan behind the tree while Bert ran, pulling, and the dog plunged after them, barking.

"Jeanette sounds like one of us," he said as they walked again side by side. "Summers in her twenties harvesting grapes—camping in the Greek Islands."

"She sounds more like us than like your father," said Trudy.

"Maybe she'll convert him." Bert laughed.

As they neared the cabin, Bert could see through the thickly falling snow a car parked in the turnaround.

"They're here!"

He smelled woodsmoke from the fire he'd set before they left, and felt a stab of pleasure that his father should find this snug harbor at the end of his journey.

He felt Trudy's mittened hand on his arm as they started past one of the windows. Inside, Walter was sitting on the couch with a blonde woman in his lap. Her upswept hairdo had been loosened, and there were lipstick marks on his father's broad, shining forehead. They were kissing, his hand moving under her skirt.

"Let's go down to Gran's," said Trudy. "We'll come back in a while."

Bert stared through the window, snowflakes blurring his sight.

"Come on—"

He could see the woman's leg bare to the lace trim of her underwear. He bent closer, like a man in a snow globe trying to see out.

FLOWERS FOR ANTONIA

As Bert rode down the hill on his bicycle, braking, looking out for loose stones, he heard Granny yoo-hoo. She was coming off her porch with a small bouquet of flowers. He leaned his bike against her mailbox and started up the drive.

They were sweet peas from her fence. She had wrapped the cut ends in a wet paper towel and put them in a plastic baggie tied with a rubber band.

"Give those to Gladys," she said, handing him the bouquet. "She knows what they're for."

Bert turned down the driveway. "I'm a little late. Maybe Trudy and I'll come down for tea tomorrow." But Granny was already headed back to the old red farmhouse. He tucked the fragrant bundle into his shirt and went on.

Bert had been working six weeks as the summer hand for Wayne Martin at the small dairy farm. The farm had been in the Martin family from before the Revolutionary War. "The War For Independence," Wayne called it. His father, Norbert, lived with his wife, Dorothy, in a house nearby. Norbert and Wayne were cast from the same mold—hatchet-faced, lean and leathery, laconic with a glinting sense of humor. Wayne's son, Henry, currently serving four years in the Air Force, had no interest in running the farm when he got out.

"That's too bad," said Bert, thinking of the long line of Martins.

"Ayeh," said Wayne. "It's a hard living. Don't know how much longer they'll pick up neither. That'll be it."

Wayne had a slight limp from a logging accident years ago when a tree fell on him. He'd rigged a kind of toboggan out of the bark of a birch and Dolly had dragged him out of the woods down to the farm.

Before haying started in earnest, Bert had spent many a day with the old man. Norbert was in his eighties. He had some trouble managing the hilly parts of the meadows when they mended fence, but he came into his own when they sawed logs for firewood that both houses used for fuel. The old man employed a peavey like a lumberjack, levering logs onto the cradle then bringing the reciprocating saw blade down on the wood.

When Bert asked about the old sugarhouse up in the woods, Norbert's eyes lit up. They hadn't made maple syrup for a few years because they couldn't find help. Bert offered to help next spring. He'd be happy to take pay in maple syrup.

"Have to talk to Wayne," the old man said. "I boil."

Bert laid his bike in the grass beside the barn and went inside.

"Morning," he said.

"Mornin'," replied Wayne

He was squatting beside a cow in his knee-high rubber boots, adjusting the milking machine.

"Granny—uh—Ms. Beston—sent these along for your wife." Bert extended the bouquet of sweet peas.

"Ayeh. I'll take them in when I go to breakfast."

Bert helped finish up the milking. Then while Wayne went in for breakfast, Bert led the cows across the road and the tracks to the meadow beside the river. He cleaned the barn, shoveling cow flops and urine-soaked hay into the trench that was scraped clean by a conveyor belt. The manure emptied into a spreader and was scattered onto the fields every three or four days.

Bert forked fresh hay and then cleaned the milking machines. The milk room was dominated by the big square stainless-steel tank, which sat in the middle of the floor. The tank truck came after the morning milking to collect. Martin with his thirty-five milkers was just able to make the minimum for the truck to stop. The milk plant didn't bother collecting from the little dairy farms anymore. There used to be eight or so between here and Burlington. Now there was Wayne Martin and one other.

Wayne came in as Bert was putting the collecting pots up to drain.

"Looks like loury weather," said Bert, liking the country sound of *loury*. "Good morning to get that lower field in?"

"Ayeh," said Wayne. "I rolled windrows last night. Hay ought to be dry."

They crossed the tracks to the lower field, Wayne driving the tractor, Bert standing on the step beside him. Bert got down and opened the fence, Wayne drove through, Bert swung the gate closed, latched it, and got back on the tractor. But Wayne had switched the engine off.

"Girl loved the farm," he said. "The horses—putting in the garden with Gladys—haying. She loved to pick berries."

There was a pause, then he said, "Antonia'd be seventeen now. Graduating high school." He started the tractor and they went on.

When he and Trudy stopped down for tea Saturday morning, Bert asked Granny about Antonia. Granny fished the last sour milk donuts out of the pot of boiling oil on the stove, laid them on paper towels to drain. She turned the stove off and sat with them at the kitchen table, steam from their mugs of tea rising in the air.

"Antonia . . ." Gran had a far-away look in her eyes. "She was a little girl about as different as that name too. So pretty and lively. Different from them."

"What happened?" Trudy asked.

"Train hit the hay wagon. I send sweet peas down every year this time."

Eleven years ago, it had been a hot dry June. The hay grew thick and high. And when it was cut, the sun dried it in fragrant swaths. Norbert baled hay from when the dew was off midmorning to last light. And everyone who could be found pitched in to bring it safe into the barn.

They were gathering hay bales from the lower meadow, right across from the house. Wayne was on the wagon drawn by the two Belgians, Prince and Dolly. While Henry, who was fifteen then, walked alongside and heaved bales up, Wayne set them in place on the wagon. By his clucks and "hi's" the team knew when to move and when to stop. The other wagon, pulled by the Ford tractor driven by Homer Kneeland, had Billy Johnson, who lived at the bottom of the hill with his mother, tossing bales up; Homer's sister, Holly, on the wagon stacking; and Antonia, six years old, up front jumping around gleefully, keeping out of the way of flying bales.

The cows were in a high meadow, so the gate had been left open up across the tracks and the road to the barn.

Wayne and Henry had loaded up and gone ahead. One sent hay bales up the conveyor while the other stacked them in the loft.

Homer's wagon finished loading, the crew climbed up on the high-piled bales, and they set off for the barn.

It was about noon, and they knew after unloading the hay, they would break for lunch. There would be a big pitcher of Mrs. Martin's Kool-aid with ice cubes floating in it. And peanut butter and jelly sandwiches.

Homer had started up the grade to the railroad tracks when he heard the train whistle. It always blew crossing the bridge below Wainwright's, half a mile away. Plenty of time, but Homer stalled the tractor. He figured to start it and get across but made the mistake of looking up and catching the distant motion of the train. He jerked the gas lever down and flooded the engine, the tractor and wagon straddling the tracks. As the kids scrambled to get off, the train hit, splitting tractor to one side, wagon to the other, and scattering the load over the meadow. The train had been slowing but still struck at about thirty miles an hour. A long freight. Little Antonia was thrown off and her neck broken. Homer had gotten off the tractor in time and the other two kids had jumped clear. Not a scratch on anyone.

It must have been a sight, the freight train stopped there, stretched a quarter mile along the track where it only ever flew by. Two cars pulled over beside the dirt road. Gladys Martin sitting among the scattered hay bales rocking the body of her daughter. The little girl looked like she was sleeping. There was nothing to be done. The black-and-white Holsteins cropping peacefully on the high meadow. Birds singing their noontime songs.

Bert never knew how to bring up the accident, or if Wayne wanted to talk about it. The last time, as they were driving the cows home over the railroad crossing, Wayne had said, his eyes sweeping toward the river, "Hay bales got knocked all down into the meadow."

BOUNTY

Granny sleeps on her yellow bed. Maggie underneath lifts her old muzzle.

Maggie, I say. She puts it down with a grunt. I go out of the house.

The vines are dead of early frost, but the potatoes are safe in the ground. The path drops steep, my feet slipping. In this brook-cut you could lick sweat off the rocks.

Don't get them no more, she said, but they are God's apples. I am coming the secret way, there will be no more sign than if a deer or coon took them.

Brook's low, hardly sounding. The pool behind Big Rock looks like a spoon on Granny's table. Smells here of wet tea bag, hemlock, pee. The air comes down against my mouth like cold breath. Spiders are quiet on the water waiting for sun to get them hitching. Trout don't eat them. Maybe they taste bad.

The apple tree grows where the brook goes under the road into the river. It is there giving apples when I was a boy and I am forty-two or three. I am almost held up by her wish, but I see Granny's face when she sees the apples yellow-striped on her kitchen table.

It's the old tree's year again. Every two it makes its bounty, the empty between so we will not be spoilt, Granny says. The pies and sauce are for me. She hardly eats, but she takes satisfaction.

I go down brook jumping rocks. This stick on my finger makes it hard, but at least no pain today. I always come by the road, but they would see me so I don't. Hadley gave the brook-edge of his hayfield for their trailer. Apple tree scratches the tin in wind. Granny says the tree is there long before them and long after. I don't like picking now, there's a power around the trailer. All I can remember is hayfield. Hadley mows it shaping around the trailer.

Kingfisher drops off a branch, goes opening and closing downstream. Laughs after a while. This brook runs right down mountain like the school ground slide. I go by a trout sunk in a pool. I don't look 'cause I ain't gonna eat him. The tree is a gift. Bounty Granny calls it. The man is there now and he looks at me. Hole under the road eats the brook, dust hangs, the milk-collecting truck goes boom.

I watched apples fatten all summer. Then saw some on the ground fallen of themselves. I came by the road and picked. He came out of the trailer, words hit around me. The girl holding the screen door half-open. I gathered apples before he was born. He took my hand, bent the fingers like they do at school, bent them till I was up on my toes. He held me and we looked into each other. Something popped. I couldn't say how I was there for apples, not for spying on the girl more than the tree was. But we had looked. I went home sick.

I leave the brook, start up the bank, crawling. I have to go for them, next year is empty branches. He don't take the bounty, why should he care I do?

I come up and stop. He is in a chair under the tree. I start back but his fingers snap—snap—his dog comes out of the grass, cuts between me and the brook. The man stands, shakes his head like a horse shakes flies. I pick an apple up near my shoe, yellow-striped. Inside an eat-hole a yellow jack too numb with cold falls out. The man shakes his head, his words thump like boulders in the March brook. Under the tree the chair is red. He knocks the apple away.

The dog is looking at me, his back feet in the water.

You got no more reason the man says. He lifts something out of the weeds, yanks, it barks alive in his hands. He goes to the tree with the chainsaw like it is me not there anymore.

WIND HARP

Bert swung down the hill road, careful to place the rubber tips of his crutches on sand that had been scattered over the hard snow-packed surface. It was Friday, fifteen degrees below zero, so dark at noon it felt like 4 p.m. And more snow on the way—as if three and a half feet weren't enough. The left crutch skidded, his cast foot struck down and he yelped. He had broken his leg Thanksgiving Day, two months ago, the beginning of their fifth winter at the cabin.

The road curved and rose slightly before running its last half mile steeply down to the river. Bert hung in his crutches, staring at Brownie Smyth's house, a conglomerate of rooms, sheds and porches which had sprouted from the core of an old mobile home, no longer visible. Tucked against a spring-fed hillside, the structure reminded Bert of a cubistic fungus. A thin column of smoke rose from a stovepipe in one of the roofs. Bert was encouraged to see Brownie's station wagon out front.

He had a toothache. He had a dental appointment in town at three. Thirty-one years old, he felt like he was falling apart. He and Trudy had saved enough money to get through this winter so he could finish the play. But then the leg. And now the tooth.

Josie, the Smyth's beagle hound, began to howl. Bert could never take a walk without being announced.

Brownie stood on the open front porch in his slippers and undershirt, suspenders dangling.

"Cold enough?" called Bert, turning into the shoveled path.

"I guess."

Brownie was a small, shy man of thirty-five with a stiff right leg from a chain-saw accident clearing brush with the town. He hadn't worked since Bert knew him, drawing workman's comp each month.

Bert carefully mounted the salted wooden steps and entered the overheated kitchen where Louise was dicing potatoes into a pot. Brownie's wife was a pale kindly mountain of a woman; her colorless hair stood out from her head in a ruff.

Bert greeted her and laid a packet taken from his coat pocket on the table.

"Little something," he said.

He leaned the crutches against a chair and, balancing on one leg, struggled out of his coat. When he finally got settled at the kitchen table, Brownie sat down.

"Last of the hive honey." Bert tapped the packet which neither of them had acknowledged. Was a simple "thank you" so much to ask? Gifts of fresh bread, homemade jam, surpluses from the garden—all vanished without a sign.

"You eat honey?" Bert couldn't help himself.

"He likes it," said Louise, setting a mug of coffee before Bert. "It gets in his false teeth."

"Fresh tasting," Brownie said.

That gave Bert the opportunity to explain how honeycomb was honey packed and sealed by the bees: "You get it fresh, pure and unadulterated, with natural pollens and enzymes which aid digestion and even help with allergies."

Louise wiped her hands on her apron and sat at the end of the table.

"Got forty pounds off the hive," said Bert. "It's about all we use for sweetener." It sounded like bragging when what he'd meant to express was his awe with the abundance.

A curly golden-haired girl appeared and leaned in a doorway. One of the Smyths' five. The face of a cherub on an old-fashioned Christmas card.

"Hi there," said Bert, forgetting her name. "No school today?"

"May's got a cold," said Louise.

The girl came out and climbed into her mother's lap, regarding Bert solemnly.

"Near lunchtime," said Louise. "Stew'll be ready."

"Oh, thanks," said Bert, "but—uh—you're not going into town this afternoon, are you, by chance?"

Brownie rubbed his chin and said, "Car's acting up. Generator light was on during the ride out yesterday."

"Ah," said Bert.

"Brother-in-law's gonna give a look."

Bert tried to fight down the rising feeling of claustrophobia and despair—he stood so abruptly that Brownie glanced up at him, sleepy eyes widening.

"Have some more coffee," he said.

"No, ah—thanks—Trudy and I—" Bert knocked a crutch over.

"Stop in anytime." Brownie stood in the open door and watched Bert descend the porch steps one at a time.

Bert crutched back up the hill furiously, twice coming down on his cast.

As he turned to go down the path to the cabin, the mailman's pale blue Rambler came over the rise.

He handed Bert several sale flyers and an electric bill through the open car window.

"I wonder, if it's possible—can you give people lifts?"

"Insurance doesn't allow," said the postman, adding, "What's killing this country."

Bert crutched down to the cabin. He sat at his desk and stared at the scene notes. Work on the play had gone poorly since the accident. Concentration snapped with the bone.

Thanksgiving had dawned with the year's first real snowfall, a couple of inches. Trudy had started a duck roasting, then they took the toboggan down to Evelyn Johnson's. Her meadow rose like a rumpled blanket from the river road up to the base of a cliff. Wayne Martin pastured his dry cows in the meadow during the summer, so the three-strand barbed wire fence was in good repair.

Billy, Evelyn's lanky son, was returning from an outing with his old Ski-Doo when they arrived. Bert recognized Homer Kneeland sitting behind Billy, glasses fogged, orange Day-Glo flap-hat tied under his chin. Trudy wished the boys a Happy Thanksgiving while Bert frowned at the clattering machine with its oily stink of blue exhaust.

"We gotta push 'er uphill sometimes," exclaimed Homer. "But it goes down *real* fast!"

The light cover of snow did little to cushion the meadow's rocks and frozen cow patties: the wooden toboggan chattered and banged over the short test run. Then Bert and Trudy pulled it to the top of the hill.

Almost immediately the sled was going too fast, and when they tried to turn, there was no snow-base to cut into; they tore on straight for the barbed wire fence. Bert eased his left foot out to brake, touched against something under the snow and pole-vaulted them, snapping his leg with a *pop*!

"*Goddamnit*!" he had shouted, spinning around on his back in the snow with his broken leg in the air. "How are we going to *pay* for this!"

Bert heard the dog whine at the door, then Trudy stamping snow off her boots.

"It's *cold*!" she exclaimed. "We only went as far as First Bridge."

"No luck."

"Did you tell them you have a toothache? You have a dental appointment?"

"Something's wrong with their car, so what would have been the point—make them feel guilty?" He sat on the sofa with his cast leg up on the hassock. “Will you please go down to Granny’s and phone the dentist and say I can’t make it? No car, no money, no telephone! You know how I felt showing up at Brownie’s with a bar of honey in my pocket?”

“Should I make another appointment?”

“*My tooth hurts*!”

“I bet you could get a lift in on the school bus that drops Brownie’s kids.”

“Insurance,” Bert pronounced blackly.

Trudy pulled her mittens on.

“Make it for Monday—around noon. I’ll leave after breakfast and *crutch* the five miles.”

Fifteen minutes later Trudy returned, followed by Homer Kneeland.

“Homer has kindly offered to run you in.”

“Got me an automobile.” Homer settled on a stool at the kitchen counter. “Nineteen Sixty Caddy.”

Trudy was slicing a loaf of fresh oatmeal bread. “My father would love it,” she said. “It must be two blocks long.”

“Rides like a loaded hay wagon,” Homer said proudly.

Trudy set a thick slice before him, with butter and elderberry jam.

Homer drove, sitting on the edge of the seat with both hands on the steering wheel. The floor was so rusted Bert watched the road streaming under his feet.

“I’d like to give you some gas money.”

“Ah,” said Homer, “wasn’t doing nothing. Besides, Ms. Beston wants me to pick up potatoes and milk.”

Homer, twenty-three, lived with his folks and three sisters in an old house below Brownie’s. He worked for a prefab house company. But there was no winter work.

The sidewalk near the dentist office had been shoveled but not salted or sanded, and Homer walked behind Bert holding on to the tail of his coat. Bert felt like a dog on a leash.

Waterbury was Doctor Marvell's first practice out of dental school. His wife was his receptionist and hygienist. He laid Bert out almost horizontal, rigged a rubber funnel-like "dam" in his mouth, and donned rubber gloves and an operating mask.

With his leg in a cast, numb jaw being drilled into, wondering how it would be paid for, Bert listened to Homer Kneeland out in the reception room flirting with the dentist's wife.

That evening as they sat near the stove reading, there came a knock at the cabin door. Alex Jensen stood in the porchlight smiling diffidently behind red beard and wire rim glasses. Fay Jensen's pretty oval face, framed in a black furry W. C. Fields hat, beamed at them almost painfully over Alex's shoulder. Beside her, Harv Moskowitz, encased in a new puffy down parka, tilted his head and grinned.

"So," he said, "are we invited in, or do we get flash-frozen right here?"

Inside the cabin, Fay shook out her hair, releasing a warm scent of Chanel. On an impulse, they'd left New Haven at five and driven up. She was a second-year acting student when Bert met her at drama school before he quit a year into the program to write full-time. Harv was a playwright and Alex finishing up his law degree. The three had been regular guests at the cabin in the time since Bert and Trudy had left New Haven.

"Yes," said Fay, "one of Alex's brainstorms. I told him you don't just burst in on people. Of course, you don't have a telephone."

"You are welcome—believe me!" Trudy laughed.

"We were bouncing off the walls," said Bert. "I was getting ready to build snowshoes for the crutches."

Alex went up to the car for their sleeping bags. Harv handed Trudy a paper bag.

"Bagels, four varieties. Not from Brooklyn, but what can I say?" He crowded the iron stove, holding his hands over it. "Christ, six hours in an unheated Volvo—I know what Sam Magee's all about. It is colder than inside my freezer."

Leaning on his crutches, Bert opened a bottle of dandelion wine he and Trudy had made.

Alex built a fire as they settled in on rug and sofa, sipping the sweet, amber-colored wine.

"We thought maybe you could use a little cheering up . . ." Fay was zipped to the waist in her sleeping bag and lay gazing into the fire. "I know about cabin fever, having spent the better part of a Montana winter holed up in one."

"It was great," said Alex. "I'd shot a deer and kept it frozen hanging in the shed. I'd go out and cut off a steak."

"The good old days," said Fay. "A steady diet of stringy meat and roots. You should have seen my figure by spring."

"It wasn't so bad," said Alex. "We had rice and flour, beans—"

"Yes, yes," said Fay. "Can I have some more wine?"

They settled into their old routine. Alex showed sketches of a chair he'd begun sculpting from an oak stump—it looked like a waiter's hand held up for a tray. Trudy read from her journal, an encounter with a doe and her fawn in deep snow. Harv acted out a scene he'd written about Thomas Jefferson's invention of the lead condom and how George Washington thereafter required wooden teeth. Bert recited a poem: the names of the vegetable seeds he'd ordered for the spring garden.

Fay yawned: "Remind me tomorrow and I'll do my audition monologue from *The Taming of the Shrew.*"

Bert poured the last of the wine. It was quiet. Once in a while a tree popped with cold. "Moon of Popping Trees" the Indians called January. Frost rimed the insides of the cabin windows and came right through the walls, sparkling on the pine paneling furthest from the heat.

Alex put a chunk of dry beech on the fire.

Harv was talking about *Mahagonny* currently at Yale Rep.

Bert stared at the blue fingers of flame curving up the log's gray back. He wished he could go back with them to New Haven—sit in Clark's and have a coffee with Harv; go to a movie; catch a jazz concert at Yale.

The dog yipped in her sleep. The brook running beside the cabin was silent under the snow. Everything out there was under the snow: asleep, dormant, suspended. Just them, close to the fire, like sleepers keeping themselves awake.

"You guys know about the wind harp?" Alex asked. He was sitting cross-legged on the rug, facing the fire. "There was an article in the *Register* a couple weeks ago, with pictures. It looked pretty neat."

"There's supposed to be a wind harp over in Chelsea, I think," said Trudy. "On some farmer's back meadow."

"Maybe we ought to check it out," said Alex. "Tie the toboggan on the car, bring Bert along."

"Now you know." Fay leaned up on an elbow, "We didn't come to visit you guys, we came so Alex could see a wind harp."

"I thought it might be something to do," said Alex.

"Do we ever do what I want?" asked Fay. "I'd like to go down to the city and see the Joffrey."

"You can go."

"I bend over backward to accommodate you—clomp around the woods, get bitten, get rashes—because I know you like it, and I want to be with you. Do you ever do one thing you don't want to?" Fay's gestures had grown sweeping; she looked like a mermaid with her bottom half in the green sleeping bag.

"All the while, I thought she actually liked being out in the woods. I do go to dance concerts with her," Alex finished reasonably.

"Oh!" Fay flopped back down.

"You can stay here tomorrow."

"That's exactly what I'm going to do. I brought *Anna Karenina* and I am going to read in peace and quiet—and warmth."

"Tempting though it is," said Harv, "I think I'll sit this one out, too, right next to old stovie here."

"Oh, no," said Bert. "If the broken leg goes—"

"It'll be great," said Alex. "In twenty years—"

"It is thirty degrees below zero," Fay's voice rose from the sleeping bag. "Do you want to freeze the man to death?"

"Bert'll be fine," said Alex. "We'll bundle him up and zip him into a sleeping bag."

"Along with a pint of Jack Daniel's," Bert added.

"Does anything change?" asked Trudy. She and Bert were taking the dog for a quick walk after breakfast.

"Punch and Judy. Last night the same as when we stayed with them in the fall."

Bert chuckled. "That's Fay and Alex. If they weren't going at it, we wouldn't recognize them."

"What's the attraction? Mountain man and ingénue?"

Bert laughed.

Trudy didn't. "Fay can be such a wet blanket. And now she's coming."

They were all standing in the turnaround waiting for the Volvo to warm up when an old Cadillac nosed over the hill pulling a homemade cart with a Ski-Doo on it.

After Bert had introduced Homer and Billy, Fay asked if they would like to join the Great Wind Harp Expedition.

Homer blinked at Fay's pretty china-doll face framed in a black fur version of his own hat. She wore a matching bearlike coat.

"Sure," he said.

"Thought we were gonna make a run up above?" Billy spoke to Homer. "We ain't got a license on the cart."

"Hell," said Homer, indicating that didn't bother him.

"That wind harp's the Ninth Wonder of the World," said Fay. "And it's just over in Chelsea."

"Might've heard of it," said Homer.

"The more the merrier. Right, Alex?"

"I'd rather ride up the valley," said Billy, barely audible.

Homer smiled at Fay: "We got about a acre of extra room in the Caddy."

"Why not keep the boys company?" said Alex who had climbed behind the Volvo's wheel. "I bet they even have a heater."

"Burn your boots off," grinned Homer.

"You go, Harv," Fay said.

"A heater?" Harv popped open the rear door of the Cadillac. "You guys wanna hear the true story how Washington lost his teeth?"

They pulled into the yard of a stark white farmhouse. Alex got out and knocked on the front door. It opened a foot and he spoke with someone who remained hidden except for once when a bare arm emerged, finger pointing to the white immensity behind the house.

Bert lay on the toboggan, cocooned in the mummy bag while Alex pulled, forging ahead through knee-deep snow. Trudy followed behind the toboggan, then Harv, and Fay brought up the rear—a hundred yards back. She'd started complaining in the car that her stomach hurt but wouldn't stay behind at the farmhouse. She wouldn't try and keep up either, and Alex didn't slow the pace. The two boys were still in the farmer's yard trying to start the Ski-Doo.

Bert leaned up on an elbow. They were crossing high, rolling meadowland; wind raced over the fields, enveloping them in whirling snow so Bert could barely see Alex's back. As soon as they had left the farmer's yard it felt like they'd been dropped into the Arctic. How like Alex to get them into something like this, with a palpable hint of danger. Last winter he'd led them up Mount Abraham, lost the trail, and had to build a fire à la Jack London. Trudy, with old boots, had almost gotten frostbite. And, finally, the view from the top: pure whiteness. They'd climbed into a cloud.

Bert felt absurdly privileged, a Roman emperor being borne along. His sense of forlornness vanished. Once again he could appreciate his life—see it through Alex's eyes. The rich, solitary, subsistence. The garden. Cutting firewood—getting "heated twice" as Thoreau put it. Belonging to the food co-op. The genuineness of the hill people. Granny. Bert laughed out loud making Alex glance back, beard and mustache frosted white.

"That harp's gonna be *singing*!" he shouted over the wind.

Bert held out the whiskey but Alex shook his head. Trudy took a swallow, then Bert.

Harv came up to them. "Jesus, how much farther?"

Alex pointed to where two woodlots came nearly together, with a passage between. "Through there, I think."

Fay managed to catch them up and Harv handed her the whiskey. "It feels like we're being followed by the abdominal snowman!"

Fay took a long pull.

"If we don't spot the damn thing in ten minutes," she said, "I'm going back." Her coat was silvered, snow driven into the long fur.

"I'm glad I wore clean underwear this morning," said Harv. "When they find us in June and thaw us out—"

Fay suddenly began to cry.

Trudy touched her coat: "C'mon, we'll go back together."

"*You don't have to do anything for me*! You're all so palsy-walsy—reading from your diaries, tromping through the woods. It amazes me *you* haven't learned to yodel," she glared at Alex.

"It was your idea to come—"

"Can we mosey?" Bert asked. "The old cold's starting to seep in."

In no time Fay had fallen behind again.

The passage between the woodlots was sheltered from the wind. A little way back in the trees stood two horses: great, shaggy-coated, deep-chested beasts with wild eyes and clouds of steam hanging about their nostrils. Alex got a camera out of his backpack, but the horses bolted into the woods.

"It feels like we're on holy pilgrimage," called Trudy, "bringing the cripple to the Shrine of the Harp!"

Alex grinned over his shoulder: "The Shrine of the Miracle of the Holy Harp!"

Bert was grinning too. It felt like he was floating dreamlike through the black-and-white landscape, safe between wife and friend.

Alex shouted.

There was the harp, stark on the crest of a hill like the figurehead of a Viking ship, long snow-white hull riding behind it. It was ten times larger than a regular instrument, mounted into the wind on an outcrop of ledge.

"Do you think Fay's okay?" Harv broke the silence.

There was no sign of her.

"Fay's fine," snapped Alex. "The best thing you can do is ignore Fay."

"It's a little cold to ignore—" Harv began, when the snowmobile appeared, running toward them over the snow like a yellow bug. They could see Fay's coat bulking out on either side behind Homer.

Homer pulled up beside the toboggan, gunning the engine to keep it running. Fay was exuberant: "It's wonnnnnderful! Like riding a magic carpet!"

"What happened to Billy?" asked Harv.

"He offered the lady his seat," said Homer. "He's coming."

"Billy's a sweet fellow," said Fay.

"What about me?" Homer grinned over his shoulder.

But Fay had seen the harp: "My God, the *Grail.* Last one to it is a rotten egg!"

Homer goosed the snowmobile and it fishtailed away, Fay whooping.

Alex followed the trail the machine had broken. He hadn't gone twenty feet before Homer and Fay were already at the harp.

Homer dropped her off and disappeared over the crest. Fay waved to them, then pantomimed playing the harp, throwing back her head as though singing.

Homer reappeared and the two of them climbed onto the machine. It fled down the steep prow of the hill, wind carrying away the sound while behind a white plume fountained.

They heard a metallic humming and moaning as they came up the hill. Half the harp's wire strings had been snapped or broken, swung in the gusting wind. Someone had spray-painted graffiti on the laminated wood body.

Alex went around taking pictures from different angles. Bert climbed out of the sleeping bag to pose in his crutches. The site had been well-chosen; he climbed quickly back in to escape the wind.

Since reaching the harp, Harv had huddled away from them. Suddenly, without a word, he started back.

"Hold on!" Alex called.

"Fuck you!" yelled Harv, turning. "You dragged us out here, now we gotta get back!"

"What's your problem?" said Alex. "I didn't make anyone come."

"Right—another *experience of a lifetime*. Here we are in the middle of a goddamn icebox."

Alex raised his voice to be heard over the harp: "Sometimes you have to give yourself to something—"

"No guarantees, right?"

Alex opened his mittened hands.

"I'm fucking *here*, that's the point! I don't wanna be!"

Harv looked like he wanted to throw himself on Alex the way he leaned into the hill, face distorting in the wind.

"You're the hero. The guy who decides what to do, then sees to it everyone has a good time—come hell or high water!"

"Fine, fine." Bert could hear Alex muttering under his breath.

"And you're so fucking nice about it, no one knows they're being jerked off!"

Harv turned abruptly and stomped down the hill the way they'd come.

Trudy pulled the toboggan with Bert on it to the back side of the summit, out of the wind.

There was a pee hole. Homer had written in the snow beside it: DON'T EAT YELLOW SNOW.

Trudy sat on the toboggan with Bert while Alex dug cheese and bread out of his pack. They ate in silence. The harp whistled and whined, thundered in strong gusts, loose wires scratching and clicking.

"I wonder if he thought about casting it in concrete?" Alex asked.

"Concrete?" Trudy snorted.

"It might last that way."

"Maybe it's not supposed to last."

"He put in all this work.... It's like leaving a piano outside."

"Maybe we ought to get going?" said Bert. He couldn't stop shivering.

Alex looked at him. "You'd be in a fix if we left you here."

Bert couldn't read his expression through the frosted whiskers.

"We live such safe, predictable lives . . ." Alex flung away a rind of cheese. "Running up East Rock the other day I got hit by a car—actually just touched—I flipped over the hood, landed on my feet and kept going."

"W—w—what's the point?" Bert said through chattering teeth.

"Bert would get back on his own if he had to," said Trudy.

She pulled the toboggan to the front of the hill where it dropped steeply, kneeled behind Bert and held the rope.

They flew down silently and fast, Trudy lifting the scrolled front so no snow sheared up over them. They flew almost as if snow were air, the waxed wood planks whispering. They could crash in this softness and not be harmed.

From the top of the next rise, they saw Harv, starting through the alley between the woodlots. Trudy yelled, but he couldn't hear. The two horses had come back as if to watch him pass. Beyond, the white fields merged seamlessly into sky.

A SMALL HISTORY

The green shoot of the onion in the water glass contrasts with the snow beyond the window. Trudy lays her brush on the palette, her still life just a sketch. The stone fireplace exudes a dampness that almost makes her sob. She dresses quickly, pulling on an old parka, and is out and running up the shoveled path. The dog follows, happy to be out. To her right, cornstalks rise above the snow, marking the garden. She turns the other way and hurries up the hill road after the fresh tracks.

The late afternoon is raw, smelling of pines and earth. As if it wanted to snow again. The brook below the road runs silent under a thick ice crust. The wedge of sky above is the color of pewter; nothing moves but she and the dog.

She sees him where the iron bridge crosses the brook, Bert's red ski hat making a protest against the multiplicity of grays. He sees her and stops.

"I thought you were going to finish," he says.

"Suddenly I wanted to come. I didn't want to be left."

Bert scrapes snow from the bridge girder and clouts it into a ball, lobs it, pocking the marshmallow top of a boulder below.

"See if you can hit it," he says. But as she is packing snow, he walks away.

She catches up and they go on in silence. From the river valley comes the cry of a train approaching the trestle bridge.

"Look," Trudy says as they round a bend and see the dog waiting, "she wants to go up on the magic carpet."

A snowmobile trail comes down through the woods to the road. They often take this shortcut to the upper valley. If they could afford snowshoes that would be better because sometimes they meet the machines on the trail. They will hear them coming a long way off like a swarm of bees and must gird themselves for the encounter: the awkward glances, the dog barking as the machines funnel past, the oily stink left hanging on the air. But today, midweek, no one is out.

They climb, following the curve of a ridge. The light seems to brighten as they rise. A deer had floundered in from the side and climbed onto the packed and frozen trail; its fine pointed tracks go ahead of them. After sniffing one, the dog goes on.

They follow her out of the woods onto a meadow. The trail runs across it like a ribbon over a white-wrapped package, interrupted here and there by dark arches of blackberry canes. Trudy slows, her eyes going out to the unaccustomed distance: the encircling horizon of mountains. As if through her eyes she was breathing deeply.

Bert has halted at the soft indentation of a cellar hole. Beside it an old apple tree, trunk riddled with woodpecker holes.

"Like it's been blasted with a shotgun," he says.

"I wonder if there will be apples like last year?" Trudy says. "We still have sauce on the cellar shelves."

High, toward the head of the valley a hawk sails.

"Ready to head back?" Bert asks.

Trudy touches the old pitchfork head sticking in the tree. She had worked on a painting of it, the five tines like curving, rusty-brown finger bones.

"The last thing Riley did before leaving—" Bert mimes jabbing a pitchfork into the tree.

Trudy says nothing.

"It was a hard life."

"They made do with what they had," she says. "They had a good life—"

"It didn't last either."

A few stray flakes have begun drifting down. The dog whines.

"God," says Bert, "it's like a walk in a refrigerator."

They continue on to the Old Farm Road, open only in summer, and walk side by side on the wider snowmobile trail.

"We could try a potato field this year," Trudy says. "Get Wayne to plow that piece below the cellar hole—"

"He won't. He'd break his equipment on that stony ground."

"But it was their old garden," Trudy insists. "I bet we could get a bumper crop out of there—sell it at the farmers market in Stowe—"

"And how would we get it there?"

Silver Farm looms beside the road: a three-story frame house of weathered clapboard, swaybacked and long abandoned. Trudy named it for the tin roof. In summer they can see it from the top of Camel's Hump across the valley: a silver chip in a green sea. It's then she imagines the broken fireplace, the stained, orange-figured wallpaper losing its grip, the rusty springs of the metal bed upstairs.

Across from the building's empty windows is a small cemetery: eight or ten thin marble slabs, more fallen and sunken into the sod. An ancient, half-dead sugar maple crowns the tear-shaped plot. In summer a man comes up from town to mow it.

"Amelia, Daughter of Michael and Jennifer Riley—Died July 27, 1846—Age Six Years, Nine and a Half Months," Bert recites almost from memory from a scaling stone propped against the tree. He scrapes away snow to read the epitaph: "Youth With All Its Bloom May Drop Into the Tomb."

The snow squeaks under their boots as they walk. Trudy can hear her breathing as if seashells cupped her ears. Their breath leaves a clotted trail on the air.

"I'm going to call Jim Bain," says Bert. "Ask him about selling the cabin."

He glances at her: "With the money we could go to New Haven. We could go anywhere."

She thinks of the windows of Silver Farm, what Amelia had seen out of them when people were settling here, how it smelled of new-turned earth, fresh boards, hot bread—and the sound of voices. When people were beginning a life here.

Ahead the dog squats, drilling a hole in the track.

Bert waves an arm at the mountain: "I haven't been able to think in months. This—emptiness . . ."

Trudy presses down on the fear rising in her. "It takes sacrifice to stay—"

"We live in a different time. We don't have to put up with this."

She thinks of high hollyhocks red and yellow under the windows, nodding across the view as you looked out. Maybe a father's pant leg glimpsed through the door of the shed where he sits on a stool milking the cow.

"I'm sick of being poor. I have a college degree." Bert stops and turns to her: "We weren't born here. All this—history belongs to, to Wayne. To Granny."

"We made a start," she says quietly. "We have a small history."

They reach the place where the road leaves the upper valley, descending into the brook cut.

They start down.

Through the trees where the road curves, she can see two oxen coming up, drawing a wagon. A man, darkly dressed, walks beside them, occasionally tapping their shoulders with a stick.

She can smell the beasts, hear the creak of harness leather, see the man's breath.

JEANETTE

The air was mild. Summer had gone but autumn hadn't quite begun. Walter kneeled at his petunia bed pinching off spent blossoms and loosening the soil with a three-pronged claw. He worked deliberately, relishing the spiced smell of the bruised flowers, the limpid notes of the mockingbird in the willow, the warmth of the sun on his back. The metal tool scritch-scratching against stones.

He laid a handful of wilted pink blossoms on the porch flagstones. Inside the bay window, Jupiter hopped and turned on his perch like a wind-up canary. Jeanette had brought him with her from Paris. Jeanette asleep in the bedroom, her gold hair spread over the lace-edged pillow . . .

A heavy machine started up and then idled down. Walter frowned. The wooded hillside across the street had been slashed by a road going up to a new house over the crest. An ancient Caterpillar appeared at the top of the cut and came rumbling down, the man they called the Baked Potato at the controls. When nearly to the street he lowered the blade and began widening the turn-in to the driveway.

Walter stood up, rubbing his knees. A thin mustache now lined his upper lip, while his sideburns, dyed dark, had been trimmed below his earlobes. He looked ten years younger than his sixty-four years, Jeanette said. He took a cigarette from the pack in his shirt pocket and lit it, watched the smoke drift in a little cloud across the front yard.

The bulldozer was pushing against a young black thorn tree, steel treads grinding around in place. As the tree went over, the machine rode up, crushing it flat.

Walter sat on the bottom porch step. He could smell Jeanette's perfume rising off his chest. He brought his fingers to his nostrils, but they smelled of earth now. She shimmered in his mind like light off water. He recalled Paris, the little restaurant . . .

They were making love in his hotel, the opened windows looking across a boulevard lined with plane trees, when Walter became so overwhelmed he passed out. "I guess we were both hungry," Jeanette laughed afterward, gartering a stocking. "You know, I haven't made love in eight months?" She had said it surprised, so ingenuous, as though usually she made love quite often, as a matter of fact, and he was utterly charmed and a little put out.

A big yellow school bus ground uphill past the house. A woman with a nimbus of frizzy hair and horn-rims drove, while an older man sat in the bench seat behind her. A new driver out practicing on Saturday. It struck Walter how much they looked like school bus drivers. Bert, on the other hand, the year he'd driven one up in Vermont, had somehow looked like an imposter. Beard and long hair. Now, in New Haven, he was a "security guard" at a college. An even more unlikely role.

Walter flicked his cigarette into the driveway where it lay, lifting a thin thread of smoke.

Bert and Trudy hadn't been over since June and the unfortunate business with Emma's furniture. But Bert had realized his blunder, done his best to make up with Jeanette. Walter felt the incident had smoothed over. He was looking forward to having the kids for Christmas. Jeanette would show off her culinary art with salmon stuffed with escargots or such, and a *bûche de Noël*! No goose with prune stuffing this year, Bert old boy.

Walter smiled, then laughed aloud. Ah, Jeanette. He was crazy for her foreignness—unshaven armpits and French *parfum*, her tiny underwear, the yellow rubber gloves she donned to wash dishes. Each new thing he discovered—her skill at chess, her love of ballet—delighted him and added to the feeling that he had struck a great bargain. Unlike Emma, Jeanette was his equal. She even made love on top!

The bulldozer had stopped. "Tink, tink, tink," went the metal cap on the vertical exhaust pipe. Baked Potato had climbed down and was kicking at the tread. He got a hammer out of the toolbox and began hitting a jammed rock. He was probably Walter's age, with a squat pumpkin head always covered by a baseball cap. His thick chest melded into a grain-sack stomach perched on a pair of thin bowed legs. A Baked Potato on Skewers. He disliked the man, who seemed inhuman—an extension of his brutal machine. And it was he, if only as agent of the owner, but it was he who had cut the gash across the formerly pristine hillside so that every time Walter glanced out his front window he felt a jab of irritation.

With a whoosh of bluish exhaust the bulldozer surged ahead. The man pulled carelessly at the levers, making the machine turn, stop, back, pirouette. The antediluvian Caterpillar with its skin of muck and rust, worn-smooth silver treads, gat-toothed bucket-maw . . . Walter caught whiffs of the thing, like rancid body odor.

"Bonjour."

Jeanette stood in the open porch door wearing the black silk kimono with huge cerise peonies. Her hair was pinned up in a bun, several strands having escaped to nestle against her nape. Without makeup her face looked almost more handsome than beautiful.

"Bonjour," Walter replied, smiling. "You're up early."

"Who can sleep with that?" She gestured with her coffee mug.

"Old Baked Potato doesn't run on Standard Time."

Jeanette carried one of the porch chairs out into the sun in the front yard. Walter took another and sat beside her. Jeanette sipped her coffee. One silver, open-toed slipper dangled off the end of her small foot. Her toenails were bright red. Her kimono had fallen open slightly, and Walter could see one of her breasts. He smiled, trying to imagine Emma sitting practically nude in their front yard with painted toenails.

The man on the bulldozer was glancing over.

"What's on tap for today?" Walter asked.

"We have to shop—your Dean of Faculty and his wife? Supper?"

"Oh, damn."

"How does *blanquette de veau* sound, a nice salad—where on earth can we find radicchio?"

"He related to Pinocchio?"

Jeanette swatted at Walter.

Mr. Gilroy's blue cap appeared to be floating across the end of the lawn. The postman came into view beneath it, laboring up the walk from the lower village.

Walter went down to intercept him, returning with several magazines, which he gave to Jeanette, and a letter.

"From Bert."

He sat and opened it. Jeanette paged through a magazine.

After a moment, Walter folded the note and tucked it into his pocket.

"They'd like to come next weekend."

"Oh?"

"We haven't seen them since—"

"Three months. It was horrible." Jeanette closed the magazine.

"I thought it was all patched up?"

Jeanette said nothing.

"You and Bert are like sister and brother. A little friction is inevitable—"

"We are *not* brother and sister. I am eleven years older than Bert." Jeanette gazed at the veins on the back of her hand. "I feel like the horse put out with nothing to do but eat all the hay. Wonderful, delicious hay, but . . . They are at the beginning of their life, struggling—it feels like I am finished, waiting to die." She paused. "All my life I worked."

"Did you trade beauty and youth for an old man and security?" Walter asked dryly.

"I love you. That is why I married. Why I left France. And you are not old—I forbid you saying that."

Walter touched his mustache with the back of a finger. It persisted above his lip like a dab of mustard. The mustache and sideburns had been Jeanette's idea; she'd even dyed them. He looked like a Spanish don, she said.

"What's the matter?" he asked gently.

"He throws his mother at me." Her voice was a little breathless. "Emma's cooking. The bundle of her wonderful letters he is dying to read to me. The wonderful vacations the three of you—"

"But that's Bert—"

"When he comes, he says, I am her son. My papa is her husband. Who are you, you interloper?"

Walter rubbed the side of his jaw.

"He makes her like the Holy Ghost—coming to appear any minute. Does he even think? I am nervous in this place. I miss my sons, my language, even my stupid little job *au bureau*."

Walter leaned across and took Jeanette's hand. "You're doing a terrific job of adjusting—"

She took her hand back. "I feel fake talking *anglais* all the time. I have nothing in common. There is no arugula, no cilantro—your professors and their little wives—I want to pull their dresses up!"

Walter couldn't help a chuckle—

"*You don't know!* I want to feel where I live is mine. I want to feel safe."

"But, darling, you *are* safe."

"Ten years ago my husband disappeared—poof! I don't know where he is to this day. I raise my boys alone. I don't want to marry anyone. I don't want to come here. I was doing fine—"

"And along I come, fall in love and—"

"Maybe it's a mistake . . ."

"Bert and Trudy adore you. They're happy I found someone."

"What about the furniture?"

Walter fixed his gaze on a blown dandelion at the edge of the lawn.

"The *look* he gives me when they walk in that door." Jeanette's green eyes flashed. "That I *antique* his mother's precious colonial furniture! I should go into a church and pee! I was ready to chop that furniture and make a fire! I can't sit on it but I want to *itch*—"

"That furniture means nothing to me!" Walter's voice rose in frustration. "It is something to sit on—eat off. Let's get rid of it—"

"How many meals did she serve on that table? How many *roast gooses*? How many times on her hands and knees polishing so she can see her round little face? I am fighting for my life—"

Walter reached for her and stopped.

"Emma spoiled you rotten. You don't know how to treat a woman. You think it's all bang-bang and then you sit back. Well I'm a human being, and you are getting off your pedestal or looking for another wife!"

Jeanette was standing, her face flushed.

Walter got up uncertainly.

Jeanette touched her throat, then ran into the house.

Walter stared after her, stunned. It felt as though a swarm of midges was hovering before him preventing him from seeing something. He sat down. The incident three months ago over the furniture. Bert, claiming he wasn't shocked by the antiquing because it was his mother's furniture, but—for Chrissake!—because—authentic colonial furniture—was not . . . Bert had actually used the word "obscene" while gesturing at the blue-and-white-streaked hutch Jeanette had painted. All he needed was a pointer to be delivering a snotty art lecture—with Jeanette boiling over.

Walter jumped as the front door slammed. Jeanette was halfway down the walk to the garage, wearing her French jeans and red silk blouse. A blue scarf around her neck as though she were one of those Apache dancers.

He watched their silver Jaguar exit the garage, tires chirping, and vanish up the hill road.

Walter went inside. He brought a mug of coffee into the living room and sat in Emma's old rocker. He had intended to sell the furniture when he moved from the old place. But this house was empty and he would have to buy all new furniture. In the end it was simpler to keep everything.

Jupiter kept hopping and turning in front of the bay window—Walter felt a sudden impulse to wring its neck—filthy bird, never sang, never sat still. Emma had had an abhorrence to caged birds. Walter pulled the rocker closer to the window, shutting the canary out. Em used to sit for hours beside the window in the old house the month before she went into the hospital. Her plump, pink-fingered hands—used to kneading dough, stuffing chickens, darning socks—grown thin and blue-veined. That was the image that most persisted of his wife who had been with him for so long, had been young with him in his youth: emaciated hands dangling off the rocker arms.

He'd been blind, assuming Jeanette was as happy as he. She'd been the one to make the sacrifices. Given up job, friends. Her mother and father still lived outside Paris, her teenage sons who would soon be joining them. What had he given her in exchange?

He loved her. He thought that was everything. Well, recognizing a problem was the first step in solving it. Perhaps a dozen roses . . .

Framed in the window, the bulldozer looked like a toy. It reminded Walter of the World War I tank he'd had as a boy. He could see it perfectly: a dark brown oval, like a large bar of soap, same top and bottom, key sticking out the side, treads like fan belts inside out. No gun. The tank ground slowly forward riding over almost anything, and if it flipped over, it kept going.

The bulldozer lurched down in front, almost lazily, but the whiplash lifted the operator out of his seat and tossed him up onto the hood. The man hung there for a moment like a fat jockey straddling it, then fell off the side onto the turning tread. The bulldozer continued forward slowly. The Baked Potato was carried along the wide steel tread as though on a conveyor belt. He struggled clumsily; he would be dropped off the front and run over by the machine. He grabbed a strut holding the blade, which was up, and hung on while the rest of him rode to the very edge of the turning tread. He looked like a man hanging onto a branch over a waterfall.

Almost the moment the man had landed on the moving tread, Walter was out of his chair. He sprinted across the lawn and reached the bulldozer as it bumped out into the street, treads clattering. He scrambled up over the back and into the seat. The man was clutching on ten feet away, staring at him with fixed concentration, kicking his legs to keep from being pulled under. Walter had never operated a bulldozer: he yanked at the levers. The thing instantly stopped and its blade rose a foot. The Baked Potato lost his hold. He was sitting dazed in the road, leaning on one hand, his hat still on, when Walter came around. The bulldozer loomed above roaring and shuddering as though it wanted to annihilate them.

"Are you all right?" Walter shouted. "Can we get you out of the road?"

The man looked up stupidly, then took Walter's hand. When they reached the bank, he sank down staring at the ground.

Walter went into the street to wave a truck around the bulldozer. He switched off the machine. When he came back, the old man was holding out a folded scrap of paper, flat and shiny from being in his pocket. A phone number and a woman's name had been printed in large letters on the paper.

Walter was sitting in his lawn chair when the Jaguar turned into the driveway.

Jeanette came up the walk hugging a bag of groceries.

"I found nice pâté and cheeses," she said, "and a frozen baguette, of all things."

"Please, come here." Walter patted the chair beside him.

"I wrote," he said. "I told them not to come."

Jeanette shrugged. "Ça va. I've gotten over it."

"I told him they're not welcome here until further notice."

Jeanette sat in the other chair, holding the bag in her lap.

"The thing is, I'm not his father anymore. I'm your husband."

The bulldozer was parked at an angle on the bank across the street. The woman on the slip of paper had come and backed it up there. A pattern of half-inch gouges was left in the macadam street surface. The woman had said nothing, asked no questions about the accident. Walter thought she might be retarded. The old man had climbed into the pickup on his own, and she drove off. Not a word from him, either.

Jeanette lit a cigarette. "He'll blame me, you know."

NEW HAVEN

NEW HAVEN

1

Trudy was standing at the kitchen window when Frank came out of the garage pulling a wagon with a pickax, shovel, and fifth of Canadian Club in it. Their landlord was small and finely boned, reminding Trudy of a midget though Frank wasn't that small. He wore a tight, sleeveless undershirt that showed his ribs thin as a chicken's. Wide-legged filthy linen pants and patent leather shoes that had once been white completed his outfit. He was sockless. Frank's five o'clock shadow had lengthened over a week into a salt-and-pepper rime. He halted under the catalpa tree that grew out of the hedge between his and Greenwald's backyards. The branches were completely sheared off on Frank's side. A month ago it had looked like a cartoon tree sliced in half, but suckers had sprouted from the amputations, blurring the clean profile.

She had to get ready for the interview. Bert had already gone to Manpower. Yesterday, with fifteen other indigent souls, he'd swept the Yale Bowl. The day before unloaded trucks at a warehouse in East Haven. Since arriving in New Haven, they had yet to turn up real jobs. Trudy was on a waiting list for work at the Yale Library and another for substitute teaching.

She heated her coffee and came back to the window. Frank was swinging the pickax plucking up little clumps of red hard-packed earth. The tool looked too big for him. Frank's porcelain doll face shone with a sickly pallor. He worked like a robot, dully, without force. He was still drunk, Trudy realized.

When Bert and she had gotten back from the movie last night, Frank was on the front porch with George, passing the bottle. His chair was propped against the door that led up to their second-floor apartment. Frank had demanded the overdue rent—or, he said, they would sleep in the street. He was doing them a favor. He didn't need to rent the place at all.

Bert said they would have the money in a week, and Frank laughed. "Maybe we ought to take it out in trade," he said, looking at Trudy. George had stood up then and pulled Frank in his chair out of the doorway.

Frank knocked himself over bringing the pickax up too fast, sat on the ground wiping his hands on his undershirt. He reached for the bottle. He'd all but told them he was drinking himself to death that night he rented them the apartment. His wife had died six months ago of cancer and since then he stopped caring about anything.

"I do three things," Frank said. "I fish, I fly, and I drink."

His flying license had been suspended because of drinking. He'd nearly wrecked a Cessna on takeoff. The closest Frank got to fishing was telling Bert he'd take him out one of these days. He was concentrating on his drinking.

The catalpa's reflection lay flat and unwavering in Frank's swimming pool. One of the big leaves floated, its stem a rudder. The tree dropped leaves, twigs, pods, bugs, bark, and once a squirrel into Frank's pool.

That spring he had announced to Greenwald through the hedge that he was cutting the goddamn thing down. Greenwald explained that the tree provided his backyard with shade; moreover, it was a kind of memorial to his wife, who had first discovered the sapling growing in the hedge and encouraged it.

"Ginny dead?" Frank had blurted stupidly.

Greenwald said if Frank cut the tree, he would sue.

Frank spread rock salt and DeCon around the base of the tree on his side and watered it with kerosene. Greenwald countered with fertilizer, mulch and water on his side. The tree seemed unaffected by either treatment.

Then Frank hired the "Tree Doctor," who performed radical surgery with a chain saw. To no lasting effect.

Trudy took her new dress out of the closet: cream-colored silk with black polka dots the size of dimes, puff sleeves. She put it on. The cut was old fashioned with a ruffled front, while the skirt showed a lot of leg. She had bought the dress, justifying it as an interview investment. Too hot for stockings. Trudy put on the white heels—her wedding shoes—and studied herself in the mirror. She twisted her thick hair up; neck and shoulders were attractively bared, but she didn't like the focus given her strong jaw. She let the hair fall. What did she look like? Beautiful, as Bert sometimes said? Ugly, as she thought, seeing her features transform with fatigue and discouragement into her mother's? How did a pretty woman like Fay see her?

"Hold it right there. Now turn around, slow." The man behind the enormous mahogany desk spoke in a hoarse whisper. The desk was bare except for a glass of carrot juice on a coaster.

Trudy halted halfway across the room and, feeling silly, turned around once: soft lighting, a bar, zebra throw rugs, chrome sling chairs . . .

"I'm Arty."

The man beckoned to a chair beside the desk. He was small, thin, Mediterranean, pitted face, olive-black eyes.

"Twenty-eight, a hundred and thirty pounds, thirty-five, twenty-four, thirty-six."

Trudy laughed. She had never been assessed quite so directly—or accurately.

"You can lose five, eight pounds," said the man. "A month of massage'll take care of that."

"I thought *I* did the massaging," Trudy joked. The dress was perfect.

The man didn't smile. "Ever work as a masseuse?" He pronounced it "mah-soooze."

"Not professionally, but—"

"You read a hippy book, worked your boyfriend over a couple times."

Arty stared at her. "You gotta have three things here: looks, give a great massage, and enjoy—I repeat—*enjoy*, treating a man like a king. Now, tell me you're a libber and stop wasting both our time."

"I can handle those requirements," said Trudy in a level tone.

He toyed with the gold medallion dangling against his hairless chest. "At Arty's Adult World, you do four, maybe five guys a shift. You move meat. Ever massage three hundred and fifty pounds?"

Trudy just widened her eyes slightly.

"What kind of client? Jew, black, dago—"

"All kings."

Arty managed the hint of a smile. "We get lawyers, bankers, and we get guys you don't ask what they are. They're all equal wore-out sons of bitches, and we renew 'em."

He let his gaze rise to the ceiling, a sea of lashing stucco. "You're gonna have to deal with hard-ons."

"My husband gets an erection sometimes when I'm massaging him. When I massage, I massage."

Arty's eyes fell back to Trudy. "What if he gets fresh? If he wants, uh—"

"I assume you have a bouncer."

"We don't insult the customer until he deserves it. You're gonna have to get your hair cut; blonde rinse; fingernails short—and lose the wedding band." Arty stared at Trudy a moment. "I started a girl at my New London club—college girl like you. She was swell until it came to putting a guy's shoes on. I think she'd rather give him a blow job than tie his shoes. Out. Whatever they want, we give 'em—within bounds."

Trudy smiled. "I was beginning to wonder if there were any."

"The state licenses us and this is a strictly massage and health club. A woman touches a guy, it's natural he gets aroused. But there's no touch-a-da-penis. I gotta tell you there are some wheels in this town don't want an Arty's. So we watch our p's and q's. There's a monitor in every room, and I'm on it. No dates. I catch a girl giving out her real name or telephone—" Arty made the throat-cutting gesture. "Legal, Peaceful, and Sexy, that's our motto."

Arty held up a nylon "baby-doll" outfit of the same light blue material as his shirt. "The uniform. Sexy but you can't see through the crotch, and the bra's snug so you can work without the boobs falling out. You play pool?"

A phone rang and Arty picked a receiver out of a desk drawer. After a few words in Italian, he hung up.

"I'm offering a human service here. That's why I'm into massage. A girl works here gotta feel the same way."

The room was tiled in flamingo-pink. A massage table stood in the middle; against the wall, a slatted bench with towels. Warm, moist air circulated. Trudy felt comfortable in the scanty blue uniform. "Take Me Home, Country Roads" on strings came out of hidden wall speakers.

Arty massaged unhurriedly, his hands seeming to sink below her muscles and lift them up toward the light. Trudy relaxed, letting go of everything but the pleasure. He unzipped the back of her uniform to massage her back.

"Take Me Home, Country Roads" flowed into "Do You Know the Way to San Jose."

Arty rolled her over and massaged her temples, cheeks and cheekbones, her eyes, pressing lightly on the sides of the balls as though he might ease them out to be cleaned. He massaged her nose, ears, chin, lips, pulling them away from the teeth so they made a faint suck. Arty rolled her head in his hands, supporting its weight.

Trudy opened her eyes dreamily: he was all concentration, shining with a light patina of sweat as he massaged her breasts, stomach, hips, the soft inner lengths of her thighs.

Frank stood in the kidney-shaped hole up to his belly, swinging a hammer, claw-end first. The almost-empty whiskey bottle lay on its side within reach. The pool's aquamarine bottom had orange spots where clods of dirt had pitched in and lay dissolving. Frank ducked and came up with a coffee can full of soil, which he dumped onto the pile. There was a new ax propped against the tree trunk; in the grass lay a three-foot chunk of root, chopped off at both ends. It looked like a human thigh.

"See any Chinamen, yet?" Trudy called. She held a *New Haven Register*, picked up on the way back from Arty's.

Frank didn't look up. He was pounding with the hammer again, clearing dirt from around another root.

Trudy went upstairs, spread the *Register* on the kitchen table, and sat, studying the Help Wanted ads. She'd circled "Hostess" at a Friendly's opening in Branford when she noticed a movement at a second-story window next door. Greenwald sat there behind the venetian blinds smoking a cigar and watching Frank.

After putting the tuna casserole in the oven, Trudy set the table. The evening sun was plating Greenwald's windows so she couldn't tell if he was still there. Frank was in the hole, chopping with the axe, each blow making the broad heart-shaped leaves above tremble.

"He could have been making love to me. It was incredible."

Bert swallowed his mouthful of tuna casserole. "Not quite your average interview."

"The man is a master, Bert. He looks like a mafioso, but with the most amazing hands. He *believes* in massage—that he's actually doing good in the world."

Bert helped himself to more casserole.

"It was like—a meditation—"

"Yeah, well, I struck out. Six hours sitting around Manpower. The guy doling out jobs works for Kafka."

"Arty said he's willing to give me a try."

Bert looked at her.

"There's a week's training—at half pay. Arty chooses eight girls from the twelve that start. The tips are where—"

"Come on. A *massage parlor*?"

"People thought chiropractors were quacks twenty years ago."

"Chiropractors don't massage you in sexy little outfits. In fact, I think they're men."

A hair was curving out of Bert's left nostril like a tusk. Trudy heard Minnie, Frank's miniature poodle, click across the linoleum in the kitchen below.

"We need the money," she said. "It's physical work. I don't see what's wrong—"

"Did you *want* the guy to fuck you?"

Trudy took the dishes to the sink and began washing them. Bert came up behind and slid his arms around her waist.

"I'm sorry. That was stupid."

"Were you ever *in* a massage parlor?"

"You're dealing with human nature. I would not get very relaxed with a beautiful woman in a nightie feeling me up."

He slid his hands up, cupping her breasts; she twisted away, spattering soap suds.

"It just seemed," she said, "for a brief while this afternoon, I had an innocent, relaxing, renewing, sensual experience. And that I could possibly do that for others. Thanks for setting me straight."

Trudy sat up in bed. She'd been aware for some time of Minnie yapping downstairs, the sound relentlessly penetrating her pillow. The dog released a string of yips climaxing in a thin howl, a ridiculous imitation of a coyote.

"Goddammit!" Bert sat up.

Frank's front door was ajar, the acrid-musky reek of his cats streaming out. Bert pushed the door open; from over his shoulder, Trudy could see Frank, who looked like he'd nose-dived into the overstuffed chair. He lay stiffly, arms hooked over the sides of the chair, and appeared to be looking closely at the seat. Frank was dressed for digging, except now he was shoeless, his bare soles red from the soil. A table lamp cast a sepia glow over the scene, like an illustration from an antique book. Minnie had been whimpering since they'd come down. Bert touched Frank's bare shoulder and pulled his hand back quickly. The side of the chair Frank lay in looked like shredded wheat from the cats sharpening their claws.

The daughter came with her boyfriend in a pickup to clean out the apartment. She had inherited the house. She planned to renovate then rent Frank's apartment. She came each day for a week and cleaned, hauling stuff away in the pickup. Whenever the furnace went on, they could smell Frank's cat-musty apartment breathing out the warm air registers. Frank's ghost, Bert called it.

The catalpa vanished. Without consulting anyone, the daughter had it removed. The boyfriend came with a bulldozer and filled in the swimming pool. She took Minnie.

A young couple with an infant daughter moved into Frank's apartment. After a month it seemed they had always been there. Or Frank never had. The two cats had disappeared.

2

"He comes home *reeking* of her! I'm in the middle of a soap opera!" Fay paused to catch her breath. "It feels like a hot mustard plaster on my chest! Alex is seeing this, this—*poet*, and—he actually said this to me—'Wouldn't it be great if the two of you could get to know one another?' He wants to be married to me and to—fuck this woman!"

Fay put her face in her hands and sobbed at the kitchen table across from Bert.

He rubbed his ear. He felt awkward because he'd known about Alex and the poet Jamie for a while.

Fay's pretty oval face was tearstained and puffy; her hair, always impeccably groomed, was a tangle. She had come over in her nightgown and robe.

She took a sip of coffee and choked: "I should be Lillian—go out and *fuck* whoever I please! How about it, Bert? Oh, but what would you want with an ugly, stupid—" She burst into a hysterical laugh.

Bert reached across the kitchen table and patted her hand. "Come on, you're an attractive—"

She snatched her hand back. "I'm not a slut—that's the problem. If this were a play—but it's not, this is . . . Alex would prefer a slut. He would feel less guilty. But, thing is, he *doesn't* feel guilty! My head's going to explode!"

Bert desperately wished Trudy were back.

"Lillian's having this *thing* with the carpenter who's renovating their bathrooms. I've seen him—tall, blond, ponytail—a Greek god. No, truly, I admire Lillian. She and Maurice have the perfect marriage—three beautiful girls, plenty of money, and Maurice is the sweetest, most decent—"

"Yeah, well," said Bert. "You gotta wonder how Maurice feels."

"He doesn't *know* anything! And what you don't know . . . Alex tells *me* everything. He thinks we ought to be one happy family. Well, let's see what happy family he gets when I start fucking someone!" Fay's face blazed: she gripped the coffee mug and glared out the window. Greenwald was raking his backyard.

A month ago, Bert passed the Lincoln Theater when Alex came out with his arm around a woman. He introduced Jamie. The three of them went to Clark's for coffee. Alex was in a goofy mood, improvising dialogue between the salt and pepper shakers. Jamie was alternately silent or hyper, talking in a tough voice with plenty of "fucks" thrown in. She'd written a book called *Whore Tense* about her time turning tricks as an eighteen-year-old. She was thin, sharp-featured with huge, deep brown eyes with long soft lashes. At Alex's urging, Jamie recited a poem. She was staring so intensely at Bert that he had no idea what she was saying.

"Did you know about this—*affair*?" Fay was looking at him accusingly.

Intending to lie, Bert told the truth.

"Jesus Christ. And Trudy?"

Bert opened his hands helplessly.

"Oh, I'm sure many enlightened people have wonderful *ménages à trois*. But I am a ridiculous—pitiful—stupid—*monogamist*!"

3

The ballet school's appearance in the weekend arts fair had been scheduled for eleven o'clock Sunday morning.

Alex picked Bert and Trudy up and they walked downtown to the Arts Center. A warm, hazy October morning. Ahead of them, a woman with three little girls in pink tutus got out of a car and hurried along the sidewalk. Alex was talking wistfully about how he would be hunting pheasants right now back in Montana. There was a distant, nasal whine of bagpipes.

Bert recognized Jamie standing on the steps of the old synagogue, the Arts Center annex where the dance concert was being held. She wore her "bag of poems," a faded Army knapsack.

"I'm reading at two today," Jamie said. "New shit."

"We'll try and catch it," said Bert, avoiding Trudy's look.

Jamie put her arms around Alex and kissed him.

A piano started up inside.

"Why don't you come in with us?" Alex asked Jamie.

She just gave a snort and walked away down the steps.

Lillian sat at a studio piano to the right side of the stage, playing a Chopin mazurka. Her eyes were closed, head nodding to the music. Lillian was the ballet school's accompanist.

Bert counted eighteen people, all parents, scattered among the two hundred chairs. Fay came out in front of the curtains to welcome them and make announcements about the winter schedule. She looked great in tights—long legs, small behind, perfect petite figure, animated oval face with green eyes, and that waterfall of chestnut hair. She was, Bert realized, beautiful. Alex, on the other hand, looked like he went to hippy school instead of Yale Law. Army fatigue pants and a flannel shirt, shoulder-length reddish-brown hair grading into a curly untrimmed beard. A lumbering bumpkin—except for the blue eyes iced with intelligence behind granny glasses.

Fay disappeared and the curtains opened: twelve little girls in pink tutus posed with arms above their heads. Lillian nodded, came down on the keys, and they began scurrying and leaping more or less to the music. At one point Fay danced with the girls, looking like a fairy godmother on points with wand and wings. She didn't look like a woman with a broken heart.

"I could get into dancing," Alex was saying as they stood outside waiting for Fay and Lillian. "It's a discipline, like running. I think I could be a professional dancer."

"Fay would just love that," said Trudy.

"We saw an Astaire-Rogers movie a couple weeks ago," Alex said. "They get out of a buggy and start dancing in Central Park. I asked Fay if she thought she and I could do that." He tugged at his beard and chuckled. "I guess I'm more the Gene Kelly type."

Fay and Lillian with her three daughters came out and they all walked over to the arts fair.

The plaza between the annex and new Arts Center had been set up with tables of pottery, batiks, carvings, jewelry, etc., all made at the Center and for sale.

Maurice showed up to take the girls to a post-performance party.

It was hot. Bert sat on a bench under a tree guarding the ceramic frog planter Lillian had bought.

He could see her across the plaza holding a tie-dye shirt against her chest for Fay's opinion. Lillian was working her way through the fair like a housewife at a yard sale. She caught Bert's eye and pointed toward the Arts Center.

"Go ahead." He waved back.

Lillian wore a long black skirt, black sleeveless blouse, her black hair flowed unbound to the middle of her back. Something of a witch, Bert thought. Lillian had always struck him as smug and superior; it was amusing to think of her having a "torrid affair" with a handsome young carpenter.

He picked up the planter and walked over to the Arts Center; inside, Lillian hoisted a huge, apple-green glazed bowl to look at the bottom. She had strong arms, blunt fingers.

"You *threw* this, Marge?" she was saying.

"Five tries," said the porcine woman perched on a stool across the table.

Lillian held the bowl clasped against her stomach.

"That suits you," Bert said.

"How do you know what suits me?"

"You look like you should be . . . bearing olives, or something." He hardly knew what he was saying.

Jamie's reading was underway in the basement of the annex. Bert slipped in and sat in the back row. There was a scattering of people, including Alex. Jamie was striding back and forth on the little stage declaiming a poem about being abused by a man.

There was brief applause when Jamie finished; without acknowledging it, she walked past the audience up the aisle and out the door. Alex followed.

A rumpled bulk of a man with nearly white hair came out onto the stage. He wore a seersucker suit with tie and looked about sixty. Hugo Penny, the program said, story writer, teacher in Connecticut's Artists in the Schools. A thin young man with string tie and ponytail came on to introduce him.

Not wanting to bump into Alex and Jamie, Bert decided to stay for one story.

Fairfield Ballentine, the young man, in a self-deprecating sort of way informed the audience he would be publishing a collection of Penny's stories. There would be a book-signing party after Christmas at the Step Down Coffeehouse. Bert caught "Kerouac," "Beat Generation," "down and out in Greenwich Village," from Ballentine's rambling speech.

Hugo Penny loomed over the podium as though he might crush and smother it, his soft white hands dangling over the front.

"I lived in 'Frisco those days. My hand had developed a semi-permanent curve from accommodating the bottle . . ." Penny's left hand came to life, curving around the imaginary bottle.

It took Bert a few minutes to realize the man was telling a story, not extemporizing. Penny remained leaning forward over the podium talking, while his hands, like Bunraku dolls, performed a sort of delicate accompanying mime. Pale and fleshy-faced, with hooded eyes, sharp nose and thin-lipped, sensual mouth, Penny's head hung above his hands like a sly Wizard of Oz. He told his tales with a raconteur's instinct for emphasis and understatement. Bert found himself leaning forward, caught up in the short fables. They didn't so much end as hang shimmering after Penny's voice had died and the hands made a little orchestral signature of *fini*.

Between stories, Bert moved several rows closer. Penny was not as old as he looked; it was startling to realize he had once been handsome. A tall young woman sat in the front row, her attention riveted on the author.

After Penny's last story, one about riding a bicycle from New York to Philadelphia during the Depression to see a girl, Bert went up and shook his hand, complimenting his work.

"That's very kind, very kind," said Penny, gripping Bert's hand while giving him a penetrating look. "This is Christine," he introduced the tall woman.

"Isn't he *wonderful*?" said Christine, a little breathlessly. "Hugo is coming into his own at last. Wait till you hear his Greenwich Village stories!" She was a head taller than Penny, a willowy, high-foreheaded woman with protuberant eyes and a full mouth. Bert decided Scandinavian. "Oh, Hugo!" she exclaimed giving him a kiss.

Hugo Penny winked at Bert. "The power of the written word, my boy—look out!" And he laughed—a wheezy, lecherous, haystack of a laugh that, when Bert laughed in response, flared yet higher and left him gasping.

He drew a handful of letters from his inner coat pocket, selected one and handed it to Bert. "Henry Miller. I'm using a quote from that letter on the dust jacket of my book. I met him a couple times in the Village, and once, when I was hitching through Carmel, he put me up. I'll never forget this—he handed me twenty dollars, and you know what he said? *Don't pay me back. Pass it on to someone who needs it.*"

Penny took back the letter, tucked it carefully back into his pocket. "You're a writer."

Startled, Bert said, "Well . . . I try."

"We're gonna grab a coffee in Clark's. You'll join us?"

"Please do," said Christine, whose enthusiasm now extended to Bert.

"I'd like to but, unfortunately, I've gotta . . . Security guard at Saint Theresa's College," he added almost apologetically.

"Ah—Saint Vaginas," cracked Hugo. "I taught a fictitious workshop there."

"It's never been the same," laughed Christine.

"Seriously, man, we've got to get you onto the Artists in the Schools gravy train. Call Barry Turpin at the Commission on the Arts in Hartford—mention my name. I'll drop him a note when I get home."

They were standing under a tree in the middle of the arts fair. Penny had taken his jacket off. The armpits of his shirt were dark with sweat, the shirt frayed at collar and cuffs.

"You know," he said, staring at the crowd, "for twenty bucks, I'd pour wine on my hair, stand out there and *sing*?" He laughed. "I'm just a third-rate hack looking for a meal ticket . . ." He glanced sharply at Bert, then a sly expression stole over his features. "I'm writing like a razor, man. I don't know whether it's good or what, but it's coming—straight out of my *cock*!"

"I'll bring the car around," said Christine. She smiled at Hugo and walked away.

Penny watched her go, speaking to Bert: "I'm almost fifty and things are finally happening. Five years ago—I'd have killed my mother for a drink. Now all I want is enough time to tell my stories. To *write them*, man. Fairfield Ballentine may be a queer little prick but he's giving me a break. A *book*. Do you know what a book is? Interviews, teaching gigs, readings, a *second book*—no one can take a book away from you. There are pricks in this world who love nothing better than destroying an artist. Her husband—" Penny indicated the receding figure of Christine—"is one, a Yale professor, a literary critic who has been sitting on the jakes trying to squeeze out a novel for ten years—" He broke off with a snort. "What do you think of Christine? She wants my body—" He laughed his wheezing laugh. "But I'm not Tarzan—I can only get it up eight times a night!" Abruptly he became sober: "She was a student of mine at Quinnipiac. I haven't had a beautiful woman look at me in . . . Christine's just a friend, you dig. Her old man's helping me out. A workshop at Yale. You'll meet Victor. One of the tenured eunuchs in a pipe and tweed jockstrap who holds forth like he got it from God. Victor would be an artist, failing that he sucks their cocks. But he's a good guy. Says I'll get a workshop up there after the book's out."

Penny was silent, brooding. Then he glanced at Bert: "Seriously, man, what do you think of her?"

4

"Always wear the cap. That way the girls know who you are. But—more important—the nuns. Nuns like uniforms. It's built into them."

Captain Wovell panted as he and Bert climbed the grassy slope toward the Victorian mansion that housed Saint Theresa's Science Department. Wovell was a short, heavy man, with a military straightness of the spine; he seemed to roll forward on bowed legs. He made a great motion of walking, without, however, advancing very quickly. A stout neck supported a round head topped by a blue guard's cap with abundant gold braid on the bill. Silver captain's bars were affixed to the shoulder loops of his uniform.

"Wait a minute," he called, and stopped to catch his breath. He was taking Bert on the official tour of the rounds of Saint Theresa's. Bert had already worked two weeks breaking in with one of the other guards. This was the first time he'd met Captain Wovell. They had spoken over the phone, during which Wovell had hired Bert right off the bat.

"Key station's in back of Science Hall." Wovell pointed at the building they were approaching.

"I think it's on the side," said Bert. He was carrying the time clock, bandolier-style. Each building on campus had a key station, either inside or out. The guard, making his hourly rounds, punched the clock with the different key at each station.

"I'm going to give you a lesson in human psychology," said Wovell. "You drink coffee out of your thermos, right? Watch this:" Wovell mimed unscrewing the lid of an imaginary thermos bottle. Then, bottle held to his lips, he rotated his head slowly in an arc of a hundred and twenty degrees, squinting narrowly the while.

"How about that?" he said. "You're checking out the situation at the same time you're drinking coffee. You know what that says, Staubie? Here is a man one hundred and ten percent on the job! The nuns eat it up."

Wovell lurched into motion again, up the sward.

"Watch yourself when you have to go into a dorm. They're full of women. You might see tits, one in her panties. I'm not saying they could sue, but—don't go into the dorms, they're off-limits."

"What about an emergency?"

"What I'm saying is you can see anything you want. You act like you don't see shit. Right?"

"Right."

"Next thing is Blacks. We're surrounded here, Staubie. Niggertown comes up three sides of the campus. This is a DMZ. Blacks and rich bitches—if you think an old brick wall with a string of barb wire across the top will keep 'em apart, well . . ."

Wovell watched while Bert punched the clock on the side of Science Hall. They walked toward the nuns' dormitory.

"I'll tell you something," said the Captain. "Saint Theresa's never had security before Wovell Systems came in. The nuns were too damn cheap—janitors had to chase the muggers."

"Trouble," said Bert.

Wovell rolled his eyes. "You probably read about the rape last spring? We've had bee-bees come over the wall. I caught the little prick. Staked him out in the car—saw the gun barrel slide out the window, one of those abandoned houses—p'too, p'too—I came out of the car like gangbusters. Nine years old."

A nun passed and Wovell touched the bill of his cap.

"It was worth your life walking around this place when the sun went down," he continued. "I told Mother Superior, put juice in the barb wire—fry the fuckers off the wall. But the nuns are too cheap." He shook his head, then brightened. "That's how they got us. I underbid everyone. I want this job, Staubie, it's my first college. All's I've had up to now is construction sites. If you think they're fun . . ."

A brief, orange sunset was silhouetting West Rock as they made their way to the last key station at Rec Hall.

"Our job," said the Captain, "is pertection. We're here to pertect the—*Holy Christ*!"

Wovell gaped at a well-stacked coed cutting across their path. "A lot of temptation on this campus, boy, that's why I'm real careful about who I—my God, will you look at that can! Just think how it must affect the Blacks. This place is a barrel of fish, and they got their spears out. Poor little rich white cakes. And they're careless. Ninety percent of them don't wear brassieres—that's a fact. I don't think nuns do, either. I'm not sure. They'd have to be black, right, everything's black. A nun in a black brassiere?"

"What if I catch someone?" Bert asked. "What do I do?"

"How much you get paid?"

"Two-fifty an hour."

"That's right." Wovell stopped and turned to Bert: "You get a call on the walkie-talkie—there's a guy seen going through a window in Rosary Hall. First thing you do?"

"Uh—"

"Call the cops. We ain't paid to get our heads blown off. Now, you'll still get to the scene nine times outta ten faster 'n them. So, use the brain. Come in slow with the roof flashers on. Take about three minutes getting out of the car. Get the dog out."

"Dog?"

"I'm gonna get a dog from the pound next week. Okay, hold 'im on the choke-chain like this: 'Hey boy! Hey boy!' Get 'im roused up. You want that son of a bitch thinking you've got a man-eating wolf. Get the walkie-talkie out, fake a call—loud: 'This is Saint Theresa Security. I'm at Rosary Hall. Squad car approaching. Ten-four.' Something like that. Ninety-nine percent of the time the perpetrators beat it out the back by the time you're stomping up the front steps. And that's the way you want it."

The color had drained from the horizon, a few big stars were showing.

"I accidentally trapped a guy in the pottery shed," said Wovell. "Place the size of a bathroom. He made a jump for me—or so I thought—and I made a jump for the door. He thought I was going for him—we practically tore the shirts off each other getting out of there."

Bert punched the clock outside Rec Hall. They went inside where the snack machines were, and the Captain bought a can of Mountain Dew. Standing before one of the big plate glass windows that looked out on the campus, and practicing surveillance while sipping, he remarked, "The nuns asked me when they hired me what I'd do to stop a man running away. Well, I said, if I had a stick, I'd hit him on the legs. I'd let him have it on the head and back of the neck." Wovell looked at Bert. "Then I asked *them*: What if he's just a kid on the track team taking a shortcut across campus? Hmm? Bet your ass. We're de-terrents. If the nuns don't like it, they can pay us five bucks an hour and equip us with bazookas—Say, there's a suspicious-looking character!" Wovell handed Bert the half-full soda and headed for the doors. "I'm gonna check him out—you watch."

Bert watched through the window as the Captain reappeared on the lawn outside. He seemed to be after a black kid in the distance who, unaware he was being pursued, gradually outdistanced the energetic Wovell and exited through the lower campus gate.

5

"*Ammunition*!"

As Bert came downstairs into the Step Down Coffee House, he heard Hugo Penny, then saw him waving one of his letters from a famous writer. He was surrounded by a group, including Christine in an off-the-shoulders green crushed-velvet gown, her blonde hair in a French twist. Pendant crystal earrings winked against her long neck as her head bobbed to Hugo's talk.

"You've got to outwit the pricks," he boomed, waving the letter and tucking it magician-like inside his jacket. "You won't believe the bad will the publication of this book will bring down on me. Where is Hans Tansky tonight? Do you see the Black Bitch? It's too much for them—Hello! Hello!" He thrust a hand at Bert between two people. "Thank you for coming, it's very kind."

Bert offered his congratulations as he shook Hugo's hand.

"My God!" Hugo exclaimed to Christine, "the man's got the grip of a lumberjack! Chopping all that wood in Vermont! Where's the better half?"

Trudy was in Troy, helping out after her father's cataract operation.

"Victor!" Hugo called, motioning.

A tall, stoop-shouldered man with a drooping mustache and three-piece suit, turned away from someone and came over.

Hugo introduced Victor Morgan, Christine's husband.

"Hugo the Magnificent!" Victor wagged his finger at Hugo. "They won't be able to ignore you after this."

Bert excused himself and went for a glass of wine. The coffeehouse-cum-art gallery was crowded and smoky. Fay and Alex had come; Fay was talking animatedly with a gray-haired woman while Alex looked on like he didn't speak English. Fairfield Ballentine, the young man with the ponytail, owner of the coffeehouse and the Matchless Press, stood behind a long table, one end of which was stacked with copies of Hugo Penny's book, *Stories from the Bottom of the Bottle*, the rest taken up with jugs of wine and cardboard bowls of potato chips. Ballentine, wearing a cardigan with holes in the elbows and the usual string tie, was filling rows of plastic cups from a gallon of pink chablis.

"You did a nice job with Penny's book," said Bert, paging through a copy.

"Mmm," said Ballentine. "Hugo tells me you're a writer. Might as well bring your stuff around."

Victor came up to the bar, took a cup of wine, and drank it off.

"Superb vintage," he said to Ballentine, holding out his cup for a refill. "About time someone recognized Penny." He turned to Bert. "It's so nice being known as 'Christine's husband.' Adjunct to the 'Lady in Green'? God. You'd think it was *her* coming-out party. But I'm at a disadvantage: you know who she is, while I have no idea who you are." He laughed mirthlessly, showing tall yellow teeth through his mustache.

"Bert Staub."

"Bert Staub. Artist?"

"I write."

"*The New Yorker*? *Esquire*?"

"Ah . . ."

"Righto," said Victor. "But on the verge, doubtless. When can we expect the miraculous birth?" He raised his eyebrows at Fairfield Ballentine.

"Don't look at me," said Ballentine, spinning the cap back on the wine jug. "Every book I publish loses money."

"Ah, but the honor—"

"Yeah, yeah," said Ballentine. "Who buys books anyhow?" He gave an indifferent shrug.

Bert noticed Hugo's wife, Pauline, by herself, pretending to be studying paintings on the gallery wall. She was a heavy woman, with the kind of corpulence that is always pink and damp. Her teeth protruded slightly and she wore glasses with outsized black frames which she was constantly pushing back up the bridge of her short nose.

"Hello," Bert said.

Pauline looked at him blankly.

"Bert Staub—"

"Of course. Bert—" She extended a small pink hand—for a moment Bert wondered if she expected him to kiss it. He shook it.

Pauline exuded friendliness bordering on hysteria: "My husband thinks very highly of you; he says we'll be seeing your work soon in the best publications. You must get him to put you in touch with Bellow and Roth and so on and so forth."

Once again Bert wondered why Hugo Penny even thought he was a writer, much less a good one. He'd never seen anything Bert had written.

"He trusts you," Pauline was saying. "And if Hugo trusts you, that's all that matters. The world, you see, Hugo's world, is divided into friends and enemies."

"You must be proud of him tonight," said Bert.

"Oh," she said, "the book. You live with someone so long—" she waved her hand as though it were obvious.

"His stories are pretty extraordinary. The life he lived—"

"Yes, yes, all the girlfriends, and so on, the whoring and drinking. Falling down and lying there. Yes, I suppose that's interesting, to someone else." She smiled at Bert, a strained smile that made her face pinken and glisten and show the tips of her teeth. "But of course that was decades ago. Decades and decades. Now all is smooth sailing." She winked at Bert. "And boring as hell if you ask me." She dabbed her face with a tiny handkerchief she'd been holding. "It's over, you see," she said.

"Over?"

"All he can do is write about it. *That's* the important thing. Relive the glory days. Pedal his bicycle to Philadelphia! If you only knew." She looked around and fixed on Hugo, who was talking to several people. "Who is that giant child hanging on his every word? She looks like a charmed snake. Just wait till you know him twenty-eight years, dearie!"

Bert offered to get Pauline a drink.

"Oh, by all means!" she cried. "By all means!!"

"Is something the matter—" Bert asked against his better judgment.

"Oh, I met Hugo at a party once, when everything was young. He only saved my life!" She laughed. "If only you knew what was the matter."

She looked around the room as if seeing it for the first time, then blurted, "I'm sorry, I had no intention of talking on like this. After all, you came to see him, not me. Who am I? And here I've been saying all these ridiculous—quite extraordinary, actually—things. Hugo, Hugo, go on with your stories, I'll just get fascinatingly oblivious."

From the corner of his eye, Bert saw Jamie come downstairs. The "Black Bitch" Hugo had referred to earlier was dressed in black, with a black cape, black lips, black fingernails, and black circles around the eyes. Alex and Fay seemed to have disappeared.

"Uh, excuse me," said Bert. "I wanted to buy a copy of your husband's book—"

Pauline laid a hand on his arm: "Get Hugo to autograph it. When he's dead it may be worth something."

Bert paid Ballentine for a copy of *Stories From the Bottom of the Bottle* and brought it over to Hugo.

"Allow me!" cried Victor Morgan, producing with a flourish an incredibly fat black fountain pen and presenting it to Hugo. "You ought to have one of these, Penny, for all the books you'll be signing."

Hugo held the pen up. "My God, where did you get this, off a water buffalo?"

"You are holding the *Montblanc*, power symbol of the age, phallus of fountain pens. Mark Strand gave a reading last year at Branford. The students flocked up afterward, and he autographed with his

Montblanc. Oh, that smart-ass, smooth-tongued—so *handsome* it's criminal!—flaunting his Jungfrau. It was—positively pornographic."

"Wonderful," said Hugo, signing Bert's book. "When I can't come, I'll squeeze the end here."

"What I love about Hugo's stories," said Victor, "is their garbage-can realism layered on top of an old-fashioned, almost prudish, sentimental morality."

"You're right," said Hugo. "There's nothing original about me."

"It wasn't a put-down," said Victor. "Who's original? It's the same old shit: man betrays woman, woman betrays man."

"I'll tell you something, my penis-penned friend," said Hugo. "Just this: sometimes a man can make a woman happy, and sometimes a woman can make a man happy." His right hand made its little signature of *fini*.

"*Well put*!" exclaimed Victor, hoisting his cup of wine and sprinkling the back of a woman deep in conversation—who merely raised a hand as though waving off a fly.

"If you think so," said Penny. "You're the critic."

Victor pulled several folded sheets of handwritten paper from his jacket pocket. "And here is the first draft of my review of your magnum opus, my friend, and it's not a pan."

"That's very kind—"

"Don't *beg*! You're the fucking writer. We're the fungi—call that your next book—*The Fungi of Yale*. We teach you, live on your carcass—especially after you're—"

There was a cry from across the room, and Bert just saw Pauline settling to the floor as though performing a deep curtsy, from which she did not rise.

Hugo was kneeling, propping her up, fanning her with a letter. "Is there a cot somewhere?"

Pauline gazed up at the ring of faces staring down at her and smiled. "Oh, don't mind me. Go on with the party." No one moved.

"Go on with what you were doing—having a gay time. I'm perfectly fine—I shall slash my wrists and be out of the way!" She laughed gayly. "A little *ouch*, a little blood, and then—" She shrugged, raised her eyebrows, let them drop, made a sour face.

Bert helped Hugo get Pauline into Ballentine's office, onto an old couch.

"Thank you," she called after them as they left her. "I have always depended upon the kindness of, of—whoever . . ."

Hugo steered Bert over to a corner.

"I'm calling my next book *Death in Greenwich Village*." He spoke quickly as though afraid of being interrupted. "I'm calling it that because after fifteen years nonstop drinking I was dead as a man, not to mention as an artist. I was going to be a writer in my twenties—set the world on fire!—but I got caught up in the party and didn't have enough discipline to keep writing through it, like some. After a while there was no Hugo Penny, just a thirst and a satisfaction of a thirst—until your liver's ham-size and one more drink'll do it."

Hugo glanced around then looked carefully at Bert. "That woman in there saved my life. I wouldn't be here talking to you—Pauline got me on the wagon. Pauline was the one person who believed I was a writer when I was a drunk."

Hugo was breathing heavily.

"I look like I'm sixty going on seventy-five. But I got some *juice*!" He nodded toward Christine. "That woman is a nympho—she looks like a cold fish, but my God . . . Victor married her when she was seventeen, a virgin. She's never known anyone but Victor. Now Victor's bored. He's fucking anything in skirts and, guess what, feeling guilty. He sics her on me. Ha ha, I should complain! Besides, he's helping me—throwing crumbs from the university's table. Ballentine's book has wrought wonders—Victor's caught himself a Live Author! And this Author is fucking his wife. Could things get any cozier, man!"

"It sounds like he's giving you a good review," said Bert.

Hugo instantly sobered. "You think so? Jesus, it did sound like it. He wants to warm his hands, the poor, frozen bastard."

Across the room, Christine was talking to some people; she caught Hugo's eye and motioned him over.

"I can't afford to make any more mistakes, man. Pauline is ticking like a bomb. I've never written better—there's Christine—I'm on the fucking rack! But I'm used to Pauline. I love her. I'm used to her. I can write. I get up every morning at three o'clock and I'm into a story. That's what's important, the work, and I'm being forced to choose. That long-legged, firm-breasted, cream-fleshed—my God, you can't imagine what it is to discover you're a man again. To have a beautiful woman in love with you—digging this carcass—loving your words, can't get enough of your cock . . ." Hugo's face was alight with anguish and wonder. "I've got to give Christine up, man. She would run away with me, you dig? I'm plugged into a hundred and ten volts—if she goes, I could go black. I gotta believe in myself. I'd wake up with her in Mexico with a limp dick, then what?" He lowered his voice, looking the while at Christine. "She is discovering her cunt at my expense. How long could I sustain that woman?" Christine started across the room toward them.

"What do you love?" Hugo asked Bert. "You gotta be careful—*what do you love*?"

Christine bore Hugo away to meet her friends.

Bert felt someone at his elbow.

"She's here!" Fay hissed. "She has actually come to this place!"

Bert tried to explain that Jamie was one of Ballentine's authors, and was probably not unexpected.

"*Author*? What the Black Bitch writes is—"

Bert asked where Alex was.

"I don't know," Fay said miserably.

"I'm about to head home, why don't we—"

But Hugo, along with Christine and Victor, had joined them. Fay forced a smile, congratulating Hugo.

"How old do you think I am?" he asked.

Fay blinked at him.

"Sixty-five? Seventy?"

"Oh, you're probably—fifty—five?"

"Forty-six."

Fay looked like she wanted to cry.

"I have sinned mightily, and I'm paying for it."

"*Je ne regrette rien*," said Victor. "You and—Pilaf."

It was very warm and stuffy down in Ballentine's den. Sweat shone on Christine's forehead, beaded the soft down above her full upper lip. Bert felt a trickle run down the middle of his back.

Jamie came up to them—Fay gripped Bert's arm.

"Hello," said Hugo, hesitantly. "I truly appreciate—"

"When are you fuckin gonna let go?" Jamie spoke to Fay. "Everyone's miserable—what's the point?"

Fay stared at Jamie in horror.

Alex went up the basement stairs just then, wearing his parka, and Jamie saw him.

WAIT A MINUTE, YOU! she yelled.

Alex kept going. Jamie ran after him.

"Welcome to our soap . . ." Fay spoke in a bright, tight voice. "Will Fay, Alex, and the Black Bitch find happiness together, or will one of them—" With a choked sob, she turned away.

"How did you like your coming-out party, Hugo?" The deep silkiness of Christine's voice lent intriguing dimensions to the most banal remarks.

"Too fucking tame," said Victor. "Hugo Penny is used to beatnik parties. Did you see anyone down on the floor *grooving*? But Penny said something insightful earlier, darling. He said a woman can sometimes make a man happy."

Christine's bulbous eyes regarded her husband with a mixture of repugnance and unease.

"Do you have the vaguest idea what makes me happy? Or, for that matter, unhappy? 'Tis the midnight hour—when the souls come out and speak—"

"You're drunk," said Christine.

"Indeed. We have to anez—anez-tatize—ourself to get to this, this—"

"Time to go home!" Hugo announced heartily, putting a hand on Victor's shoulder.

"That's right!" cried Victor viciously. "We'll all climb into one big bed—"

Hugo moved with surprising agility, putting the refreshment table between himself and Victor.

"Easy, man," he cautioned.

Victor had seized a handful of Hugo's books.

Ballentine continued sitting with one booted foot up, smoking a cigarette-sized cigar.

"Just speaking metamorphically . . ." mumbled Victor. He put down the books, leaned heavily on the table, sank into a chair.

Christine went for their coats.

"Well," said Hugo. "I best gather Lady Blanche and warm up the troika for the ride back out to the estate. Can't have the menials slacking off the water wheel."

6

Bert was in the patrol car with the engine running and the heater going full blast. In the frigid light of the February afternoon, he was trying to read *Tristram Shandy* propped against the steering wheel. He had parked on the hill next to Science Hall, with a maximum view of the quiet, snow-covered campus. A foot of snow had fallen the day before and then the temperature snapped arctic, freezing a crust that could almost be walked on.

Bert was only half reading; the other half of his mind was rehearsing the notice he planned to give Captain Wovell. In addition to teaching at the Arts Center, Trudy had gotten an artist residency at the elementary school in Wethersfield, thanks to Hugo Penny. The guard job could go. Bert could use the spring to finish his play on Custer and get it to the dean of the drama school. And polish a one-act for Fairfield

Ballentine, who was publishing an anthology of short plays, including his and one by Harv Moskowitz.

A quarter mile away, down the slope, he noticed two black kids climbing over the gate he'd locked. When they were over, they lifted the gate by the bottom so a small black dog could squeeze under.

Bert put the car in low and started down the slippery road. The dog was attached to a rope leash and one of the boys had picked up the end of it. They were headed for Rec Hall.

Bert intercepted them in the parking lot and got out of the security patrol car, a five-year-old Gremlin with two emergency lights clamped to the roof like Mickey Mouse ears.

"What's your dog's name?" he asked casually, allowing the impression of uniform and walkie-talkie to sink in.

"Queenie," sullenly answered the one holding the rope.

"We ain't doin' nothin'," said the other.

Bert reached down to pet the dog which was sniffing at him.

"She bites," warned the smaller boy.

Bert asked what they were doing there, trespassing.

"Ain't," said the older boy.

"Yeah," said the younger, bolder now. "We walkin' the dog."

Bert knew about these two and their dog. Captain Wovell had caught them in Rec Hall on two occasions. He was sure they were responsible for much of the petty thievery that the students reported. While the dog distracted the girls, theorized the Captain, the boys filched items out of their purses and backpacks. He had escorted the trio off campus, placing them on "final warning."

"No one's allowed on campus after the gate is locked," said Bert. "I saw you climb over."

They said nothing.

"Out," said Bert. "The way you came."

He walked them to the exit, his ears, exposed beneath the guard's cap, stinging with cold. They waited for him to unlock the gate.

"Go out the way you came in," he said.

With impudent slowness the boys climbed back over. Queenie, left with Bert, was torn between growling at him and whining anxiously through the gate at the boys. They lifted it and she shot under, scraping her back.

"This is it," said Bert. "I catch you in here again—"

The boys with the dog between them were already walking away.

Bert took the time clock out of the car and started back up to Science Hall. He liked walking the rounds to break up the monotony of the long shift.

He punched the clock and started across to the nuns' quarters when he saw the two boys and Queenie in the parking lot behind the cafeteria. Half a dozen cars belonging to the food service people were parked close to the building. The boys were peeking into a tan station wagon. One tried the door and opened it.

Bert swore and ran, the snow crust breaking through with every step. As he descended the hill, he could see the older boy go into the back seat, while the other, with the dog, kept lookout. It was amazing—infuriating—that they didn't see him coming. Bert reached the patrol car and started it, hit the flashing roof lights, and rounded the corner of the cafeteria, sliding broadside. The three scampered to one side, where the snow was pushed up in a long dirty wave. Bert got out and stood in the open car door.

"Get over here."

Incredibly, as if he hadn't spoken—as if he weren't there—they turned their backs, climbed over the snow wave. They reappeared on the other side walking on the crust, which supported them, heading toward Science Hall.

"YOU KIDS COME HERE!"

Their unzipped jackets fanned out as they ran, laughing, slipping and sliding.

Bert yanked the walkie-talkie out of his peacoat pocket and called the New Haven Police. He unlocked and swung open the south gate.

It became nearly dark as he stood outside the gate waiting for the cops. If they didn't get here in another minute, the boys would slip away, and Bert wanted them taught a lesson.

A squad car swung through the gate.

"I think we can catch them," said Bert, getting in. "Take a left uphill to Science Hall."

The cop was young and baby-faced with a drooping blond mustache. His manner affectedly hard-boiled.

"I got the guard," he said into his hand speaker. "Perps at Science Hall. Proceeding."

As they ascended the hill, a second squad car with two cops in it shot through the gate. It sped across the lower campus and started up the far side, tire chains spinning.

"*Two* police cars?" said Bert.

"We'll get 'em," grinned the cop.

The radio came alive: "Perpetrators running across campus, headed for south gate, bottom of hill."

The cop got the car turned around and they went fishtailing back downhill—then skidded off the icy road into a snowbank.

"Goddamnit!" The cop banged the steering wheel.

Bert jumped out and went plunging across the Great Lawn, sinking through the snow with every step. The two boys and dog had nearly reached the open gate when the second cop car cut them off.

The boys fought the men who dragged them, kicking, to the car. They fought and cried and implored, and finally the cops jammed them into the caged rear of the vehicle. The men were furious, one kicking the boys' legs inside before slamming the door. The younger boy cried and banged on the window.

Bert could barely bring himself to look at them. The windows of the cop car were steaming up.

A heavyset blonde woman in a tweed suit came out the back door of the cafeteria, accompanied by a janitor.

"The security guard put the call in," he said, indicating Bert.

"It was my car they broke into," said the woman, Mrs. Deitz, Dietitian, according to her name tag. "They didn't take anything—I don't leave temptations around."

The one cop asked if she wanted to press charges. She looked at the boys, the smaller beating rhythmically against the glass with his open palm, the other sitting stoically on the far side of the seat.

"I think they've learned their lesson," said Bert.

"Perhaps if you could take them down to the station," said Mrs. Deitz. "Impress them with the gravity of what they did?"

Queenie was dancing on her hind legs, trying to see her two young masters.

"If you want to press charges," said the cop, "we'll take the suspects in and book 'em."

"Please," said Bert, "I feel responsible for this whole mess."

Mrs. Deitz fixed her small eyes on him: "You are to be commended, Mr."—She leaned in to read his name tag—"Staub. Quite frankly I am astounded that a culprit—*two* culprits—have actually been apprehended—"

"What do you wanna do, lady?" interrupted the cop.

"Who *are* they? Where do they live?" she demanded. "I would be satisfied if you take them home and speak with their parents."

The cops got into their patrol car and left.

"I will certainly mention this to Mother Superior," Mrs. Deitz said to Bert. "And she will, I'm sure, pass it on to *your* superior." She went back inside.

Bert picked a small, black sock hat off the ground. Queenie had gone over to the dumpster and was licking something in the snow. She still wore her rope leash. He called her, wanting to take it off so she wouldn't get tangled in something, but she slunk away as he approached. Suddenly aware of how cold it was, he ran around to the front of the cafeteria and went inside.

7

Bert handed Trudy the note written in his father's clear, cursive hand:

> *Dear Bert and Trudy,*
> *This letter is not intended to be philosophical, neither is it explicative. It is merely a directive. Whether you understand the reasons for it or not is of no moment. It is necessary, to insure and secure Jeanette's and my marriage and our marital happiness at this time. To this end, keep out of our life. Do not visit, phone nor write us. Under these circumstances if things change we will contact you.*
> *As paradoxical as it may sound we love you and wish you success in all your undertakings.*
> *Dad*

"Can you beat it?" said Bert. "A *directive*?"

Trudy handed the note back.

"She gave him an ultimatum—us or her. And he caved in."

"He should give her up for us?"

"The honeymoon got over pretty fast."

"It's got to be hard for her," said Trudy. "Your father—charming and innocent, and completely used to having his own way."

Bert said nothing.

"You remember how she was last visit."

"But I don't *care* about the furniture—I just reacted to seeing it painted over—"

"Why do you think she painted it? It's your *mother's* furniture."

Bert folded the note and thrust it back in the envelope.

"They can go to hell. It's him I blame, not her. This is so stupid. What are we—*excommunicated*?"

He tapped his palm with the edge of the envelope.

"Jeanette's had to give up everything in this marriage," said Trudy. "Maybe she's at a place where she can't give anymore up. He has to be the one."

"I'd like to drive over there, knock on their door—"

"And what?"

8

On a sweltering August night a week after his birthday, Bert stopped by the Arts Center. He walked his bike behind the building where he could see through the big windows a line of little girls practicing ballet. Lillian was playing for them. Fay wasn't there; she'd gone to California to her brother's wedding. He sat against a tree and watched.

"I happened to be passing by."

Lillian, unlocking her bike from the rack behind the Center, glanced at him and smiled.

They walked their bikes out to Orange Street. The night was cottony and humid.

"Actually, I wanted to see you," he said. "At my birthday party you were lying on the blue rug in the candlelight. Looking sad and regal—a queen."

He knew, through Fay, that Lillian had broken up with her carpenter.

"When you were leaving you kissed me and said, 'Happy Birthday, Bert!' You know, that wasn't exactly a motherly kiss?"

"I'm sorry. I was being irresponsible."

They walked on for a while without speaking, lawn sprinklers going in the dark, people sitting on their screened porches with iced drinks.

"Care to go for a swim?" Bert asked.

They biked out Orange Street to East Rock. A lopsided moon was rising through the haze. The smell of the sea was thick and heavy. They left their bikes and Bert led Lillian down through dark woods. He could smell sweet fern; it was a way into the reservoir Alex had showed him. They crawled under an old wire fence. Lillian stripped and was in the water; he followed, immersing in liquid tepid as the air, in the darkness almost indistinguishable from it.

They swam under the low over-arching trees. Bert floated on his back, looking at the moon, flattened and lemony, which had cleared East Rock.

He came out of the water after Lillian, the white of her buttocks rising into the dark under the trees. She lay back on the bank and he entered her.

He told Trudy he was wet from riding home through the lawn sprinklers.

One night he walked over to Lillian's house. Standing outside in the dark he could see Maurice working at his desk upstairs; downstairs the three girls watching television, and in the kitchen Lillian washing dishes. He startled her, tossing a pebble against the window. She came out into the yard: he backed her against the elm—he had to put a hand over her mouth to stifle her cry. They were giddy with their daring, and Lillian had run up the porch steps, her light dress floating a moment in the kitchen light.

"We're good for one another," Lillian would say. "We have good body chemistry." But sometimes she worried. "I think I must be a nymphomaniac. I should be satisfied. This is selfish, but I love it so. Who am I hurting? Who am I being unfaithful to? I love Maurice. I'm a good mother. I cook and clean house, write Christmas cards. I take the girls to ballet. I'm nice to my mother-in-law—I really like her. I belong to the Audubon Society. I'm a vegetarian. It doesn't make sense not to be lovers, does it?"

Hands spread on her slender buttocks as she rose in the air above him, he believed there was nothing to regret, everything to be grateful for.

9

"Maybe it was foolish to come and talk with you. But I think of us as, well, practically sisters—"

"Yes, yes . . ." Trudy found herself saying. "I guess I supposed something was happening . . ."

It had blindsided her. Bert and Lillian? This woman who was talking to her. Earnest and pleasant—concerned—naked—*fucking Bert*? Trudy caught the back of the kitchen chair and sat down. Lillian was looking at her gravely.

"It's okay, really . . ." said Trudy. Images surged and swamped her, receded. They'd been making love a lot lately. *Passionately*, tenderly. Because of Lillian? What was she saying—*sisters*? "I have to go now. I have a class at the Center, uh—Still Lifes."

"It means nothing," said Lillian. "Bert and I found a certain . . . pleasure in each other. I don't know how to say it—it sounds stupid. Believe it or not, I wrote down what I was going to say—"

Trudy had gotten up. "Do you love one another?"

Lillian looked at her blunt fingers. "I think of love as duty. Maurice and the girls—something I have to spend my life doing. Bert . . ." She shook her hand. "It was very nice. Something extra. Don't tear your life up because . . ."

I'm not. I didn't realize I had to consider it.

Trudy put on her backpack filled with art supplies. She clipped her pant legs to her ankles with the bicycle clips. Why wouldn't Lillian leave?

"I'll tell Maurice," said Lillian. "I always do. He forgives me. It keeps things honest."

"You always do?"

Lillian looked at her. "You wish I hadn't told you."

Trudy waved her hand vaguely. "Does Bert know you've come here?"

"The last thing either of us wants is to hurt you."

Either of us? As if it was them and her—and where was Bert? Fucking this woman and then coming home and—

"I have to go—really," she said, pushing past and out the door and down the stairs, leaving Lillian standing in her kitchen.

"What was it? Why did you do it?"

Before he could answer, she said, "*I don't want to know anything*! Was it one of those things you had to experience? As a writer? *Why*?"

In the middle of the blue living room rug where they sat opposite one another, was a basket of fruit: apples, a hand of bananas, blue plums.

"That you came home from her and, and we made love. I feel—I guess I feel that—as if you were trying to—mix us up—or tainting or blending or wiping me with her. *Why*?"

Bert opened his hands and could say nothing.

"Do you want to leave me?"

"No."

"Why?"

"It's over with Lillian. I'm sorry—"

"I wish I could go away. You wish these things . . . You can't go back. What we had. Where do you go?"

"I love you," he said, staring at the bowl of fruit.

MAMAUGUIN

Mamauguin was a mistake. But then, where could they have gone? Actually, Mamauguin was perfect.

They had abandoned New Haven in September looking for a place to start over. Trudy wanted to live by the sea—thoughts of walks on a winter beach, quiet times in a stormbound house . . . What they'd been able to afford had been a cottage in Mamauguin, the run-down, half-deserted beach town east of New Haven. Whatever Mamauguin meant in Indian, for Bert it meant swamp—muck—muggy place. Place where you got stuck.

It was the last of April, with a month to go on their lease. Though he hated the place, it rankled that they were being kicked out. Rhoda and Eli had rented to them to have someone in the place over the winter, so it wouldn't get torched. Then they reclaimed it for the three months of summer, moving out of their house in New Haven. The previous September Trudy and he had been happy to sign the short lease: their own house on the beach.

Bert sat at his desk beside the window and watched Eli backing down a double row of young beets, lifting and dropping his hoe in measured chops. The old man's flaccid behind was aimed at Bert, Eli always orienting so as not to see him sitting there, idle at his desk, watching. Eli wore his usual straw hat with the green plastic visor-brim: it gave his sweating face a croupier's green pallor. His chambray shirt looked like it was falling apart on his humped back; he wore old gray pants, suspenders, red tennis shoes. He had been hoeing an hour, starting the same time Bert had sat at his desk.

Bert couldn't write. The old man's activity, which seemed real, invalidated his own, which seemed imaginary—worthless. He had watched Eli putter in his garden since the middle of March. At first, he came out once or twice a week, but now it was practically every morning—as if the old man were shepherding, driving them with his hoe toward the uncertain fields of summer.

Trudy was gone days, commuting to the art gallery in Hartford. Sometimes she even slept over. The job, writing grants, had begun part-time in November. Now it was full-time and included hanging shows, designing publicity, and teaching a life-studies class on Saturday mornings. Recently Trudy had begun renting a studio in the art gallery building. She planned to live and work there over the summer.

Bert had not been invited. He tentatively planned to go to Montana. Alex was building his house on a hill outside Missoula and had been urging Bert to visit. He and Trudy would join up in the fall—maybe Hartford, maybe New York City. But plainly, for now, she was looking forward to being on her own.

Eli's head looked like an egg resting on its side on his shoulders. The head of a praying mantis. He'd been a tailor, had risen to head tailor at Tillingers on Whitney Avenue. He had once been able to measure, cut, and sew a man's suit in three days. He could take one look at you, Rhoda had told Bert, and make you a suit.

Eli reached the end of the beets, fifteen feet from Bert, shifted a row over and recommenced hoeing, moving forward now, maintaining his back to the window. Bert felt a sudden fury that dissipated at once. Why shouldn't an old man have his own place, uncompromised by begrudging strangers? Rhoda said Eli was eighty-eight. Ripe and ready to drop. Rhoda told Bert all he knew about Eli. The old man hardly spoke. When they came—she was usually with him but had stayed behind today—he would shuffle out back to the shed, unlock it, get his tools, go to work in the garden. Rhoda would sit in a folding lawn chair in the shade of the cottage and read women's magazines. Eli gardened, laid out lines like once he'd chalked serge; dropped seeds, hoed weeds, watered. Usually they would be gone by two, when full sun fell into the garden.

Eli had stopped and was wiping his forehead with the filthy rag he kept in his back pocket. He was on a row of bush beans now. It should have been a pleasing sight, a spring garden, an old man hoeing.

When Bert looked up again, Eli was gone. He went to the front of the house where he saw the old man through the porch window sitting under the big, untrimmed hedge that hid the garden from the street. He looked like a small heap of used clothing, and was smoking one of his filterless Camels—would take a drag and gaze at the cigarette smoking between his fingers.

Bert went out back and sat on the porch steps, the cool of the concrete penetrating his shorts. Here he couldn't see the old man, but click, click, click, could hear him hoeing again.

Trudy had made new friends in Hartford. Mira Hagen, in particular. Mira was a photographer Trudy met while helping to hang her show at Asylum Art in January. *Body Parts* consisted of large-format photos of human feet, knees, hands, breasts, knuckles—posed cleanly against white backgrounds. Cool and artsy, Bert felt, but Mira was an immaculate Swede, one of those cool, graceful women of a certain age, of independent means. An established artist, she had taken Trudy under her wing—had liked her painting and encouraged her. It had been at Mira's suggestion that Trudy rented the studio.

Mira had done a series of photographs of Trudy, extraordinary pictures that caused Bert to see a woman he had not known. In one, Trudy sat in a high-backed wicker chair wearing a yellow sarong, one bare foot cocked up on the seat, staring off beyond the camera. She looked moody, sultry—and Bert felt a pang of jealousy. What was the nature of her and Mira's relationship? Mira was helping her, opening her in a way he couldn't. Trudy had described being shot—over and over—until she felt as full of holes as a paper doily—the primitive's fear of the soul being stolen, replaced with the delicious sense of the body being subtracted in little bites and replicated elsewhere as something else. Bert had seen contact sheets of the film Mira shot, and saw Trudy, as it were, in hundreds of pieces. He recognized her parts almost with nostalgia.

"I admire Mira," Trudy had said. "She burns with a clean flame. It's the first real friendship I've had with a woman. She loves me for my better self. Go further, Mira says. Be extravagant."

Away from him, from their habit of poverty, she found she loved having a little money—earning it and spending it on clothes, eating out, taking a cab. And not suffering his disapproval.

Trudy had made attempts to include Bert in her new life—inviting him to gallery openings, concerts in the park, parties at Mira's. But he felt awkward, as though trying to horn in on what was hers. They were her friends, excited about the Hartford art scene, *their* scene. He was losing her and couldn't lift a finger—because it was necessary, inevitable, terrifying.

"Hello!" Bert spoke loudly. "How grows the garden?"

Eli glanced up from under his green shade, smiled tentatively. Pocked with craterlike pores and blackheads, his large nose appeared to be melting in the heat.

"Where's Rhoda?" Bert shouted.

"Too hot."

"Ah. Could you use a glass of water?"

Eli waved a hand as though warding it off.

Bert walked back into the house.

He sat at his desk, took a sip of lukewarm coffee. Did Eli bury fish heads in his corn hills? Bert remembered the corn he had grown in Vermont. Tall, long-leaved, rustling in the lightest breeze. He would go sometimes and sit in the corn patch. He had grown a black-kerneled type that went all the way back to the Aztec. Dried and ground, it had made sweet, nutty, gray corn bread.

He watched Eli pull a couple of green onions and retire to the hedge. The old man sat and took a sandwich out of a paper bag. He ate as deliberately as he smoked: bite, chew, swallow—a slug out of the thermos. Another bite, chew—*look out old bastard or you'll be buried with that mouthful!*

Bert got up and went into the bedroom on the other side of the house and, cross-legged on the bed, began a letter to Alex.

He'd been writing for a while when he heard a knock at the entry door.

Eli stood on the stoop. He had the house surrounded and was at the gates.

"That glass of water?" He asked.

Bert invited him in and the old man seemed grateful to sink onto the front porch sofa. His bleached blue eyes blinked slowly under the green shade, like an old tortoise's.

Eli took the glass of water and drank it slowly, without stopping, his Adam's apple going up and down. He exhaled as he finished and handed Bert the glass.

"More?"

Eli made a small negative gesture.

"Would you like to come inside? It's cooler."

"Thank you. I'll rest a little here, if you don't mind."

Bert stood a moment, not knowing what to do.

"It's hot as hell," he said.

The old man took his hat off, ran a liver-spotted hand over the eggshell cranium.

"Would you—a piece of cake or something?"

"No."

"You actually hear pretty well, don't you?" Bert said, and laughed.

Eli smiled. "Poor man's hearing aid."

"What's that?"

"Stick a piece of straw into a cork. Stick the cork in your ear. It will improve your hearing."

The old man looked at Bert, his eyelids drooping, his white face, blotchy and wrinkled with its great chop nose blackhead and pustule-covered, fleshy ears with melting lobes and white hair tufts sticking out, wisps of white hair plastered on the egg-dome skull. It was a mask Bert was looking at—and something living staring back at him through the eye holes.

"That actually works?" Bert could only think of a kid's tin-cans-and-string telephone.

Eli smiled faintly. "People see it and talk louder."

Bert gaped, and then laughed.

"A tailor I know did it," said Eli.

Bert went back inside and continued his letter. When went out to the porch, Eli was gone. The maroon Chrysler parked out front was gone. But Eli had left his hoe in the garden, and his lunch bag by the hedge. Bert put the tool away in the shed, locked the rusty padlock. There was half a meatloaf sandwich in the bag; Rhoda had trimmed the crusts.

When Trudy returned from Hartford that evening, Bert told her he'd decided to head out to Montana for the summer, see what Alex was up to. She seemed unsurprised.

MONTANA FIX

The sound of the Willys' four-wheel came from the woods below the house; the old pickup emerged into the sunlight and stumps of the slash and ground up the last pitch to the woodshed. Alex got out hoisting a case of Olympia beer onto his shoulder.

"Something for you—" He scaled a letter up onto the roof and went inside.

I laid the hammer down beside the bundle of shingles.

"Dear Bert," Trudy's clear, open hand began,

I'm learning a lot about running an art gallery. Two of the grants I wrote came through. Mario has been letting me design the posters for shows, doing the artwork and graphics. So, I've been pretty busy with hardly a breather to write. I don't know what to say. I'm involved with Mario. He put me in the group show at Asylum last year and we hit it off—that's why he hired me. It seemed like a good working relationship. Neither planned for this to happen. I hope you are well. It sounds great out there, all the fishing and backpacking. I don't know where this will go, Bert, I can't think about it. Mario is married and it is very difficult. I haven't felt this alive in a long time. I feel a little out of control, a little crazy. I can't care about anything—forgive me. I love you,

Trudy.

Alex came through the open skylight with a six-pack.

"Ran into Jeremiah in town. Rainbows are hitting flies at sundown up by him."

I opened a can and took a pull.

"Jeremiah got me started on the chimney," Alex said. "Only outside help I used on the house. He's a stonemason. But I finished it myself." He was looking at the chimney, a massive, curved wing of fieldstone that soared up from the end of the house.

"I don't feel much like fishing," I said. "You go ahead."

Alex's red Feed and Read cap pinched his thick shoulder-length hair like a headband. With his overalls, untrimmed beard, and wire-rimmed glasses, he looked like an aging hippy. Alex had looked that way studying at Yale. He was medium height and strongly built, walked lightly, sort of slump-shouldered like he was stalking something, and talked in a soft joking way that I thought of as western. I noticed his face had started to crease like an old cowboy's.

"Too fine an afternoon to spend shingling." Alex had taken out a piece of dental floss and was working his teeth. "There are some bragging fish up—"

"I don't feel like doing a goddamn thing. If you don't mind."

He looked at me.

"She's fucking this guy in Hartford." I held up the letter. "How can she get any perspective about us if she's fucking this guy?"

Alex shrugged. "Maybe that's what she needs to do."

"All I know is I'm out here two months, and I can see we've got a future. She goes and does this. It's really finished."

Fireweed bloomed all over the hillside, among the stumps. Alex's house looked out on Missoula Valley, and far across to the gray teeth of the Idaho Bitterroots. He balled the floss and tucked it into his pocket.

"I sometimes wonder about Fay and me," he said. "If it mightn't have worked out . . ."

I almost laughed. "If ever there was oil and water."

After a moment, Alex said, "Trudy would have liked it out here. She could have done some painting."

"Yeah, well, she's into interiors these days. Light in empty rooms."

"I could see it," said Alex. "Trudy would make that interesting."

It felt like she and I were the surviving pair of an endangered species. Find your way back together or become extinct. I loved her, but that had sunk so far into the grain I hadn't been able to see it or feel it until I got away.

"Let's go fishing."

"For Chrissake, Alex—"

"Jeremiah invited us to stay for supper. You can see their tipi."

Downstairs, he dug an elk roast out of the freezer as our contribution to the meal.

The road off the interstate followed a small river into hills thickly wooded with fir. The macadam turned to dirt and we overtook a gaunt man on a bicycle pulling a homemade cart full of groceries. Alex stopped on the shoulder and Jeremiah pulled up on the driver's side.

"Thought we'd take you up on your offer," said Alex.

Jeremiah was over six feet and sat on the bicycle seat with his boots flat on the ground. He had a reddish beard streaked with gray, thin lips, and mournful eyes—a face for El Greco. And body odor that climbed into the cab.

"They'll be hitting about the time you get up there," he said.

Alex introduced me and I reached across to shake Jeremiah's hand through the window.

"Ever see a chimley like that?" he asked.

It took me a moment to realize he was talking about Alex's chimney.

"Ain't built for drawin' curved like that. Big bird wing. You're gonna regret that fancy idea come winter."

"We'll see," said Alex. The truck almost stalled. He gunned it. "Bert's from New York City."

"Not quite," I said. "Let's not rush it."

Alex offered Jeremiah a lift.

"Na. I got this far, ain't but a couple more miles."

Alex parked beside an old concrete abutment. The bridge was gone; a single rusty cable bellied thirty feet over fast water. Alex loaded our gear onto a wooden platform slung beneath the cable on pulleys. We climbed on. Kneeling on this cable car, he let go the strap that held it: we fell toward the river, swooping up the far side.

I stuck the three six-packs of Olys in the river. Alex was fishing already and had gotten rises. He tossed me his fly box and said tie on the gray and brown one with the yellow tail and douse it with dope. We were fishing dry flies which had to float on the water like winged insects.

I waded out. The bottle-green water, icy and fast, leaned into my legs; it felt like the bottom was cobbled with greasy baseballs. I rooted my sneakers as best I could and began whipping the long rod overhead, back and forth. The line snaked out over the river and dropped the fly onto quiet water behind a boulder. No sooner had it dimpled the surface than it was gone. I hauled back on the rod and it bent jerking like a bull terrier. The fish jumped—a foot and a half out of the river—and fell back with a splash. I whooped.

I was playing the fish, backing onto the shore when I noticed Jeremiah squatting on the opposite bank, watching.

Without a net I would have to lead the fish in and beach him. He hovered in two feet of water, nearly invisible in the shifting browns and golds of the river bottom. I could see the fly hooked through the cartilage of his lower lip. Alex had filed the barb so the only thing holding the hook in place was the tension on the line. I drew the fish in until his nose almost touched sand—then dropped the rod and scooped with both hands. I pounced on the flipping fish and held him up, victoriously.

"Fair brown . . ." came dryly from across the river.

Jeremiah disappeared. He emerged a moment later from the brush behind me carrying a fly rod.

"Keep it hid there," he said. "Handy to fishing."

"You wouldn't try that in New York," I joked. I hooked my fly into the cork handle of the rod and laid it in the grass.

"They're hitting the gray-ruffed midge," I told him.

Jeremiah continued tying on a small black fly.

"Give up already?" he said.

"Thought I'd see how the natives do it."

"I don't see no natives," he said. "I'm a white man from Eugene, Oregon."

Jeremiah had a fish on in three casts. He played it right to him, picked it out of the water by the gills, unhooked and tossed it up the bank. He moved upstream fifty yards and cast again. Another fish—up onto the bank. He could have been picking cabbages.

It was twilight as we followed Jeremiah up a path into the woods, me then Alex. The air was warmer away from the river and smelled of pine.

"You sure do love to fish," Jeremiah called back to Alex. "Seven keepers."

"Some great action," said Alex. "Too bad the sun had to go down."

"Yep, along with my four—and your friend's one big one—ain't a bad supper."

A tipi appeared through the dark boles, sitting in a clearing like a sepia photograph, with a woman standing in front of it.

We went inside, then Alex and Jeremiah left to clean fish and build a fire. I was wet and shivering from being in the river. The woman, who introduced herself as El, gave me a pair of moccasins and an old blue parka.

"I've never been inside a tipi," I said.

El stood sideways, picking herbs from a basket and hanging them on a line strung between tipi poles. The old Crosby, Stills & Nash T-shirt stretched tight over her large breasts.

"All I know from these things is what I've seen in the Natural History Museum," I said. "Those life-size displays with the tipi sliced in half. Same as yours—except they don't have a stove and Kashmir rug." Then I noticed the rug was threadbare, gone through in places.

El was hanging sage. It smelled like turkey stuffing in the tipi. Each time she raised her arms, tufts of armpit hair showed. She was strong and thickset and looked like the picture of a squaw, even to the single heavy braid down her back. In the close space I was aware of her smell, compounded of woodsmoke and cooked food and sweat.

"Have you lived here long?"

She put the basket away behind the stove. "I started in the old logging bunkhouse till it fell down. Someone gave me the first tipi. This is the third."

"It's yours?"

She didn't say anything.

Alex came back with the cleaned fish.

"You give her the elk?" he asked.

I got the roast out of the backpack. It had begun to thaw and a pool of blood lay in the bottom of the plastic wrap.

"You guys keep it for later," Alex said to El. "We got enough trout for supper."

"Meat won't keep," she said. "We'll cook it up."

Jeremiah had a fire blazing a hundred yards from the tipi, against a stony hillside that rose steeply out of the light. Alex set a couple of heavy iron fry pans on top of the burning logs, cut some elk fat and put it in to melt. Then he laid the fish in, sputtering. Their tails curled up as they began to fry.

"I'm bottling this smell to take back with me," I said.

"Why go?" grinned Alex.

We settled our backs against a log and sipped beers, waited for the fish to cook. Sparks flew up mixing in with the huge stars. This is the life, I thought. Trudy would love this.

El sat on the ground, leaning against a backrest she had woven out of green willow. An Indian design, she said.

"You did some nice stonework on Alex's fireplace," I said to Jeremiah. "I guess you've built a few."

"Yeah, I worked for the professor. He paid good wages, but he cut the job short." Then he added, "You learned off me and let me go."

"I intended finishing it myself. You knew that."

Jeremiah just grunted.

When the fish were done, Alex put one on each plate and handed them around. He laid the extras on a clean slab of firewood, then cut the elk roast in halves and started cooking each in a pan over the fire.

I'd never tasted better fish—firm and sweet, flavored faintly with a musky elk taste. I was hungry but Jeremiah ate like a starved man, eyeing the elk hunks while he chewed. He caught me looking at him.

"Guess you've a good time out here," he said.

"I've got a few stories to tell folks back—"

"Imagine what it'd've cost if you'd had to pay for it—first-rate guide, canoe, camping gear, four-wheel-drive vehicle. Bet that nice fly rod ain't even yours."

Alex turned the roasts; fat spattered, igniting in little bursts.

"How much you make?" Jeremiah asked. "Eighty grand a year?"

I laughed.

"Bert's a writer," said Alex. "He hasn't been discovered yet."

Jeremiah took another fish in his fingers and began gnawing it. Alex offered one to El; he and I each had another.

"Jerry's a writer." El's voice was startling. She'd hardly spoken since we'd come up to the fire. "Got a story this thick he typed in the tipi."

"What's it about?" I asked.

Jeremiah slung the fishbone into the dark. "A little something."

"About a murder," said El.

"Don't give it away," snapped Jeremiah. He took the last fish. "I don't know how anyone can write with freezing fingers in that goddamn tipi."

"He brought it to the university, see what people thought—"

"One of Alex's asshole friends," said Jeremiah. "Well, fuck him. I think it'd make a movie. The shit they make movies out of. You know how much movie-writers get? Beau-coo. Even if they don't make the movie."

Alex went off to pee in the bushes.

Jeremiah lowered his voice. "Hired me to learn enough stonework, then I'm gone. Had me pretty pissed there. He's got the bread—works at the university—fifty, sixty grand a year—"

"He wanted to do it himself."

"He didn't know how. He would have fucked it up, that big motherfuckin' chimley. You know how much they weigh? You gotta dig, lay foundation. Select stone. You gotta do it right—"

"I guess you'd be satisfied if the thing fell down?"

Alex came back.

"Got me a gig playing a roadhouse to Hungry Horse," said Jeremiah.

"All *right*!" said Alex. "Bert 'n me'll come by."

"Thursday nights, ten on—come one, come all."

"Who's for a taste of elk?" Alex grabbed a corner of one of the roasts like you'd grab an ear, and sliced it off.

"That the one Jerry missed?" said El.

Alex chuckled. "A nine-hundred-pound bull coming out of thick brush at twenty feet looking to mate with you can perturb the aim—"

I let out a cackle.

"I'll get one this year," said Jeremiah. He took a piece of meat from Alex. "Then I'll bring *you* the roast."

We chewed the hot meat, juice on our hands. We ate like we'd just killed it with spears and rocks. It tasted like rich, tender beef.

"Jerry shit his pants." El was smiling at me. "Fired off five rounds and killed a tree."

"I wish you'd a been there, Ellybelle. That big fella would've had a ball." Jeremiah looked at me. "Ever see a bull elk? Got a pizzle on him satisfy the worst woman."

"Mebbe you ought to eat one?" said El. "Grow you a cock like a bull elk. It got its work cut out."

I laughed, I didn't hold it back.

At Alex's urging, Jeremiah brought a banjo up from the tipi. He also brought a nearly full bottle of I.W. Harper. He tuned up standing back from the fire, the damp night air soaking up the plunks of the banjo. A heavy dew was glistening on the weeds and leaves when you looked away from the light.

Standing with his weight on his back foot, Jeremiah played the banjo. He played jigs and reels, and Alex accompanied on spoons. I stretched out on the ground. El was sitting against her backrest, eyes half closed, lips shiny with elk grease. She could have been an Indian; she could have been thirty or sixty. When I drank and passed the whiskey, she drank without wiping the mouth of the bottle. Her feet were drawn up under the hem of her skirt so I couldn't see them. I remembered the Indian story about Deer Woman. So beautiful no one ever looked at her feet and saw she had hooves. She appeared only at night during tribal dances, and would lure a young man into the woods. In the morning he would be found trampled to death.

Jeremiah was singing in a toneless, nasal voice, a song about a cowboy betrayed by a whore and dying out on the "prayer-ee." His thin voice slipped in and out of falsetto like a loose gearshift. Every now and then he yodeled. The whiskey kept going around. The song was endless. After a while El's feet came out, fat and dirty as a child's.

"Know any Dylan?" Alex asked when Jeremiah had finished.

He retuned and began "Blowin' in the Wind."

El got up and went into the bushes. Jeremiah stopped singing but kept the banjo going softly.

"You want her, Hemingway?" he asked. "Ever had a squaw woman?"

Alex stretched.

Jeremiah passed me the bottle. "You've scaled peaks, run rapids, reeled in bragging fish . . ." He grinned showing his crooked teeth. "You was lookin' like you wanted to eat her 'n lick the plate—no need apologize. Wide open spaces, all that—fella ain't had full value till he shot his wad. Am I right?"

I wiped the bottle mouth and took a drink. "You offering me your woman?"

Jeremiah looked at me with a flat grin. I couldn't tell what he was thinking. I was too drunk to care.

"My woman?" He laughed. "Not for free. Not by a damn."

Trudy was free, wasn't she? We both were. Alex had gotten up to move the roasts back from the fire.

"How much?" I said.

Jeremiah looked like he was thinking. "Five hundred."

I laughed.

"Fifty. Quickie in the tipi?"

I was fumbling for my wallet when Alex stepped between us. Then we all stopped. El was standing on the other side of the fire coals.

Jeremiah chuckled and picked up his banjo. He began slowly to pluck out "Irene Goodnight." Then his queer voice started, "Last Saturday night I got married . . ."

The driver-side wiper smeared arcs of dew and road dust across the windshield. The old Willys had no wiper on the passenger side.

"I thought we were gonna take that goddamn cable car straight into the river!" I yelled over the wind.

Alex grinned, guiding the truck down the mountain road. "Two of us full of whiskey—"

"I expected that bastard to start taking potshots at us!"

The moon was coming up somewhere; I could see a bone-white cliff turning above us.

"I would have done it—I would have gone into the tipi with her—"

Alex switched off the wiper.

"She was ready, man. I mean, who gives a fuck at some point—right?"

"It wouldn't have been a great idea," said Alex.

"Can you imagine what's going on back there? I hope she doesn't slit his scrawny throat."

Alex chuckled.

"You ever sleep with her?"

His bearded features were soft in the dashboard light, eyes old and bright behind his glasses.

"Trudy and me . . ."

Something small ran out in the road and hesitated. As if it had been thrown in front of us. Alex pumped the brakes; the creature whisked off with its tail up.

"Time you went to California for your play," he said. "She never told you?"

The road had left the river, climbing, and came back, high. The water breaking below showed silver.

"I drove up to the cabin one weekend," he said. "Something between friends, maybe a little more—in a way, something to get past." He glanced over. "I never felt bad about it. It felt like a good thing between us."

"Trudy."

He exhaled through his nose. "Yeah, I guess so. Someone we both cared for."

The moon, about half full came out from behind a shoulder of mountain. Alex switched off the lights and ignition and we coasted, just the skurr of gravel under the tires, wump of the chassis taking ruts. Alex with his big hands rolling the steering wheel.

We hit the macadam and traveled in sudden silence.

LIVE WITH ME

The night before Christmas Eve. Bert watched the taillights of the Amtrak *Bankers* fade up the tracks toward Springfield. No one had gotten off in Hartford except him. It was clear and still and cold.

Union Station was deserted. He was disappointed Trudy hadn't met the train. In a way glad, too—still to be alone, still moving toward her.

He carried his suitcase down Railroad Street to Asylum. A liquor store was open and he bought a pint of Jack Daniel's. Tomorrow they would drive to Troy for Christmas. He was looking forward to seeing Mom and Pop Steiner.

He opened the whiskey and took a drink.

Bert watched Trudy through the plate glass door descend the long flight of wooden stairs. She hugged a cardigan to her. She looked thinner. Trudy unlocked the door, entrance to both the Asylum Art Gallery and her studio, on the second floor.

"Hello," she said, kissing him quickly. She bent to relock the door. A cab went by, reflecting in the mirrored sides of the Civic Center across the street.

"How've you been?" asked Bert.

"Okay. Pretty busy."

"I brought Pop a kielbasa from the Polish butcher on Second." Bert tapped his suitcase. "I guess I didn't think—everything's gonna smell like garlic."

Trudy smiled. "He'll appreciate it."

Bert followed her up the stairs. He wanted to stay easy, keep the good feeling of the train ride.

As they passed through the darkened gallery, Trudy hesitated and said, "It's a beautiful show, almost pure color. In the light . . ."

He knew she was talking about Mario's paintings. His show had opened the week before.

They passed into a long-darkened hallway; at the far end a rectangle of light falling in from an open door.

How many times has Mario stood here before going to her?

The bank of windows looked out across a flat roof and parking lot to Bushnell Park. Dark woods on a winter night. Bert could make out the hatbox shape of the new carousel. On the far side of the park a few houses were decorated with colored Christmas lights.

"Sorry it's cold," said Trudy. "It's a commercial space; they cut the heat at night."

"So, you go to bed early, right? I brought some stuff." Bert opened his suitcase, taking out half a broccoli quiche, pecan tarts, pears.

"Leftovers from the bakery," he said. "Everything's either overbaked or stepped on or something. But basically good."

Bert laid the food out on the rug, the old blue oriental with the dog-chewed corner. They'd splurged—thirty-five dollars—to "furnish" their living room in New Haven.

He took a fat green candle from his suitcase, lit it and set it on the rug. Then he turned out the lights.

Trudy put a record on—an Indian raga, just the sitar. She sat opposite him and began to roll a joint.

"Look what Santa brought." Bert held out the whiskey.

"You go ahead."

He drank and then she took the bottle.

When Trudy offered the joint, Bert said he'd stick with the whiskey.

The tempo of the raga had been increasing; abruptly a tabla entered, ticking and gurgling.

"You look good," said Bert. He lay on his side, arm over one of the big pillows. Trudy wore sweatpants and had put Bert's old red and black wool shirt on over her sweater. Her hair was in a single braid.

The candle glowed green; the flame burning deep inside looked like a little campfire in the dark room.

Trudy dragged on the joint and grimaced as smoke went into her eyes.

She looks oriental. Who is she?

"I've been working kind of hard," said Trudy. "A new show comes in after the First."

Bert cut the quiche and put wedges on napkins. "Did the gallery get that NEA grant?"

"No."

"That mean you're out a job?"

Trudy shrugged. She took a bite of quiche.

Bert got up and lifted the needle off the raga. The music seemed to be racing headlong. He switched to FM radio and Nat King Cole in the middle of "Oh, Holy Night."

Bert felt the whiskey warm in him. "You know," he said, "I heard a dog bark 'Jingle Bells' on the bakery radio the other night?"

Trudy had stretched out on the other side of the food, almost his mirror image.

Nat King Cole sang "I Saw Three Ships." When "Chestnuts Roasting on an Open Fire" began, Bert stood and held out his hand.

He didn't try and hold her close as they danced, and Trudy began to relax. Bert felt better and better. He kissed her neck and she stiffened—he tried to go on dancing but she pulled away, went to the window.

"Mario didn't think I ought to stay here tonight."

After a moment, after letting his anger subside, Bert asked why—or what that had to do with anything.

Trudy shook her head.

"Do you want to be with him?"

"He's with his family."

Bert pressed his fingers against his whiskey-numbed temples. "If you want to be with him—"

Trudy touched his arm, pleadingly. "I didn't think it was such a good idea, either, your coming here."

Pop Steiner was framed in the kitchen window slicing a ham. He pinched a fatty scrap between his thick fingers and put it in his mouth.

"Save the bone for soup!" Bert called as he and Trudy came up the stairs into the kitchen.

Pop turned, carrying the refrigerator's reflection across his glasses: "Well, for God's sake."

Trudy kissed her father on the cheek.

"We'd about gave up on you for lunch," said Pop.

"Please, no," said Bert. "We caught a bite in Great Barrington."

"Your mother's in the parlor," Pop said to Trudy. "I'll set the table."

Mom Steiner was slightly breathless as Bert pecked her on the cheek.

"I've had the runs all day," she said. "I wonder if it's that darn bacon?"

She seemed heavier and grayer than Bert remembered from last Christmas.

Pop took beers out of the refrigerator and popped them open. Mom got a glass of water. They ate ham sandwiches with bread-and-butter pickles, and a lettuce salad Mom drowned in oil and vinegar.

"I didn't see a Christmas tree on the front porch," said Bert.

Pop accidentally set his beer can down on the edge of the ham plate—and grabbed it before it went over.

"Two Guys had a sale," he said. "I bought an artificial tree."

"We always had a real tree," said Trudy.

"You can't tell the difference. They're very believable."

Trudy started to say something, but Pop cut her off: "Who vacuums up when the goddamn thing sheds? You can build it to four, six feet—whatever you want."

"It packs away in a tube," said Mom.

"You can *grow* a tree in your house," said Pop, screwing the lid back on the pickle jar. "By the way, when are you and him gonna start acting like you're married—you in Hartford, him in New York City?"

Bert took their luggage up to Trudy's old room. Mom Steiner kept it as her daughter had left it: high school snapshots under the vanity glass, crucifix over the bed, graduation tassel hanging from the mirror knob, nursing books in the pine bookcase Pop built. There was a framed picture of him, around twenty, on the vanity. He stands with a foot up on the running board of an old truck with wooden spoke wheels. A sign on the open slats of the body reads: EDWARD STEINER, FREIGHT. Pop has a hard, glassy look. He wears a bow tie and white shirt with a black mourning band around the left sleeve. His father had died two days before. Pop will let you know how he'd bought the truck that morning, Ed Senior no longer there to stop him. The first truck in Troy, New York.

He woke in the dark, Trudy curled away from him. It was impossible not to touch in the hammocking mattress.

Mom Steiner was asleep, breathing heavily as Bert passed her bedroom at the head of the stairs. He caught a whiff of damp potting soil from her houseplants in the dormer window.

Down in the parlor, Bert plugged in the Christmas lights. Trudy and he had erected the new tree, up to six feet, and trimmed it. The presents lay open in their boxes. Bert ran the back of his hand over his gift of flannel pajamas. Mom sewed either pajamas or a shirt for him every Christmas. He picked out one of the hammered gold earrings he'd given Trudy; on her card he had copied out the Donne quote:

Our two souls, therefore, which are one,
Though I must go, endure not yet a breach,
But an expansion
Like gold to airy thinness beat.

The three bubble-lights, warmed up, began to bubble.

Bert lay with his head under the tree, staring up at the lights, the little double-sided mirrors, an old hand-blown Santa Claus, his own face looking down at him in a large golden globe.

What was he *feeling*? As though there were some lost emotion to be found in these old ornaments.

Pop was watching *Donahue* when Bert came into the parlor from breakfast.

"Parade's on at one," the old man said. "They have elegant floats, elegant."

Bert sat on the sofa, balancing a cup of coffee on his knee. Mom's Hummel crèche took up the coffee table. There was a basket of Christmas cards on the television and a white poinsettia from Buddy and Stephie.

Pop snorted when a woman in the TV audience said that she suffered from toxic shock syndrome contracted from a tampon.

"It's all they talk about," he said. "A priest was on the other day telling how he was attracted to women. I'll give them credit, though, they didn't show his face."

Trudy passed through on her way upstairs.

"I'll be ready in five minutes," she called to Bert.

Mom's sewing machine could be heard from her nook in the kitchen. She was making aprons for Sacred Heart's January bazaar.

"Looks like one of your maples lost a big limb," said Bert.

Pop had dug the two trees out in the fields in the twenties and planted them in the tiny front yard. Their roots had buckled the side-walk and made a familiar bump when you drove in the driveway.

"I'm cutting the damn things down," said Pop.

"That'll be the day. Summers you have it twenty degrees cooler than anyone on the block."

"I had a fella in the end of summer—Holy Christ!" Pop laughed as Donahue lifted a woman by the elbow and said, "What if I was the family doctor—delivered you—still care for your children—and I say you can use this tampon?"

"Toilet kept backing up," Pop went on. "This fella sends a long cable in—next thing I've got a six-foot trench in the front yard and a four-hundred-dollar bill. *Roots*. It's the old sewer pipes—roots grow right in, attracted to the shit."

"Did he solve the problem?"

Pop looked over: "Those damn things are alive."

It was cold with snow predicted, the bare ground frozen solid. Bert and Trudy walked down Pauling Avenue toward the city.

"Ma wants us to pick up half a pint of heavy cream," said Trudy. She wore her maroon parka and the old yellow Vermont ski hat. Her face looked puffy and stern.

"Want to stop at the Old Rubber?" Bert asked. "Have a couple for auld lang syne?"

Trudy didn't smile at their name for the Trojan Hotel. "I just feel like walking."

They waited for the light to change at the Point, where Spring crossed Pauling.

"So, what's happening with you and Mario?"

Trudy toed a piece of frozen slush. "We're not seeing one another. His wife threatened to take their little girl."

They crossed and walked along beside the iron fence that encloses Emma Willard School.

"Were you—planning to . . ."

Trudy glanced at Bert. "We didn't think about anything. It happened. It was impossible, we both knew that. We had no expectations."

The creche looked like something abandoned on the bleached lawn of the school. The foremost Wise Man tilted back from the cradle, as if surprised, the work of a frost heave.

"Come to New York,"

Trudy shook her head.

"We were good together."

Suddenly she gestured angrily: "Why did we come back here?"

"It was always good—"

"For you."

They overtook and passed a woman in a tweed coat carrying a booted chihuahua under her arm.

"The only way I can bear them is with you between us."

Bert stopped, facing Trudy: "Then why did you agree to come here?"

"Part of me wants things to be the way they were—familiar, safe. But we stopped living together. Things have changed—no matter how much you want them to be the same."

"I *don't* want them to be the same! I've changed, too, you know?"

They were facing each other on the sidewalk, breath clouds mingling.

"Are you in love with this guy, for Chrissake?"

Trudy looked at him sadly.

"Do you love him—just answer me that!"

"Mario was a small part of it. For the first time in my life, I'm free. I have my own place, job, friends—"

"*Lover*. Sounds like you've been sprung."

"I don't think we're right for each other now."

"You kill me when you say that." Bert jammed his gloved hands deep into his pockets. "It just gives you an idea what it cost our parents to stay together."

"Was it worth it?" Trudy asked gently.

Skaters were out on Mount Ida pond. Far below where Bert and Trudy stood, a kids' hockey game was in progress. A man swooped around the perimeter on racing skates, hands clasped behind his back. They'd skated here. The sound of whacking sticks ratcheted up. Bert gazed at Trudy's profile as she watched a girl in pink tights and short pink skirt practicing spins. Cassiopeia would have been ten, about her age. If their daughter had lived, who knows . . . All at once she pulled in her arms, whirling like a drill.

They walked up a side street to where it dead-ended at a cast iron cemetery gate.

Pop's mother and father were buried near an old marble angel; their marker a flat granite slab.

"The thought of being with you—in that tiny apartment in New York—" Trudy pulled her hand out of her mitten and touched her cheek as though it were hot. "I wouldn't blame you if you left me."

He could hear water trickling under the ice. They had gone into the woods behind the cemetery, down a steep ravine, and were following along the frozen stream in its bottom. A mattress of dead leaves underfoot. Trudy followed twenty feet behind Bert. It had started to snow, he couldn't remember when, cold pellets, like tiny camphor balls.

They walked until a fallen tree blocked their way.

He heard her come up, felt her touch his sleeve.

They lay down in the leaves beside the frozen stream and he made love to her.

They lay for a while after, warm in their heavy coats, snow rattling in the cups of dead leaves.

A ROOM OF HER OWN

1

Stars like diamonds—and cold! I remember Vermont Junes. Greg and Jo wanted me to sleep at the farmhouse, but I needed to be in my own shelter this first night. Neither of them ask why I am doing this. I don't want to try and explain to anyone.

I dragged the tent up onto the high meadow, to the corner where it angles into the woods. This is where I'll live.

Reading the directions by Pop's kerosene lantern, I set up the tent. At one point there was a snort in the dark—Belle and Lulu, Greg's Morgans. We share this meadow. Their company gave me courage and I finished almost whistling. The tent sagged and was lopsided—Bert wouldn't have approved—but it stood, and it was mine.

I left the lighted lantern inside and went down to the car for some things. Coming back I could see the tent up on the meadow, a fairy's green lantern.

My home now is an eight-by-twelve-foot room of heavy canvas that cost a hundred and sixty-five dollars, new. A whole house for less than a month's rent in the city! It is big enough to stand in, and I have a cot, a card table and a chair. It smells of hemp and canvas, bringing back memories of summer camp. I woke during the night and saw the moon blurrily through my roof, and woke this morning within a green translucence. Is it not perfect that a painter live in a canvas house?

I thought it would be difficult leaving Hartford. "Do what you have to do," Mario said when I told him I was going. Not that I ever asked anything of him. But this sad ending, as though we're strangers. Oh, Mario, that we loved at all was a miracle. This truck driver's daughter never felt such joy, pleasure, freedom from who she was. I don't wish to hold on to anything. It's the beginning of summer. Like the cricket, I want the whole eternal time to play.

2

Greg appeared one afternoon at the tent. Luckily Trudy had clothes on. He was embarrassed by the utter privacy he discovered her in—the open journal, frypan with leftover scrambled eggs in it, female undergarments drying on a line. He explained that the cut hay was dried on the meadow and a storm promising—would she help them get it in? It sounded odd when she spoke—she hadn't said anything aloud in a week it seemed—her voice harsh and rusty—and loud.

Greg drove the hay wagon clucking and talking to the horses while Jo and Trudy walked along opposite sides forking up hay. It was pleasant easy work, the hay light and fragrant, dried baby's breath, daisies, black-eyed susans mixed in. They joked and talked as they worked. The horses would fart, leaving a rich, fermented odor on the air that was far from unpleasant. Gathering hay alternated with rides back to the barn to unload. As the afternoon wore on there was less talk; they were bound by the rhythm of work, and then by urgency as thunderheads built in the west. They finished up as the first drops of rain fell.

Greg and Trudy made ratatouille from fresh-picked garden vegetables while Jo fixed an apple crisp. Greg brought up bottles of home brew he'd been aging in the cellar—strong, thick, black stuff that was supposed to be English porter. The storm beat against the house while they ate. For the first time since coming Trudy was glad not to be alone.

After dessert and coffee, Greg played his violin—Bach, Vivaldi. Jo laughed and said he was much sought after for barn dances—if they only knew! Greg played some Mozart, and Trudy found herself almost weeping for the sheer pleasure of it.

It was after midnight when she headed back up the meadow. The rain had stopped but the air was heavy as though there were more to come. She climbed, pausing now and then to glance down at the lights of the farmhouse. There was a life. From Greg and Jo's union good things had come: hearth, house, barn, animals, fields. They owned their life and were owned by it. She felt like a moth beating against the lit lantern, except she was forcing herself away from the light which drew her, which seemed life itself, out into the dark.

She sensed the presence of the horses. They seemed inhospitable, inhuman. She couldn't see the tent until she was almost on it. There were flickers of lightning, distant rumbles. She zipped up in her damp bag, slept curled in a ball.

3

I dreamed of her—for the first time since that autumn eleven years ago. Two nights in a row. In the first she is lying in a crib wrapped in a blanket, looking up as though expecting me. She speaks though her lips don't move. She is too young. In the morning, I can't remember what she said. Maybe it was only my wish to hear her. I cried that day in odd moments. Gratefully.

I had a daughter. She would be eleven, nearly. My life would be different. Yet she could be here with me, it's not hard to imagine. Cassiopeia Bert named her. He'd been studying astrology. The Queen. Not a real name.

What would I have called her? I never held her, never saw her. She lived in me six months, then while I wasn't looking, disappeared—utterly. I can look up these nights and see Cassiopeia, that W of stars lying on its side. Sometimes Bert calls her Cass, as though he'd gotten to know her that well.

In the second dream we are walking in the woods. I'm taking her to school. I turn to say something and she isn't there. I'm frantic. There's an old woman talking to me in our New Haven vegetable store—a witch—"Is she yours?" "Yes," I say. "Watch out," she says, "they snatch them to sell in Mexico."

I wake up—and desperately try to go back, will myself back.

What does her absence mean, since that's what I have? I feel blessed to have found her in the dream, even if I lost her there.

4

After drawing in the woods in the afternoon, Trudy stopped by the pond for a swim. It was nearly dark, but lighter than when she usually came. She felt uneasy taking off her clothes. She'd never met anyone at the pond—or on her rambles. She felt like a deer that comes out on the meadow at twilight.

The pond was warm with icy spots where the springs came up. She imagined them rising on clear stems to the surface where she swam through the shocking blooms, cold that took the breath.

I float, looking up at the stars, huge and close—lift my hand thinking to pick one. It's the beginning of stories, the world young and mysterious: woman in the pond picking stars . . .

She floated, breasts awash in the dark light. She almost slept, if that were possible—when lifting her head she saw a shape, someone standing over her clothes.

"Warm night . . ." Greg's voice came to her, intimate in the dark. "Thought I'd take a dip myself."

He was naked, penis dangling pale in the shadow of his thigh. He waded in and dove with a heavy splash.

Trudy came out and dressed without drying herself.

Greg swam, kicks and arm strokes shattering the pond. He reached almost to the opposite shore and stood, water to his navel, blowing air out and combing back his long hair with both hands.

"Nice."

Trudy hugged her knees, watching him.

Greg swam back. He dried himself with a towel and sat ten feet from her, staring out at the water.

"You looked like the belly button of the pond out there," he said, and chuckled. "You're a pretty swimmer."

An owl hooted in the woods.

"I've seen you before," Greg said, "without your clothes. You're not altogether careful."

"I didn't think I had to be."

"You're like a kid let out of school, aren't you? Except you're a woman." Greg paused, and added with a hint of invitation: "I can't help my feelings."

They were silent until Trudy couldn't stand it and blurted out that she couldn't bear to have anyone touch her now. She was in a kind of chrysalis. She went silent at once, aware how naive she must sound, how off the wall. A little like a crazy woman. Like Crazy Mary long ago at Dyken Pond they all used to joke about. Crazy Trudy. Maybe that's how Greg saw her. A thorny temptation. He didn't say anything. After a while he went back into the water.

She could hear his splashing as she walked, then lost it to crickets and night birds and the damp absorbent silence of the woods.

The image of a Bride of Christ stirred up in her—and she laughed in exasperation. Strange fulfillment of the "calling" she'd experienced for a few months during her senior year at Sacred Heart. Holy Virgin of the Pond.

5

Trudy watched Mira Hagen coming up the meadow. Mira wore slacks and a light blouse and carried a small blue duffel bag over one shoulder. Her blonde hair was mannishly short, smoke trailed from the cigarette in her left hand.

Trudy ran down and hugged her—almost fiercely.

Mira laughed. "You haven't seen a human being in a while!" Her glance took in the tent, the circle of fire stones, the primitive kitchen under the maple. "My God, you *are* camped out."

And suddenly it seemed mundane, slovenly. Eden? Trudy felt almost ashamed. The descriptions she'd written to Mira seemed wildly romantic—worse, sentimental. Mira could never see the place, mystical and haunted, as she did. It was ordinary sunlight falling rather hotly on plain meadow grass. The horses were horses. Had her friend even noticed Lulu and Belle standing like boulders in the deep shade below?

That evening, the valley spread purple below them, the two women sat before the tent drinking the wine Mira had brought. An evening like the first Trudy had spent on the meadow, writing in her journal. But two months had passed.

As they talked, Mira would reach across and touch Trudy's arm—naturally enough—but Trudy was painfully aware of it. No one had touched her so easily, so intimately since Mario—it made her want to cry out with gratitude.

They spent mornings around the tent reading and talking, making pots of coffee on the camp stove. Trudy would go off after lunch to draw, Mira often accompanying her, camera in hand.

Once, Trudy brought Mira down with her to work in the garden, but Jo had been there and it was oddly constrained. Jo made an excuse to return to the house. Mira had laughed, saying she probably thought they were lovers.

Mira was looking at Trudy's portfolio of summer work—some watercolors but mainly pencil drawings, carefully detailed toadstools, ledgestone with lichen, wild thyme in bloom, pond lilies, a bullfrog.

"Quite nice . . ."

Trudy could detect the hint of uninterest.

"I wanted to look closely at things. Themselves, not my interpretation. I wanted to watch the frog breathing, his sides going in and out, the fly coming closer . . ."

"Back to basics," said Mira.

"I love being in the woods. Drawing's an excuse to go."

"Well, very nice," Mira repeated. "Reminds me of Dürer: lines, shading—kind of a silky feeling . . ."

She was studying a drawing—a decaying log lying in deep woods, lush with fungi, toadstools, mosses.

"Is this a doll?"

At the side of the picture, almost incidentally, a small white figure lay at the base of a tree. Unlike the rest of the drawing, which had been rendered in detail, the figure was vague, not quite focused. Mira was squinting at it.

"It's a spirit," Trudy said.

Mira's blue eyes regarded her; long-lashed, almond eyes with a quality of sleepiness that disarmed, until you realized they were taking you in like a camera.

"Well," she said, "Shakespearean. Fairies . . ."

Trudy wouldn't try and explain that she'd been working on the drawing at the time she'd had the dreams of Cassiopeia. The figure had simply appeared in the picture, Trudy unaware of having drawn it.

She took the portfolio back, gazed a moment at the figure, brushed it lightly with the ball of her thumb.

"Where will you go from here?" asked Mira.

"Go?"

"Your work."

Trudy laughed. "I thought you meant where would *I* go."

One day it rained and they were confined to the tent. When evening came, Mira suggested they drive somewhere for dinner.

There were no guests at the old inn on a rainy weeknight; their host lit a fire for them in the parlor and served after-dinner drinks.

"Civilization . . ." Mira murmured swirling her cognac.

Trudy smiled, lifting her glass: "To illusions. Where would we be without them."

"To more and better illusions," Mira toasted.

Over dessert she asked about Bert. Trudy said she hadn't heard from him since the beginning of summer.

Which wasn't true. Bert had written often. Letters filled with his New York life, the bakery job, new friends, the off-off theater scene—his longing for her buried in the glitter. She had not been able to respond.

One evening while Mira was there Bert phoned. Greg came up to fetch Trudy. She listened to his voice far away in the city, like the voice of an old radio announcer. He was making a life for himself, he said, apart from her—working nights in the bakery, working on Vermont stories, going to museums, concerts, plays. New friends. "I've got a life here," he said. "It's a real change." Implicit was the hint—or threat—he wouldn't wait for her forever. That there might be other women. It was almost unbearable hearing him brag about his independence and freedom.

Don't wait for me, she said at last. There was no place for him in her life—he couldn't accept it. Nor could she explain to this man she'd lived many years with, for whom she cared deeply—except in a kind of coldness, a paralysis of the heart.

He talked on and on, as though frightened a silence would cut the line connecting them. Trudy felt like she was turning to stone with the receiver in her hand. She could not respond to him for fear of betraying herself.

"No," she said quietly when he asked if he could visit, and she felt his hurt as though she'd hit him.

He asked if Mario had come there. She could feel the hysteria in him then, threatening the little beachhead he was trying to establish in the face of self-loathing, failure, loss of her. It was all she could do not to slam down the phone and run, hearing that wave of their past, that terrible amorphousness out of which she had so awkwardly and painfully crept, which she could not slip back into.

"How much time will you need?" he asked.

He couldn't see her face grown vague with her loss of how to speak to him. She looked like an Indian, taken over with an emptiness beyond sorrow.

Walking back up to camp Trudy thought about the life they'd had together; a story she knew by heart, a fairy tale set long ago. Vermont and the cabin . . . Maybe it had become that for Bert, too, the stories he was writing.

She had previously visited him in his apartment in the East Village. What he'd extolled as cool and funky and in the middle of what's happening had only depressed her. The storefront was long and narrow and dark; steel bars covered the front and rear windows; cockroaches moved like a nighttime army. Her breath constricted thinking of it. The two of them in it. When you sat up in the loft bed, your head hit the ceiling.

But where would she go? The cricket's summer was ending. There was no returning to Hartford. Pop had hinted, sardonically—but meant it—that she should come home. Seductive! Come back and resume adolescence. Admit the experiment had failed, she had failed. Come back and suck her claws in the tomb of the ancestral home.

They were in the woods behind camp, Trudy sketching a stone wall, Mira shooting her. Mira worked rhythmically: nearer, farther away, different angles, shooting the whole while, adjusting speed, changing filters, never studiously composing a frame.

Trudy had been flattered that Mira liked to photograph her, but she never got comfortable with it. Herself as a series of pictures of herself. The actual shooting was nice, like a massage, light touches as Mira ranged over her clicking and clicking. Her life here was the opposite of this fragmentation and analysis: a kind of unknowing wholeness. She could feel her balance in her drawings, in weeding the garden, in swimming, in sleep, in dreams. She sensed that Mira wanted to surprise her, catch her in absolute candidness in order to understand her. She was a kind of mystery to the older woman. How did she look to Mira? Fixed in a series of moments: Trudy moody, Trudy laughing, Trudy with her eyes closed. It seemed the more there were of her, the more unreal. Who were these detached women, each a little different? Mira would say: "Now, *this* is you." Or, simply, "Nope." Yet they were harmless, dropping away like sheets of tracing paper. She did not have Mira's compulsion to *understand*. Her drawings were not attempts to understand anything.

Back at camp, Mira announced that she was going to leave. She was studying Trudy through the camera, screwing her into focus in the lens. Then she didn't snap the picture, dropping the camera into her bag.

"I'm bored," she said. "It's been great."

She held Trudy by both arms and shook her gently as though settling her. "Good seeing you this way. Strong."

Trudy stood in front of the tent watching Mira descend the meadow. Her slacks, her shoulder bag, her short silky hair. Life running backward. Either you were leaving or being left, aching that the two of you could not be one forever. And great relief of course. Her friend's visit had caused her to withdraw from the intense, private life she had been living. Their time together colored by the older woman's gently ironic objective style.

Mira's receding form blurred, changed into Bert's. He had gone away from her so many times, but always as preludes to returning. She needed not to run down the meadow after him. It wasn't so hard; the sense of having passed beyond the narrow defile of their life frightened and filled her with exultation. She wanted to burst into something like a hymn of praise—like the hymn that pealed forth from the old Sacred Heart organ concluding mass. Tears blurred her vision as Bert dropped from sight below the hill and she was alone.

JOURNAL 1979–1980

11 AUGUST

In tent, a.m., hill above Shuman's farm for Bread and Puppet *Resurrection Circus* weekend.

Yesterday train to New Haven, thumbed up from there.

North country, rain and cool. Blueberries, sharp dark firs.

Found Trudy and Mira on hill.

Trudy slept with Mira in her tent while I slept alone in mine, which seemed natural, under the circumstances. The two of them drove up together.

Beautiful talk by Helen and Scott Nearing. He over ninety, so clear and steady and sane. "If you can't afford it you don't need it." "If you can't do it yourself, don't do it." Felt like Thoreau was there.

15 AUGUST

At Gran's, gentle rain. For breakfast whole wheat pancakes with blueberries and maple syrup. Painted pantry floor in the forenoon, spaghetti for lunch and apple pie.

Yesterday weeded flower garden beside house, painted mailbox white, walked up brook from swimming hole below Gran's—Old Farm Road and hill road back.

Fried chicken, potatoes, garden squash for supper.

The Hill very busy since our day: new year-round places, new side roads, a lot of lumbering. Bryant who sold his old farm and moved to Iowa is back and building above First Bridge, and Gran heard Hadley's going to build houses on his old hayfield.

Ten years later . . . little ruddy-faced Janice L is married, lives in Barre and has a baby.

When Gran saw me on the road below the house with my pack (coming from Bread and Puppet), she hollered, and I watched her bearing across the lawn in a wide-brimmed straw hat turned up in the front like Cisco Kid. Ken recognized me too. Right away I was home with a cup of tea and gassing with Gran.

Left Trudy and Mira after buttermilk pancakes and coffee at Saint Johnsbury House, they continuing on down I-91, me thumbing west on Route 2. Walked the river road to Gran's, getting a blister on right toe.

Old Norbert was sitting at his window. I waved but don't think he saw.

Gran told me of her grandfather Morse: "He wore a beard and a big hat like he meant business, and I thought him the handsomest man around."

16 AUGUST

Reading Nearings' *Living the Good Life.* Autographed copy!

Clear morning and cool; after pancakes and coffee, set off for the Hump.

Howard's face shows at his camp window—he waves me in. Only reason he stays there is "to be around Miz Beston." Howard paid $500 last winter for oil, gas, and electric for his camp. He can hardly bend to tie his sneaker. He could get wood, have a garden, couple of chickens, an old pickup truck. But his spirit has run out—were it not for

Gran he might quit altogether. He is warmed by her, beams and chuckles as we talk. "You walk in on Miz Beston after being gone a while, and she looks like she's expecting you."

Howard drives me up to the foot of the trail, and off I hike, fresh.

Up Dean Trail, past the beaver pond and steep climb onto the paws of the Couching Lion, tiny sweet blueberries. Stand on the cliff looking out across to New Hampshire. How many times this hike. Maybe last one with Trudy and the dog. We tried to put down roots; we left. The child didn't live. We've failed to make a home somewhere. Our marriage has either failed or is transforming (what does that mean?).

Adirondacks and Samuel de Champlain's Lake from top of the Hump. Then down and down—past the wreckage of the Army plane that crashed in World War Two. And out finally at the Dog Cemetery.

Home by 6.

17 AUGUST

Porch in the warm morning sun.

The deliberate scheduled planned meticulous quality of the Nearings' endeavor.

The solid satisfactions.

The hard work with results yielded and benefits along the way—health, a life.

The meaningful activity and direct experience.

The satisfaction of doing for yourself.

Independence.

Cultivating a philosophy by living it.

Necessity—sticking to it.

The process of many projects in various stages of completion (duration).

Taking time to do things well. Taking time to work deliberately while taking pleasure in the work.

Subsistence economics.

Lining up priorities determining projected duration of projects. Thus digging a pond takes fourteen years, and a garden right away.

18 AUGUST

Berrying before noon, clearcuts up behind Evelyn's where someone had logged. Two quarts of blackberries in no time. Ate ham sandwich Gran had made for me, tomato from her garden. And fig Newtons. One I tossed away—for next time. A fox slipping through the shadows.

Gran's daughters, Mariann and Catherine, visiting when I got back—they hoped I might stay the winter, keep Gran company.

Got a knapsack full of Duchess apples from tree beside the brook. Which I cut up—two packs frozen and one large pie immediately! Incredible warm pie for which Gran magically produced vanilla ice cream from her freezer.

Brook is cold from recent rain, so I didn't go in.

Gran hasn't been up to fishing much.

19 AUGUST

Manhattan.

Thumbed off from Gran's yesterday morning.

Ride into Montpelier with guy in a van fragrant with apples. Bryant's as it turned out. Friend of his bought Bryant's place and lets the trees go for cider. This guy lives year-round in a tipi up there.

One ride from Montpelier to Hartford with a couple of motorcycle guys in a truck, drinking beer and tequila.

Train from Hartford to New York City.

1980

12 MARCH

Gran's.

Took the 10:45 pm Montrealer Monday, was 7:30 Tuesday morning in Waterbury. Left the city in a rainstorm and it was snowing up here. First light around 6 at White River Junction. Stark early morning sight the flying snow and white Vermont houses against a hill. Like I'd opened the pages of an old book.

Got off at Waterbury in the cold and flying snow, walked up Main Street and stopped in a new restaurant. Early morning road crew and one old guy with a cup of coffee in booth chain-smoking, and a fine older waitress handling things, knowing most of the men, pouring seconds of hot coffee. Had two eggs with sausages, hash browns and rye toast.

Hiked river road to Gran's. Bad wind in open places so I walked with hands over face, and tucked long johns down front of pants to cover legs. It let up after Wayne Martin's. At Gran's I tapped on the front window, she came from the kitchen and let me in, saying, "Well, you must have known!" She happened to be making catfish chowder. I'd brought a bunch of fresh greens from the First Ave grocery, a kielbasa and pumpernickel bread from the Polish butcher, Trudy's collection of cabin poems, and seed packets saved from my city roof garden.

Howard came down and we had amazing catfish chowder for lunch (someone had caught an eighteen-pounder at the Waterbury dam and *somehow* Gran got a couple of steaks—which she froze).

Everyone's water is frozen and some wells are dry. The Kneelands are having a bad time, Gran says. The old man is *sick* sick and off his head to boot. Ma Kneeland has to take it. Holly is home but walks with a cane and is very heavy. Ma has to haul water down from their spring. (Later, taking a walk uphill past their dilapidated house I saw her humped form dragging a litter of five or six plastic gallon milk bottles tied together, downhill on the end of a rope, over the fresh snow. She had her back turned so I slid by, resisting an impulse to stop.)

Evelyn Johnson is just the same, "only a little more so."

Ken is gone, caught or ate something. They all speak fondly of him.

Gran: "He was no sooner to the vet when three or four dogs were ready to move in."

Howard: "It won't do but you've got to have an animal. Folks won't leave you in peace."

Gran's granddaughter Brenda dropped by and stayed for dinner. She was pleased to see Trudy's poetry collection, reading through it after we ate. Thought *How Homer Got a Girlfriend* especially good.

Brenda is really of Gran's line—a strong, generous, good-willed person. Bought an old farmhouse she's fixing up. Teaches art to grades 1–6 in Burlington, new car, one of Ken's puppies. While we lived here she was attending the University of Vermont. It was Brenda who'd loaned us snowshoes.

13 MARCH

Slept good under electric blanket, upstairs over Gran's bedroom.

Wheat cakes and Harrington's bacon for breakfast, then helped Gran by rolling out dough for four pies (three apple, one blackberry, from the freezer from my August picking!) The incredible winey-pungent flavor of wild blackberries . . . in a March pie! Then rolled and cut sour milk donuts, which Gran deep-fried. And we ate with mugs of Red Rose tea.

I went a'walking with three donuts and an apple in my pocket. From Old Farm Road tried to cut over the hill to Wayne Martin's back hill pasture, but snow too deep. So beautiful up there, deep blue sky and sun and pure white snow and hemlocks and birches and the wind and me toiling upward. Finally gave up and ran plunging back down my broken trail to Silver Farm. Where it used to be—now the whole thing collapsed into a cellar hole, under a blanket of snow. Silver Farm, our old marker in a sea of green seen from the top of the Hump. Hung my last donut on the branch of the apple tree, still there, head of rusty pitchfork stuck into it.

Would it be possible to come back here after ten years gone? Be back again in this world of natural things? But own a car! Have a telephone! There are many ways to go about living here. But simplify your life. Heed the Nearings. You put yourself into a situation, and consequences and solutions follow. It is possible to survive, to thrive. What is plain to me right now: I am in the City—everything the opposite of here—and need to be there until my obligations are done. To my grandmother, to involvement with theater. To Trudy. Then I could come back here, resume a life interrupted?

14 MARCH

Howard: "He was already a full-grown man. He says I'll get rid of them kittens for you. He got out his shotgun, put down a pie tin full of milk and he set them all around it. That way he thought he'd get rid of them all at once. Well, sir, he shot the middle of the pie plate out and didn't touch a one of them."

Brenda: "Before the oil stove, a big old wood-burning stove sat right here. Gran'd be mopping the floor and she'd hit the stove and boy would it sizzle!"

Ten above last night. Icicles in sun dripping from front porch roof this morning. Chickadees and downy and hairy woodpeckers, and jays, at the suet bags on the clothesline.

Visited with Ma Kneeland, then Brownie and Louise. Good people. Their lives not easy. Brownie: "Think you'd buy the cabin back?"

No energy for walking. Sat for a long while in sun at the Shamrock deer camp on Old Farm Road.

Cut Gran some budded hobblebush to jip out. Holly was visiting with her Polaroid and took a picture of Gran and me with a loaf of fresh-baked bread. A mellow oversize girl/woman. Asked about her brother—Homer is living with a woman in a trailer in Richmond. Had been working at a lumber mill—got laid off.

Played Scrabble with Gran. Catherine came by about nine p.m. and drove me in to Waterbury to catch the train. Train crowded; dozed uncomfortably.

Back in slushy, snowing Manhattan a little after seven a.m.

NEW YORK

SWISS

I went to the play reading because I knew the director, Greta Tanzer, and because Max Frisch would be there. The chance to meet a writer I had long admired—ever since my father played The Professor in *The Firebugs*, twenty years ago—was not to be missed. In anticipation I'd been reading *Montauk*, Frisch's memoir/novel.

The small lecture room in NYU's Deutsches Haus was crammed. I was standing pressed against the rear wall while Trudy had found a spot on the floor in front of the stage. I recognized Frisch from his book jacket photographs, seated in the audience. A younger red-haired woman sat beside him, and I wondered if she was Lynn from *Montauk*.

The play, a monologue by an "emerging Swiss writer," was read by an actress with a thick German accent and a bad cold. She kept wiping her red nose with a handkerchief held in one hand. She was supposed to be a schoolmistress lecturing a class of imbeciles (us), and almost did too good a job: without dropping out of character, she barked "Shut up!" at a woman who had asked her to please speak more clearly.

A panel discussion followed on current German and Swiss drama. The panelists, including Frisch, my friend Greta, the playwright, a critic, and the actress, sat shoulder to shoulder at a table which filled the tiny stage.

At one point the playwright declared with a red face that he had "gone beyond Brecht." Max Frisch sitting at the right end of the table looked like a somnolent bear unearthed for the occasion. He remarked that what interested him was not repeating himself. He hadn't written a play in a while because of this feeling of following a known route. But he liked writing for the stage, was attracted by erotic bodies and by the language of speech. "I see good-looking actors," he said good-naturedly, "and I want them to play me." He had been jotting down dialogues, waiting to see if they would lead somewhere.

The reception upstairs, though in a larger room, felt more crowded than the reading. The audience had gotten to their feet and spread out, and were acting up a storm: reciting lines, pulling faces, posing, drinking. Windows had been propped open and smoke funneled out as though we were a ship under full steam on the March sea.

Trudy took a glass of wine from my hand and vanished into the crowd. We were on the outs—a minor disagreement over something or other. All our tiffs seemed to come from a general irritableness. We'd talked about splitting up, almost, it seemed, since we'd begun living together again. A year and a half.

German was being spoken on every hand; though I knew barely a word, it was in the blood, and I had no trouble imagining I understood it, standing there soaking it in by osmosis.

"You copped out, old buddy—gave up on them as human beings and turned the story into a Rube Goldberg machine: *if we go fast enough, no one will notice we're not moving.*"

Harry Saint James had squeezed past a large woman to join me. A few weeks ago I'd made the mistake of showing Harry a story, and every time he saw me he offered another insight:

"Instead of allowing your characters their ragged, unpredictable humanity, you subject them to some a priori *theory* you've gotten infected with—Sartre, Robbe-Grillet and so forth. My friend—" Harry squeezed my arm—"you've turned them into *puppets*. Stories are people."

A woman passed us, seemed to float, cradling a white lily in her arms. She looked like a figure from a tarot card. It was the suggestion of a smile: private, self-satisfied as the Mona Lisa's.

I escaped Harry to get a refill.

Trudy was in a conversation with Greta and I steered the other way. There's not much to say to the director if you don't like the play or the acting.

A group stood around Max Frisch; his large head was inclined as he listened to a woman who spoke directly into his ear. He held a plastic cup of white wine. Lynn stood on his other side. I began imagining they'd just driven back to the city from Montauk—straight out of the book. *Montauk* seduces you into thinking you know the author. His words have that unpracticed quality of life. You feel a third party sitting on the beach with "Max" and "Lynn" listening to them, privy to his thoughts. And here they were. No surprise perfect strangers come up and speak familiarly with him. No wonder Max had developed that impenetrable look. The least I could do was leave him alone.

I looked for Trudy, couldn't find her and started for the stairs.

"You're leaving?" It was the woman with the lily. "You don't know the saying?" She spoke with a slight German accent: "He who stays to the end of the party rules the world."

I asked about the lily, remarking that she "looked like a vestal virgin"—whatever I meant by that.

She laughed a soft, merry little laugh. "It's my birthday; someone gave me the lily. My name is Leela Marqua. And you must be a writer—why else would you be standing around like a storm cloud? Come, I'll introduce you."

And there I was shaking the hand of Max Frisch, being considered by a pair of shrewd, polite eyes. I blurted out my appreciation for his writing, mentioning my father playing The Professor in *The Firebugs*.

"Ah, Beiderman," Frisch said, seeming to soften at the mention of his old play. Did *I* write? Yes, in the midst of, of a collection—"In the autobiographical mode," I stuck on, thinking of *Montauk*.

Max Frisch was very kind to a young man who, if nothing else, exuded sincerity. He would hope, he said, to see something of mine one day.

Did that mean I could send him something?

Leela Marqua brought me over to the Swiss playwright who was holding a sort of opposing court to Frisch's. He shook my hand. "So, who are the hot new American writers these days?"

Other than myself, freshly confident from Max's handshake, I didn't really know any other American writers. However, extrapolating from my own experience, I thought we were a private, fearful, backward bunch working alone in rooms, unconnected with anyone. I resisted asking if he'd gone beyond Frisch.

"You looked interesting standing there brooding," Leela said when we were alone again. "I decided, if he doesn't say something, I'm going to be bold. But, you know, if it hadn't been my birthday . . ."

We sat on a couch talking near one of the open windows. Leela told me she was a sculptor.

"I refuse to call myself an *artist*," she said. "There are too many *artists*. There is something too practical in my nature. I make things."

That sounded Swiss.

She laughed. "Swiss, yes. Cuckoo clocks and immaculate bathrooms. I hate the Swiss. Children are old by the time they're three. You see them walking down the street with their nannies, little clockwork soldiers. Those who rebel are crushed or, like me, escape."

"And Frisch?"

"Max has made his peace. He has lived all over the world in order to be Swiss. Or, should I say, to be able to write and be himself."

Trudy had come up and stood behind the couch.

"I forgot my keys," she said. "I can't get in."

Without introducing her, I gave her my keys; she departed without a word. I felt angry, awkward. We had both stopped wearing our wedding bands.

Leela invited me to join her and Max and some others at the Cedar Tavern.

"I can't," I muttered. "I have some work to do."

She smiled sympathetically.

We walked downstairs; I helped her into her coat. Max and the others were waiting outside. I felt utterly wretched and inept. I managed to get it out that I had to see her again.

A woman I took tai chi with was selling her Honda 350. An old bike but in good shape. She let me try it after class one night, with her on the back. I wanted to twist the throttle and keep going—take this woman I didn't even know and *go*—another city, another life. She was willing to take two hundred down and the rest in modest monthly installments.

Next class I brought the money, but the bike had been torched two nights prior in front of her building.

There was a crowd. Leela had set a long banquet table buffet-style with salads, cheeses, cold cuts, breads, fruit. There was a case each of red and white wine. Vases of flowers, lit candles. Her basement studio felt like a Swiss chalet.

Leela wore a pleated black skirt that brushed the floor, a white silk blouse, her arms bare, her black hair pinned up. Sophisticated and practical. She was busy playing hostess: bringing out platters of warm hors d'oeuvres, visiting with guests. She introduced me. I spoke again with Max Frisch, again no less awkwardly.

"I'm glad you came," Leela said, pressing my arm. "I hope you're having a good time."

"It would be better if I had a minute with you."

She smiled and drew me over to a small Slavic-looking man who stood by himself.

David was Hungarian, in his mid-fifties. He had made the pumpernickel bread for the party, Leela said as she left us.

It was good bread. I asked his secret.

"How do you like her?" he asked. "Obviously she's in love again." And he chuckled. "We made the furniture here, Leela and me. Banquet table and benches, the bed. How do you like the bed?"

The bed was huge and piled with coats.

"We would go out late at night and steal wood from construction sites. I built the things, Leela carved the bas-reliefs. This used to be my place. I let her have it when I moved to Paris. Stupid, eh?"

He reached out and unbuttoned the bottom button of my sports coat.

Across the room Leela had seated herself in Frisch's lap and was whispering something to him. She lifted her head with a laugh and Max looked up at her with a sly expression.

"Wonderful lover," said David. "Completely focused, makes you feel like you're the most important man in the world."

"Oh, Max, *you*!" Leela cried out.

"The secret's in the sourdough starter," said David. "It's been in my family centuries. I brought a vial over on the boat. I'll drop some by for you, with Leela, along with my recipe."

Some of Leela's sculptures were displayed on a table and the floor, roped off against the wall. Abstract shapes carved out of white marble showing the chisel marks. And one piece the size of a football in pure black stone polished to a high sheen. *Egg at the End of the World* a tag before it read.

The party was breaking up and I hadn't spent five minutes with this woman all evening. She walked me to the elevator. She pressed into me as we kissed.

"I wanted to do that all night," she said.

We kissed again and my hand went to her breast and she trembled. The elevator door opened and as if on cue there stood Frisch and Lynn. Max said something to Leela in Swiss and she said something back. It was not hard imagining them father and daughter.

Looking down on Saint Marks Place I could hear Trudy washing supper dishes in the back of the apartment. We would be married twelve years in September.

That time seemed both without limit and unreal; being with her had become one of the conditions of my life. I had known her forever. We had no future. No plans. I worked nights in the bakery and wrote; she'd found a job through Mario, a friend of his running a music studio on the Upper West Side.

There were a lot of people out walking; the action never stops on Saint Marks Place. After a while Trudy came into the dark room.

"I think I'm going to have a relationship with this woman," I said.

She said nothing.

A week later, she moved out.

I thought of David building the huge bed on which we had just made love and now lay resting.

"David is my best friend." Leela snuggled against me. "You're not jealous, are you? But, that was seven years ago."

Jealous? I'd made love to her half a dozen times. They had been lovers for years, built furniture, eaten meals, traveled to foreign countries. They had lived together. Gotten sick together. I didn't know how I felt about David. I had never made love more passionately to a woman—nor felt it more reciprocated. As though we had been waiting for each other, hungering for what the other could give.

"David is special," Leela said. "He was in a concentration camp in the war. I learned so many things from him. I would like you to get to know him."

"I'd rather concentrate on you."

She took my face in her strong hands. "Who are you, you strange man? Were we sister and brother? In the same womb?"

We made love very slowly and for a long time, with great curiosity and tenderness. I was on top, barely moving as we stared into each other's eyes.

"I hope," she said, "we never become a burden to each other."

"Am I squashing you . . ."

"Vor dem Essen, hängt man's Maul;
Nach dem Essen ist man faul."

Gram looked at me expectantly, and I translated. "*Before eating, a man's jaw hangs down; after eating, he's full as a tick.*"

"Tick," she said. "Let's have those donuts Otto brought."

Astoria, at my grandmother's for Sunday dinner. Ninety-one, she had lived by herself since my grandfather died eight years ago.

Gram had roasted a chicken while I shopped on Steinway Street: Benkerts for Kaiser rolls and coffee ring; Shaller and Webber for cold cuts; coffee, canned foods, bananas, etc. at The Associated. Our routine twice a month since I'd moved to the city.

"Don't get the wristwatch wet," she joked as I dunked a donut.

Afterward, we had cigarettes. I would put two in my mouth at once and light them, handing Gram hers like we were in a noir film. She would smoke, relaxing in her rocker, one foot up on the footstool. And that is the time I remember, the quiet, the mantel clock chiming, the smokes rising from our cigarettes. No future beyond the next puff.

My old "box of tricks" had stayed in the bottom of the coat closet—as though awaiting the return of the man. When we visited when I was a child I would go right to the closet, take out my box and dump it into the middle of the floor: wooden blocks, hard rubber cars, a stamped metal dump truck, World War Two soldiers. And the cast-iron brewery wagon with eight detachable iron horses. Gram had provided empty thread spools for beer barrels.

"A letter from Walter," she said, reaching it over to me from the side table.

I hadn't heard from Dad since the directive to stay out of his and Jeanette's life. Seven years. Through Gram I knew he'd retired and they had moved to the village outside Paris where her mother still lived. They spent their time working on their old house and wintering in the South of France. Gram kept a recent picture of Dad in her dresser drawer under the handkerchiefs. He'd gotten heavier and sported a short thick mustache.

"He looks awful," Gram says whenever I get the picture out. "Hitler." Adding, "Your mother was good for him. But this one . . ."

I now have their address and phone number.

Gram exhaled a slow stream of smoke. "I had a dream," she said. "We were getting married."

"You and me?"

"Uh-huh."

"But grandsons can't marry their grandmothers."

"The pastor said it's been done before. And he married us."

The freight elevator stopped on the top floor. At the far end of the factory loft Leela was disk-sanding an eight-foot-high mushroom. She looked like an Arab in a babushka, goggles, and dust mask—and even at that distance I could see she was furious.

"What are you doing here!"

"It's half past five—"

"OH! I can't believe it—ten hours breathing this plastic dust. This thing will give me cancer!"

Her sculpture, *Hands of God*, consisted of three polyurethane mushroom-like forms of different sizes. The piece had been commissioned by a woman in Westchester who wanted an "environmental artwork" for her outdoor garden.

"Hey, Bert!" Sammy Singh came around a stacked pallet of plastic chairs. He'd been hand-sanding one of the other Hands, but wore the only protective gear he ever wore, a big grin.

"My friend," he said, shaking my hand. "You must take Miss Leela away. She is not acting very peaceful making God's Hands!"

Leela frowned, pulled her mask and goggles down and went back to sanding.

Sammy drew me away from the whine of the machine:

"You must come see the elephant. This high now—" He held his hand up to his thick eyebrows.

Sammy worked part-time in the chair factory on the floor below. When Leela had run out of patience with her project, Sammy offered to help. He was an expert in papier-mâché and was presently building a life-size baby elephant in his small apartment.

"You make anything with papier-mâché," Sammy was saying. "Cheap, easy, strong—except to not leave out in the rain! But, you know, I can fiberglass—make a house!"

"What about papier-mâché umbrellas?" I asked.

"Sure—hats—pants that can also be a pissoir—"

Leela lost her temper: "Sammy, we fiberglass these blasted things Monday!"

Popping his eyes at me, Sammy went back to his work.

Leela sanded up and down the long arc of the stem, then abruptly turned off the machine and tore off her mask and goggles.

"Instead of getting better, it gets smaller. I would like to reduce the whole thing to a pile of dust!"

We left Sammy hand-sanding, singing falsetto to himself, and Leela took me down to the third floor to see the fiberglassing equipment which would coat God's Hands with a finish like that of the chairs. It looked like a car wash.

Maud wouldn't eat, just lay around. I was keeping her until Trudy got a permanent address. The cat was Trudy's. She had found her as a kitten in New Haven the week we'd moved down from Vermont.

Trudy stopped by and we took the cat to the vet's: feline leukemia. There was nothing to be done. We came back downtown without Maud.

We sat on the floor on pillows at Trudy's place eating left over Yankee bean soup. One more bridge to the past was gone. Trudy read from her journal about finding Maud rummaging in the garbage can in front of Frank's on Cottage Street.

It was hard crossing the courtyard, leaving Trudy. She wouldn't have minded if I'd stayed.

Leela was modeling something with clay. I hadn't called and she was pleased to see me. I licked her throat. Half embarrassed she tried to push away. I held her, unbuttoning the chambray shirt, kissed her breasts. Her hands were covered with clay slip and she didn't want to get it on me. I slid down her shorts.

"Let me shower, at least."

Her panties were on the floor and already she was moving against me.

"I smell like a pig . . ."

"God has the most intelligence, then man, then sparrow. Sparrow comes with feathers; man has to think to keep warm. So, you see, with intelligence comes responsibility."

Sammy was holding forth to Mohammed and me, while the rest of the party milled around us. Mohammed was a young Arab who owned Pharos's Cab Company, one old Checker which he drove. Mohammed had beautiful eyes, dark and liquid, with which he gave undivided attention to Sammy. The fat Indian was practically his guru.

"What do you want from life, my friend?" asked Sammy.

"Lots of girlfriends," said Mohammed. "Second of all, money. A Mercedes 300 SL. Nice apartment with cable TV, Jacuzzi—"

Sammy was regarding the ceiling patiently.

"What do you want, Sammy?"

"To want something—is to be lacking something. I do not feel I am lacking something."

I noticed Leela talking with the Harrises of White Plains. We'd installed *Hands of God* in Mrs. Harris's sunken garden earlier that day.

The garden was an inverted truncated pyramid sunk in the ground and lined with grass. White marble steps decreasing in width came down one side, about fifty feet. The garden had been designed by an architect, pure and simple, and not meant to have anything in it.

Hands of God had been fiberglassed and looked like three shiny white aliens. Leela, Sammy, Mohammed, and I had packed the Hands carefully and transported them in a rented van to Westchester. Then, in the hot forenoon, we men adjusted the three pieces in the bottom of the garden while Leela directed from above. Then Mrs. Harris appeared.

"Oh, no," she exclaimed, opening her arms. "They must *breathe*."

Leela explained that precise spatial relationships had been worked out among the three pieces.

"Yes, yes," said Mrs. Harris, waving to Sammy and Mohammed who stood by the largest Hand. "Put it over there."

I watched Leela considering saying something; in the end she walked away.

We spent an hour sweating and shifting until Mrs. Harris was satisfied. Then we dug holes, mixed cement, and planted *Hands of God*.

On the ride back to the city, Leela said, "I suppose you despise me. The piece is ruined. But I tell you, I was not opening my mouth to end up dragging those blooming things back to New York and shoving them under my bed!"

"The air," Sammy was saying, as he made a gesture of air rushing up his nostrils, "comes and goes; so Sammy, too, gets taken care of by God." He hefted his stomach and giggled. "I will tell a story that illustrates. I am washing pots in the restaurant, and I am done quite late. I am walking home and a car stops. 'Hop in, I'll give you a ride.' Well, I think this is very nice—"

"No!" exclaimed Mohammed. "You must be crazy."

"What have I to be afraid of? I get in. 'How much money you got?' says the man. 'Four hundred dollars'—"

"*You told him*!"

"It's the truth—"

Leela interrupted, saying I had a phone call.

It was Otto, Gram's neighbor. I had left Leela's number as I was at her place a lot lately.

"I had to put your grandma in the hospital. She can't keep nothing down, she's had the shits for a week, I guess you know."

I didn't know.

"She's in Boulevard." He gave me the address and Gram's room number.

After three days they hadn't determined what was wrong with Gram, nor had they been able to stop the diarrhea.

"I wish this tour was over," she said. "I want to go home."

Her eyes were rimy from sleep and tears. They gave the impression she was turning into crystal.

"If I die, take the apartment."

"You're not going to die."

She squeezed my hand insistently. "You can't beat the rent."

After leaving, I went over to Gram's apartment, watered the plants, then picked up the phone and dialed France. Dad answered, voice as familiar as though it were a minute ago. And for a moment I thought he had died and I had gotten through to another place. He was as flustered hearing me. I told him what was going on, and couldn't resist adding that maybe Gram wasn't going to pull through.

He didn't say much. He thanked me for looking after Gram. He asked how I was doing. Pretty well, I said and then felt myself running out of breath. We left it that I would call again when the prognosis was in.

"It's been good talking with you," Dad said. He seemed to linger for a moment. "Mother's been more or less keeping us apprised of your doings . . ." He hesitated and said goodbye.

Leela was leaving unexpectedly for Switzerland. Her father had had a stroke. It was time to go back and face the past, she said.

We had gone late that afternoon to *Art On The Beach*, a dozen or fifteen conceptual/environmental sculptures, scattered over a sandy landfill beside the Hudson near Battery Park. We had both liked *Blocks of Sidewalk*, forty large, jagged chunks of New York City pavement that had been stuck on end in the sand in a large rectangular pattern. Blowing sand had almost buried some of the pieces while the bases of others were so eroded, they'd tipped over.

Afterward, we strolled to West Broadway and decided to eat in a Greek restaurant.

"You frustrate me," Leela said. "You're content with what the world brings you, but I must go out and take. I want to be appreciated for my work. You could have such success and you do nothing. Would it kill you to extend yourself to people? While over there I'm talking to a gallery in Zurich that wants to take my work. I'm impatient with anything holding me back—"

"Am I holding you back?"

"I married a Swiss airline pilot when I was seventeen—just to get out of that blooming country! He brought me to America and left me in Brooklyn. For weeks at a time. I didn't know English. I watched television all day. A man delivered groceries. I was going out of my mind; that's when I started playing with clay. To make a long story short, Paul left me and a Jewish doctor married me. An American. He wanted a hausfrau with a hobby, but I began to have success. My clay sculptures sold, I was asked to teach in the local art club. Life became very ugly with my Jewish doctor. I walked out with just the clothes on my back. I came to Manhattan. I was already thirty-five—but to have your destiny in your own hands! I lived in an attic, I met David, I found the Swiss community. Two galleries here handle my work, and I'm starting to get commissions."

"I'm not trying to interfere with your career—"

"You know the next step is us to live together. I have not let someone this close since David."

Though we'd finished a liter of wine and drank a couple of ouzos, it was a sober ride back to Leela's. She seemed untouchable. Her past, like a wave spiked with husbands and lovers loomed over my short time with her. She would be gone until September; it wasn't my imagination that she'd already put distance between us.

When she said, jokingly, "Sex is so great with us, I don't trust it," she became angry: "You think I fall in love with anyone? Respect yourself! You're alone, you know!"

I felt like I'd been kicked in the gut. Lying in bed beside her I thought of her lovers—lit by these stalagmite candles, breathing the musk of her body, their skins cooling with faint sweat, feeling as omnipotent and well-loved as I: swarthy David with the wood shavings of their mutually wrought furniture; Henry the museum curator and all the exact-replica jewelry he'd given her; Richard the Jewish doctor; the airline pilot; the actor from *Star Trek*; etc., etc. Lying there alone in all that company . . .

"I was standing in a field of little trees. One grew out of my hand. Then a lot of trees were growing out of me, all over."

"Was the dream scary?"

"No . . ."

Gram looked like a mummy lying on the hospital bed with her eyes closed, hands crossed on her stomach.

I told her Trudy and I were getting divorced.

She opened her eyes and looked at me. "For me, there was only my Emil."

I wanted to explain but she had closed her eyes.

"I have schnelekatrina," she said.

Under the bed was a pan of brown-colored sludge.

I helped her up and we walked slowly down to the smoking lounge, sat on a couch that felt like it had been covered with linoleum. Gram shivered and I put my arm around her; she snuggled in like I was a mother hen, turning up her old face:

"What would I do without you, my Albert?"

"You'd do fine."

"You're the only one."

I asked if she would consider living in a retirement home when she got out of the hospital.

"With those old fogies? They're got one foot in the grave and the other on a banana peel!"

I told her I'd spoken with Dad. "I thought he ought to know what's going on."

"He's no son of mine. You're my son."

"It's hard keeping in touch from over there."

"Why did he marry that woman? He should have stayed with your mother."

"But Gram—"

"He'll never see me again before I'm dead."

As we were walking back to her room, soft feces fell out the bottom of her nightgown and left a train of patties down the corridor. Gram didn't seem to notice, or didn't care. I mentioned it to a nurse who raised her eyes.

Gram drowsed off doing a crossword puzzle; I left without waking her. Her doctor, a small Indian man, was at the nurses' station studying a chart.

"Ah," he said seeing me. "Your mother has the liver stone. This we found by sending down an underwater camera at the end of a cable. There it was, a coffee bean."

I asked what could be done about it.

"She is very old; we do not wish to risk an operation. We will, therefore, be patient and wait for the stone to dislodge. If blockage? Of course we must operate. Please sign."

He pushed a permission form at me.

As I walked to the subway I thought about the previous afternoon. Standing naked in the doorway that opened onto Leela's outdoor patio. She was in the bathroom putting in her diaphragm. A slight breeze was playing over me, over my half-aroused penis. Outside, in the sunless rectangle deep between buildings, blades of grass nodded between the flagstones. I was thinking of Leela in a moment crossing the studio, naked, dark hair loosened, feeling her smooth warm legs against the backs of mine, her hip, a breast, nudge into my side. And as I'd stood there I realized the moment was already becoming memory. I would remember forever the waiting in the open doorway, the breeze playing over my nakedness, anticipating her.

Leela threw a graduation party for her three sculpture students, all well-to-do Swiss. They brought their Swiss husbands. Leela outdid herself with salmon mousse, vegetable pate, and so on and so forth. Flowers, candles. The whole Swiss shebang.

Afterward we all went to a bar in Chelsea. I wasn't feeling sociable. Leela was leaving in a couple days for Switzerland. I drank and stayed out of the conversation. After a while they stopped trying to include me and jabbered in Swiss.

We lay side by side in her bed not touching. Leela fell asleep after a while, but I couldn't.

The sky was brightening as I looped back through Central Park. A few people were out walking their dogs.

"Where were you?" Leela was making coffee when I got back.

I told her I couldn't sleep.

"Why, what was the matter?" Heavy sarcasm.

I didn't say anything. She snapped the lid back on the coffee can.

"We don't have to fuck all the time."

"I guess I'm feeling a little—like it's the end of something—"

"The way you acted with my friends. I was humiliated—"

"To hell with your friends—what about *us*!"

"You son of a bitch! If you can't fuck me, you won't sleep with me?"

"I don't want to fight."

"You are incredible. Everything is you, you, you—"

"Maybe I should go."

"Yes, you should."

There was an old man in the smoking lounge. He wore a hospital gown and corduroy slippers and a faded newsboy cap; tufts of hair came out of his ears.

Gram steered us to the opposite side of the room.

I lit cigarettes. Gram related a dream from the night before in which my grandfather was chasing her:

"I stopped running after a while. I knew he could catch me."

Shrunken and white she sat smoking while another evening backlit Manhattan across the river. Time was swallowing her. I wondered what it would be like without Gram. To no longer be grandson.

"How old?"

The old man had dragged his chair over.

Gram looked as though she might ignore him, but then relented. "Old enough to know better."

The old man shook his fist approvingly. Then, in broken English, he told the story of the hundred-and-five-year-old man. He had helped this man's father with farm chores back in Italy, a real worker, and it seemed like he would go on forever. Then a cow fell on him: one of the old man's hands rose over the other, then fell crushing it.

"He was lucky," I said. "A clean death."

"Lucky?" cried the old man. "He'd still be here!"

Gram, who hadn't attempted to follow the story, had a fixed, querulous expression on her face, hoping to drive the old man off.

The phone rang when I got home. Sammy inviting me for Indian food and a discussion of God. I wasn't in the mood. *Stormy Weather* with Lena Horne was on TV. I was watching it when Trudy stopped by to pick up some clothes. She hadn't expected to find me in. We watched the end of the movie together. I made an omelet with broccoli; we ate it and after a while Trudy left. Lying on the sofa reading, I fell asleep. The phone rang after midnight. Leela had finished working and wanted to come down. Twenty minutes later we were making love.

On my birthday Trudy brought three pieces of sweet potato pie to the hospital. She stuck a tiny candle in each, lit them, and I blew them out. Gram and Trudy sang Happy Birthday, then Gram had an attack of the runs and we rushed her to the toilet.

Trudy and I rode our bicycles back across Queensborough Bridge. We bought Vermont cheese, a baguette, wine, a mango, and rode to Central Park's boat basin.

It was very hot; the only thing on the pond was a little fireboat moving in one direction and then another. It would pause to squirt water from the hose mounted on the bow. We said little. It was so hot. It wasn't strained between us. We loved each other and were parting and there wasn't much to say. I would be going shortly to Leela's. It almost seemed incredible that we weren't choosing to go on together.

Gram passed the liver stone and two days later was home. I went to The Associated for a chicken and other supplies, and when I got back a cake was baking. Gram was rejuvenated in the little apartment of her things and memories. "There's no place like home," she said more than once. Wearing an apron she strolled through her two rooms like Tallulah Bankhead, trailing cigarette smoke. I did a load of laundry, vacuumed the place, hung summer drapes. When the chicken was done, we had a feast, complete with glasses of Liebfraumilch, yellow cake, coffee and cigarettes. Before I left, Gram had sewed up the tear in the seat of my biking shorts.

Trudy and I had supper in Hwa Yuan's on East Broadway. That morning we'd concluded divorce proceedings with a firm I had found in the *Village Voice*. The firm was a heavy sweating man on the twenty-third floor of a building on 42nd near Grand Central. In addition to cheap divorces he was a private eye. Trudy and I joked about it over whole yellowfish in brown sauce. We were almost giddy. The divorce was uncontested, me being the "plaintiff" whom Trudy had "abandoned." Standard terminology the fat man assured, not to be taken personally. Two hundred dollars.

After signing the papers, we'd biked out to Riis Park and swam, walked the beach gathering shells.

"Funny," I said. "Here you and I are officially finished, and it's over between Leela and me, too."

"Oh?"

"The next thing was to be 'serious.' She doesn't want to be serious."

"Do you?"

"I might have been stupid enough."

"Do you love her?"

"I thought so, for a while."

"I'm sorry."

We finished the meal. I hadn't gotten divorced to marry Leela. It was a thing Trudy and I were doing to get on with our lives.

HOME

The train came out of Penn Station into night. Snow had already begun to fall. Trudy hoped Pop wouldn't have trouble getting down to the station to meet her. He was eighty-three. He had driven all his life: horse wagons for his father's carting business, the first truck in Troy, chauffeuring a beer baron through the Depression. The paper mill had made him park his Mack cab for the last time when he was seventy.

A man carrying an attaché case took the aisle seat.

"Looks like we're in for it," he said, cleft chin jutting at the window.

Trudy took out her paperback.

He asked where she was going and she told him.

"No kidding? I once dated a girl from Troy. Emma—Willard."

"She'd be a little old for you."

He laughed: "You're the real McCoy."

She began to read.

"What do you do?" he asked. "I bet you're a nurse. You strike me as a—"

"Sorry," Trudy said, "I don't feel like getting picked up tonight, okay?"

He raised his hands in mock innocence. Then he took a sheaf of legal-size papers out of the attaché case.

"No rest for the wicked," he said giving her a wink, and she had to turn away to keep from smiling.

Snow flew nearly horizontal past the window. She imagined it quiet out there, falling on the river. She missed seeing the bays with ducks on them, the reeds, lighthouses. When she was little she thought they were dollhouses floating on the river. She could almost live in one now, no phone, her own boat. But no one lived in them now, they were automated.

At Poughkeepsie the man got off. Snow was building on the platforms and station roof. He was met by a woman with a black Lab on a leash.

Trudy found the bar car and ordered a Manhattan. She'd never had a Manhattan; a character in the book she was reading drank them.

Pop had called in the middle of the morning:

"You'd better get home, my girl—I'm putting her away!"

Her mother had had a mild stroke six months ago. The numbness in the left side cleared up, but she had stayed muddled. Pop had to take over the cooking and cleaning, and oversee Ma's medicines.

Trudy asked if he'd talked to Buddy.

"That useless son of a bitch."

"He and Stephie live eight blocks away, Pop."

The phone was silent.

Trudy called her brother's house and Stephie answered: "Your father is off his rocker. He threw us out in the middle of Sunday dinner—in my condition!"

"How is Ma?"

"I boiled water for tea—you know your ma's whistling kettle? Out came a hot dog! She'd put a frank down there. Your pa acted like it was my fault. It coulda been in there two weeks. Buddy stuck up for me and I thought I'd have to get between them!" Then she said, "They're going into their decline. It ain't fair depending on Buddy and me just because we live close. You're the daughter."

The '60 Caddy gleamed under the arc lights, snow bouncing off its dark blue polished surfaces. Pop put Trudy's suitcase into the trunk. An electric motor whirred, drawing down the lid and locking it.

"How about that?" he said.

They were crossing the farm flats when he spoke again. "She don't know me." He was staring into the snow funneling at the windshield. "At breakfast last week I seen her looking at me. Next thing I'm sitting in the front room hearing her say, 'There's a strange man in my house.' She's talking to the precinct. She called the cops."

Pop glanced over: "Can you beat it? Reported me!" He tried to laugh. "My own house—I worked fifty years, and that—"

"Did they come?"

"Flashing lights, sirens—the neighbors were out—Gilinsky hanging on the fence sucking his pipe. I tell you, my girl, I could have gone through the floor."

"What did Ma do?"

"That bird don't know what she does. Them coming was a big surprise. But two days later she's next-door telling Marge there's a strange man in the house. I ain't gonna put up with it."

His huge, blunt fingers, bent sideways with arthritis, opened and closed on the steering wheel. When Trudy was ten, he took a cat by the tail and banged it once up against the brown shingles of the garage. It was a stray, he told her, it didn't belong anywhere.

"Have you taken her to the doctor?"

"You fart and it's twenty-five dollars. She went through them tests four months ago. They said she'd bounce back. She's worse. I see to it she eats her medicine. I can't handle her, Trudy. You got to come home."

The dash light reflected off his lenses, thick and smudged.

"There's jobs in J. C. Penney downtown. You can have your old room."

"I have a life in New York, Pop."

"You're forty-two. You quit nursing school—lost a kid and an old man—and now you got a life. What did you ever have you didn't walk away from?"

Cherry Street wasn't yet plowed. The single set of tire tracks coming down had nearly filled in. Pop followed them into their driveway, two houses before the block ended in the fields. The parlor light was on. Ma used to wait up in the rocker for Trudy to come home from dates. Whistler's Mother, Bert had nicknamed her.

"Did you tell her I was coming?"

"I don't tell her nothing."

Ma was sitting on the sofa under the Hummel figurines. Her big body, always held erect, slumped against the cushions. The deep lines of her fleshy face looked like they had been lifted and smoothed. Her hands were folded in her lap and she was gazing at them.

Trudy kissed her cheek.

Ma looked up: her expression hardened. "Who are you?"

"Trudy."

"Trudy has long hair."

"It's like it used to be," said Pop. "Like she had in high school."

Ma continued to stare. "Who do you think you're fooling?"

"I'm tired," Trudy said. "Let's talk in the morning."

She started for the stairs, but Ma got up and blocked the way, stretched her arms between the banister post and the wall. Baby pictures of Buddy and Trudy looked down from silver frames on the landing.

"That's Trudy's room!"

"But, Ma, I am—"

"If you don't get out of this house, I'm calling the police!"

Pop took Trudy into the kitchen.

"You see?" He was almost gleeful. "She don't even know *you*."

"Why don't you put her to bed, Pop. I'll sleep on the cot in the cellar."

He gave Trudy a set of his pajamas, sheets, pillow and a blanket. Where her dollhouse used to be under the cellar stairs, Pop now kept a case of Carling Black Label. She could smell the workbench against the far wall in the dark; the oil-wiped tools on the pegboard; the big vise clamped on one end. She opened the cot and set the legs. Before they were married, she and Bert would sometimes sneak down and make love on this cot, Ma and Pop right overhead watching TV.

Morning sun slanted into the kitchen lighting a row of old green patent medicine bottles on the windowsill. She and Bert had found them on a hike in the Lebanon Mountains. Trudy poured coffee from the electric coffeepot.

Pop was out clearing the driveway, guiding the snowblower up and down like a farmer cutting furrows in a white field. Snow spumed against the green board fence he'd put up to hide the DeAngelos' backyard parties. Pop wore his mackinaw and the new Roosky hat of fake lambswool Buddy had given him for Christmas.

It hurt Trudy's eyes looking out, the sun so bright reflecting off the snow.

Pop set his galoshes beside the refrigerator on two sheets of *Troy Record*, hung his coat and hat on their hook.

"Driveway looks good," Trudy said.

"I thought we'd take a drive." Pop pulled out a chair and sat at the kitchen table. "That snowblower's a honey. Fifteen years old and starts like that. I can't change the height it throws, but that don't bother me."

"Where will we go?"

"The mall. Grace likes that."

"Do you walk around?"

"No. We used to go to the Trojan and take in dinner. They served an elegant chop."

Pop polished his glasses with a handkerchief.

"I saw Marge hanging clothes and stuck my head out to say hi," Trudy said. "She told me Ma is running away now."

Pop put his glasses back on, fixed on her with his magnified eyes. "Gilinsky found her down on Pauling. Brought her back and lectured me, the Polack bastard. She does that again, I ain't letting her in."

"Pop—"

"Next time she runs away, I'll let the cops handle it."

"You could put locks on the doors."

"Yeah."

Ma came into the kitchen in her nightgown. Her dry, gray hair was flared in back from being slept on. Trudy got up and she sat in the chair.

"How about some OJ, Ma?"

"Thank you."

"I thought you and me and Trudy would go riding," said Pop.

"Where?"

"We'll stop down the mall, get those little franks. Maybe after lunch. You ain't been out in a while—"

"What's for breakfast?" Ma asked Pop.

"Trudy's cooking bacon and eggs."

She looked at Trudy as if noticing her for the first time, and Trudy got busy.

"It's sunny," said Ma, staring at her hands in a triangle of sunlight. "Maybe we could go for a drive."

"Where are you going?" Pop asked as Trudy put on her parka.

"Out."

"Take the car."

"I feel like walking."

"It's raining." He dropped the ring of Cadillac and house keys into her pocket.

"Are you giving her money?" Ma was watching them from her sewing nook in the kitchen corner. The old Singer machine had been folded into its cabinet, the dress and shirt and pajama patterns put away in shoeboxes. A lifetime of sewing had stopped six months ago.

Trudy followed a path up and across the fields to Lookout Hill. Pea Soup, the hill they used to sled as kids, stood across the gulch. Today, in the rain, no one was out. She wondered if they even sledded anymore. She and Bert had taken the toboggan down it a few times over the winters they visited.

When she came out on Pauling her boots were soaked through. It was getting dark. She walked six blocks to her brother's house.

Buddy was sitting at the kitchen table in his underwear. Trudy looked at him for a moment through the window before knocking on the back door. It was surprising how much he resembled Pop when he didn't think anyone was looking. The same indifference under that always-trying-to-please face.

"Hey, Trudy! Stephie said you were coming."

Buddy put Trudy's boots on the radiator and gave her a pair of his slipper-socks.

"Steph's not here right now; she's at cake-decorating."

Buddy lifted a pan down from the top of the refrigerator. The cake was half-eaten; it was Big Bird.

"Last week she did Mickey Mouse. He was the best. George Washington—I don't know."

"Stephie's feeling ok?"

"Yeah, great. I'm the one with morning sickness. Geeze, sis, can you imagine me a pop?"

Trudy laughed. "No, I can't."

"I want a boy, but a girl'd be okay. How about a piece of cake?"

"I've got to get home to supper."

Buddy cut a hunk and ate it out of his hand.

"Guess you heard about the latest blowup. We ain't talked to them in a week. The old man won't call. He can go to hell. He tell you he's gonna put her in McCarthy's?"

"He's not putting her anywhere."

Buddy went to the window, staring out, munching cake. There were nose-prints on the glass. The streetlights had come on.

"Seven thirty they call me at work—I don't know, a month ago. Mrs. Bacardi down the corner. Ma goes visiting and won't leave. The old man won't go get her—he's abusive on the phone to Mrs. Bacardi. Dinnertime at the restaurant, I have to leave the sink. Okay, I pick Ma up, bring her home. He won't let us in. I'm so friggin' mad, I bust in the back door. He comes out with a tire iron—I grab the snow shovel—" Buddy started to laugh—"Ma jumps out of the car—goes running up the driveway—"

He was laughing so hard he had to stop talking.

The rain had turned to sleet. Buddy wanted to drop her back at their folks, but Stephie had the car. Besides, Trudy wanted to walk.

She passed the old Albia Paper smokestack, all that remained of where Uncle Zak had worked for sixty years. But the Pine Tavern was still across the street; the sagging two-story building looked like a rotten molar capped with aluminum siding.

Three men were watching a basketball game on the TV over the bar. The place stank of stale beer and Pine-Sol. Trudy regretted stopping in, but the whiskey warmed going down.

When the nearest man offered to buy her a round, she realized she knew him: Joe Sullivan, a driver with Pop at the Mount Ida mill. Joe had spread and turned white. He didn't recognize her. She was probably seven or eight last time he saw her in the Pine. Pop used to take her on his Saturday run to Saratoga. She rode high in the cab beside him. They would get back in the afternoon and stop at the Pine. Pop would plop her on a stool and she'd order a Shirley Temple. She had long golden hair which Ma made into ringlets with newspaper strips.

When she got back, Pop was doing supper dishes.

"Where've you been for Chrissake? It's after eight."

"I had a few down at the Pine. Joe Sullivan was there."

"Sullivan? You could go to a higher-class joint, my girl. You'll pick up a reputation."

"I'm not your little Shirley Temple—"

"Shut your mouth. I'm telling you what this neighborhood is like."

"You're a son of a bitch."

Pop looked like he was going to hit her, then he laughed.

"You're like me! You're more like me than Bud'll ever be. You don't give a goddamn—you've got a head hard as a Saint's!"

He rapped her head with his knuckles and she knocked his hand away.

Trudy took Ma to see Doctor Fisher. His office was up by RPI and she parked the car so they could have a little walk. Ma liked to walk but Pop insisted on driving her, even to Phelan's Drug Store at the corner of their street.

"He thinks he knows how to cook a pork chop." Ma laughed scornfully. They were passing the old field house. "I want to live alone. Like Aunt Rhoda did."

"There's not enough money, Ma. Rhoda was in a private sanitarium."

"I don't like him."

Trudy tried to say he was doing the best he knew how.

"What do you know?" A car passed, fanning slush. "It'll be sixty years in May I put up with him. I don't know why I have to."

"He's all you've got, Ma."

"Who are you to talk? You have a fine life. No home. No family. What are you doing in New York? I can't look in the newspaper because—sometimes I think—because if you haven't got anything, they'll take the only thing you have."

They were walking faster, Ma's attention fixed on the pavement ahead.

"It's not right," she said, "to make us feel our life ended with you. You're alone because you pushed us away—"

"I had to find out what my own life was about."

Ma glanced at her with a mocking smile, and Trudy felt like she'd been knocked flat in the slush. Her life was plain wrong to Ma, without moral value or justification. It didn't seem to matter that she'd given birth to Trudy. That Trudy had sucked milk from her breasts.

After the examination, Trudy left Ma in the waiting room and went back to see Doctor Fisher. He didn't know what was wrong, he said, she was in good physical shape. Trudy said she didn't think Ma wanted to get better, if it meant going on living with Pop.

They could see Ma through the half-open door all the while, sitting back on the couch so her feet were off the floor like a kid's.

"I'm going to make an appointment for a brain scan," said Fisher. "It could be a tumor causing pressure. Her coherence comes and goes. If it's not that, we may be looking at dementia. Alzheimer's."

A salt-streaked Chevy was parked in front when they got home.

"Oh," said Ma. "Buddy and Stephie."

The kitchen smelled of cooking pot roast. The three of them sat at the kitchen table, Stephie's chair pushed back to accommodate her pregnant belly. She and Buddy were drinking Amaretto out of wine glasses while Pop swigged a can of Carling.

"Look who's here," he said.

Ma kissed Stephie's cheek and kissed Buddy on the mouth. Pop got down two water glasses.

"So, how'd it go at the doc's?" asked Buddy.

"She in great shape for the shape she's in," joked Pop.

"Is that Amaretta?" asked Ma. "I want that."

Pop chuckled and poured a glass half full.

"Beer for me," said Trudy.

"You and me, both. This stuff's for the girls."

"They're going to run a test next week," Trudy said to Pop. "Ma has to go to Albany Medical Center."

"Yeah—and they'll find out she needs another test costing twice as much. Bloodsucking bastards—"

"Who are you?" asked Ma.

Pop looked at her and then grinned. The rest of them vanished in that intimate, terrible grimace. But Ma had picked up her glass and drank off half of it, paying no attention. She ran her tongue over her lips.

"What are you doing here?" she asked Buddy, brightly.

"I invited 'em to supper," said Pop. "The gang's all here."

"Past, present—and future!" exclaimed Buddy.

"We brought you a present," Stephie said to Ma. "Close your eyes."

Ma closed her eyes and held out her hands. Stephie got a cake box out of the refrigerator, opened it and put it in Ma's hands. Ma stared at the cheesecake topped with pineapple.

"It's from Tarducci's," said Buddy. "Your favorite."

"I like cherry," said Ma.

"Be grateful for what you get," said Pop.

"I don't like pineapple."

Pop had a butcher knife in his hand. He took the cheesecake to the garbage can and scraped the topping off. Then he got a jar of cherry preserves off the shelf, unscrewed and dumped it over the cake. He set it back in front of Ma.

Pop had set the dining room table with Aunt Rhoda's lace cloth. The best dishes and silverware were out. There was a half-gallon of Gallo burgundy on the table. Two candles burned in Ma's rooster candle holders. Buddy leaned back in his chair and flipped the lights off. It was quiet for a moment in the candlelight.

"Can we pray?" asked Ma.

"Good drink, good meat, good God, let's eat," chanted Pop. He couldn't see to carve, so Stephie turned the lights back on.

Buddy filled their glasses: "I'd like to make a toast: To Trudy—"

"Light the candle under the gravy there," said Pop. "I can't stand lukewarm gravy."

"You're here a few days, sis, and we're sitting down together like human beings."

"Like family," said Stephie.

"Trudy's been kicking butt around here," said Pop.

"And when I go," Trudy said, "you're gonna do your own kicking. How about some gravy on your potatoes, Ma?"

"I like butter."

Pop stuck his finger in the gravy and sucked it. "It ain't bad, my girl. Not like you used to make, but you ain't making it."

Ma smiled. "That's right."

They ate for a while. Then Buddy said, "This is the way things oughta be." He refilled his wine glass. "There's my father at the head of the table; there's Ma. Honor thy father and thy mother!" He drank and set the glass down. "When our kid comes, I'll bring it over—let it mess around in the cellar with Pop, smell Ma's pie cooking upstairs. I want the kid to know where it comes from."

"I don't bake pies anymore," said Ma.

"I bet you would if little Ed junior was asking you," said Stephie. "We're gonna call it Mary Grace if it's a girl—after my mom and you."

"Why do you want children?" asked Ma.

"I don't know . . ." Buddy looked like he'd never thought about it. Then his face brightened: "I'm taking a test end of this month for the county. Fixing roads, plowing snow—"

"Last year you were gonna be a mailman," said Pop. "You were gonna be a goddamn fireman—"

"Come on," Trudy said.

"He ain't got a trade. You had your chance ten years ago. Zak got him on as an apprentice at the mill. Look where you'd be today."

Buddy said nothing.

"Zak was a foreman when he retired. Sits up at the farmhouse in Poestenkill, and all he's gotta do is walk five hundred feet to the mailbox once a month for a check. Not bad for someone with no brain."

"I couldn't stand the noise," said Buddy.

"Stop fiddling with your glass—drink it or leave it alone!"

Buddy stood up: "Why can't I even not drink my wine right? I COULDN'T STAND THE GODDAMN NOISE!"

"Sit down," said Pop. "You think you're here to have a good time?"

"If you want a nice family, that's what you should have," said Ma.

"I'm full as a horse." Pop waved the cheesecake off.

Trudy poured coffee.

Buddy asked Ma if something was wrong with the cake. She was pulling her piece apart with a fork.

Trudy gave Buddy a look, and he snapped: "That cheesecake cost thirteen bucks!"

"You enjoy it," Trudy said. "She doesn't have to."

Buddy abruptly picked the cake up by the cardboard bottom and brought it into the kitchen. They could all see him from the table except Ma. He set the cake down on the linoleum and stepped into it.

"Wait for me!" called Stephie.

Pop and Trudy followed her into the kitchen. Buddy was treading up and down with a broad grin, squashing the cheesecake.

"You damn fool," said Pop, grinning. "You ain't even got your socks off!"

Trudy set the plate of scrambled eggs in the middle of the table. There was no bacon. Then Ma said she believed Trudy was a friend of her daughter's, and Pop had taken her in. Her face darkened:

"You slept with her, didn't you, Ed?"

Pop said nothing.

"Don't lie to me."

"That's right." He turned to Trudy. "I hope it wasn't too crowded in my closet with the other three."

"Don't pay him any attention, Ma—"

"I have the blonde on Saturday, the redhead on Sunday, but the Jap I use all week."

Ma was panting: "I want to go home—"

His fist slamming the table turned the creamer on its side: "Don't start that!" The tongue of milk reached the edge and went over.

"I want to go home," said Ma with dignity.

"What the hell do you think this is!" shouted Pop.

"I don't want to stay here anymore."

Pop walked out of the kitchen.

Ma leaned down where Trudy was sponging milk off the floor and whispered: "It's not your fault, but you better not stay here. You can't trust him."

"Ma—"

"Trudy's gone. She lives in New York."

Trudy took hold of Ma's hand in her lap: "I'm Trudy. I'm your daughter."

Ma stared at their hands.

"Remember Dyken Pond? The summer I was five or six, I fell out of the rowboat with cousin Mikey? Pop dived and swam out from the dock, went down and brought me up. I would have drowned. Remember? Pop saved my life."

Ma took her hand back. "I wouldn't know about that." The family history was none of Trudy's business. "I want you to leave after breakfast. My husband will drive you to the bus—"

"You're my *mother*! I'm *here* because of you!"

Pop came back in. There were tears of bewilderment in Ma's eyes.

"She is going to live with us, Grace," Pop said softly.

Ma watched through the living room blinds as Pop and Trudy pulled out of the driveway.

"I'll drop you to Buddy's," said Pop. "She'll get over this."

"Take me to the train."

He pulled over to the curb. "You ain't gonna leave me with her."

"She wants to be in a home, Pop. I'm going to look into Saint Michael's."

He stared at his hands on the steering wheel. "She wants to leave me. Where she's been all her life."

Mr. Gilinsky was chipping ice on his front walk. Smoke from the pipe in his teeth floated on the air.

"What am I supposed to do?" Pop looked over at Trudy. "There's money enough, you wouldn't even have to work—"

"Come home and take care of you like Ma?"

His eyes got a bright hard look and then went dull. It was quiet except for the chip, chip, chip.

"I ain't dead yet."

He put the car in drive and they left the curb.

EMPTY ROOM

Dad,

Gram's in an assisted care facility out on Long Island, The Jewish Institute For Geriatric Care—the resident shiksa. After four months she hasn't gotten her bearings. She rolls off in the wheelchair and can't find her way back. Her roommate is a bedridden woman who cries at night. Gram pulls the divider between them and says she never slept better. She doesn't complain, is liked by all so far as I can tell.

Nurses call her Smokey the Bear because of her cigarettes. When she wants one, she must go to the nurses' station and ask, then smoke it there in front of them. She hates this and bums cigarettes from visitors on the floor—and sneaks smokes. And of course is found out. The nurses routinely check her drawers and pockets for butts.

She has quit trying to use the walker except when I'm there making her. She wheelchairs around. There is a big color TV in the lounge and Gram likes to watch bowling, golf, baseball. Still a Mets fan. We do crossword puzzles. I bought a whole book. She knows an astounding number of arcane words. Meals are bland, for old stomachs. Half an hour before serving time there begins a slow mass movement toward the dining hall. A lot of walkers and wheelchairs.

Men are scarce here. It's apparently true women live longer. The men have their own table in the dining hall: an island in a sea of women. There was a new old man—no place at the boys' table so he has to sit with women. He is somewhat paralyzed and out of it. One of the women at the table wipes his mouth for him. We bring Gram's meal down to her room and share it in private. I eat most of it.

Coffee Klatch is on Tuesdays. Everyone who wants can have a cup of coffee and donut or Danish for twenty-five cents. The Activities director plays records. I have been there during entertainment. A woman comes from the outside and plays the piano, songs like "Take Me Out to the Ballgame," so everyone can sing along. Most do in some fashion, but it is not like a roomful of people singing, but of individuals half-remembering, singing to themselves.

Gram's Social Security plus Medicaid meet the bill here. There is enough left over for manicures, Coffee Klatch, Bingo. Last Friday she won forty cents. She gets her hair washed and permanent-waved. They make it very curly, but she has fine hair like me, and it is soon straight and limp. It helps her spirits though.

I encourage Gram to phone or write me but she won't. "I'll see you soon enough," she says. I've been getting out most Sundays, but it's a four-hour round trip by subway and bus and you pretty much give up the day. We sit for long periods staring at the tree line. Jets cross the window. Clouds. The sun sets. She—the two of us—waiting it out.

I bring carnations (they last), cigarettes, chocolates—usually a Whitman's Sampler. Once I forgot them—had to leave without taking off my coat and hunt up a box in the neighborhood.

Gram pretty much accepts where she is. I ask her about the past, and I'm learning some things. Poppy was an athlete—a "Tournfereiner"—won first prize on the "horse" at a Saratoga meet back in the day!

I am writing this from Gram's apartment. It's empty now—I'm sitting on the bare parquet floor. I kept paying the rent when I knew she wouldn't return. We pretended for a while that she would. She doesn't mention it now. I held a rummage sale for the neighbors, sold the glass china cabinet and her Singer sewing machine to an antique dealer, took four loads to Goodwill. I kept her rocker and footstool and a few things. I think she is in as good a place as possible.

Please drop her a note. I've included the address.

I was reading the letter over when Otto let himself in. He carried a newspaper and a bag with something in it.

"I'm going out to see her," he said. "You want I should bring something?"

"Cigarettes."

"Sure. She wouldn't let me in."

Our voices were loud in the emptiness.

"Your grandfather was a whistler," Otto said. "I'd hear him in the hall coming up the stairs. A nice sound that whistling." He gestured at the blank walls. "Where'd it go, a lifetime? My place'll be the same. Places don't hold no memories."

"Thanks for visiting her."

"I got nothing better to do." He held up the bag: "Nice piece of baklava. She didn't like it at first, now she asks."

We were quiet for a while. Silence settled in the emptiness like it was the rightful owner. It grew fat until it seemed another word would be forever out of the question.

"I wonder who'll move in?" Otto spoke. "It makes me sick to think of. It's like being married, living in this building. I'd like to move to a place with walls this thick. Just hear your heart."

He started for the door, then turned back:

"C'mon over, a little ouzo before I go."

WOMAN DANCING

Bert recognized her at a distance through the new leaves and Sunday strollers. He hadn't seen Trudy in nearly three years. Since Gram died. Her hair was cut short and dyed red, and she wore a green dress shimmering with sequins. He stood next to his bike, balancing it by the saddle. He had ridden down to the Battery to take a break from correcting papers. The air was soft, caressing in little puffs; the smell of grilling shish kebab drifted to him.

He walked his bike closer, hugging the fence. Trudy stood near the snack booth where benches enclosed a natural performing area. As he approached, she began to dance, or to sway rhythmically. He heard the guitar then, a low thrumming Spanish guitar. Trudy picked up the front of her flaring skirt and began to swish it from side to side. Bert stopped and watched over the heads of a Chinese family. A small Hispanic man with an Afro was sitting on one of the benches, playing the guitar. Then he began to sing in Spanish. On the ground beside his leg a guitar case was open for contributions.

Trudy had started a syncopated, flamenco-like stamping to the guitar's rhythm. She wore green high heels. Suddenly she ran half a dozen steps, whirled, making her skirts flare, stamped, ran and whirled again. It was thrilling, barely controlled. Bert felt his grip tightening on the saddle. The guitarist cried out Olé! Trudy swayed, raising her hands above her head.

Bert was feeling slightly breathless. He wanted to go down by the water where the old men sat on benches, white breasts lifted to the sun. He wanted to smell the sea air, watch the ferry—he wasn't responsible for Trudy.

She stumbled and kicked off her heels—to claps from the audience. *Please let there be no broken glass*, he thought. She closed her eyes, making little stamps with her bare feet, turned in place holding her dress up.

A man who had been sitting on a bench, a large man wearing a black silver-brocaded costume and a black sombrero got up and joined Trudy—began stamping a counter circle around her, their eyes locked. The crowd loved it.

The man was not very young. He wore black pointy boots with silver tips and metal taps: the bricks chattered as he stamped. Abruptly he raised his hands over his head, potbelly joined with barrel chest, and began rattling castanets. Clapping from the audience, whistles and laughter.

The musician meanwhile had stood, one foot up on the bench, and was playing fervently, rapping the guitar with his knuckles, giving out with *Olés*! Trudy broke away from her partner and danced with increasing abandon and wildness, while he remained in place, arching his back, clacking castanets, stamping, and regarding her with what looked like disdain.

Bert couldn't help grinning.

Trudy, who had paused at some distance from her caballero, now began performing a motion somewhat like harp-playing. The man appeared to take heart and stalked her, clacking and stamping. She deigned to notice him. He took her in his arms, and they whirled around to music that now sounded like a polka.

Applause, the sound of coins dropping into the guitar case, the small crowd melting away as the caballero passed his sombrero. Several tourists lingered to chat with the guitarist and Trudy, who sat beside him on the bench.

A one-man band out beside the main promenade began to play. His trumpet languishing over "It's Cherry Pink and Apple Blossom White" as his drum thumped. Apparently he took turns with the trio so they wouldn't compete.

Bert could feel the tension easing in his shoulders as he walked his bike back through the park. Rastafarians were playing soccer where big metal sculptures leaned in the grass. It seemed to him Trudy had gotten about as far out as she could. Dancing the past out of her—Mom and Pop, Troy, Catholic school, him. She had looked like a little girl who'd dressed up in her mother's dress and heels.

Washington Square was a carnival on this early spring day, performers everywhere, people hanging out. Bert coasted through clouds of marijuana smoke.

Susan was sitting on a shady bench near the statue of Garibaldi, the baby asleep in the stroller.

Bert laid his bike on the grass.

"Have a good ride?"

"Great. No traffic."

He sat back against the bench. Across the way a man in a stovepipe hat was tying a rope between two trees.

"I rode down to the Battery," Bert said. "We'll have to take her nibs out to the Statue one of these days."

"A weekday." Susan had been reading a spy novel which lay open in her lap. "I'm about to fall asleep. This air—"

"I saw Trudy. She was dancing. The man she lives with, I think, was playing guitar. Another guy, dressed like a caballero, danced with her. He had castanets."

Susan dog-eared a page and closed her book. "Will you ever be through with her?"

"We didn't speak. She didn't even know I was there." Bert toyed with a tassel on the baby's blanket. "Seeing her was—I didn't want to talk with her. About what? The past is—"

"Everything you write is about her."

"Hardly everything. I'm just trying to get some things right."

"Look at you. You're sad because you saw her."

"It struck me as a little sad—"

"Pathetic, I'd say. You're still taking responsibility."

"Because I wish someone well, someone I once knew?"

"You were married for twelve years."

A tall man passed wearing Shakespearean garb. Bert watched his purple velvet cap cross the plaza where the fountain played.

"I'm glad you told me." Susan pressed his hand, briefly. "Yes, I find it upsetting. She's here in the city."

The baby was awake now. She lay in her stroller, looking up at him with her mother's eyes.

THE BATTERY

They were kissing under a tree a hundred yards away, the boy with a thick black pompadour, the girl, a sea of blonde curls, beneath him. Trudy could barely see her. She looked flattened into the dry grass.

Warren's face was all concentration as he sliced the salami with a red-handled pocketknife. A sweat bead on his broad forehead slipped and ran down beside his nose.

"The original, from Katz's," he said. "'Send a Salami to Your Boy in the Army'?"

Trudy managed a smile.

Warren laid the slices on opened hard rolls, then unscrewed the lid of a small mustard jar. Potato salad and coleslaw sat on the blanket in plastic half-pints. The paper plates had dancing cows on them. Warren had brought an Entenmann's coffee ring for dessert.

The girl was pretty in a delicate bony way that reminded Trudy of Bert's Gram Helen. Pictures of her as a young woman. The boy had hunkered over the girl like a beast over its prey. Trudy imagined him shaking her in his teeth.

Warren poured more wine into their plastic cups; sweetish and warm it clashed with the salami. Trudy recalled with a pang the icy taste of Pouilly Fume, her and Bert's favorite.

"What is a picnic not a picnic without?" Warren asked, taking a small package wrapped in butcher paper from his shopping bag.

"Ants?"

"Ants? No. A pickle—from Gus's!"

He stood the fat pickle on its end on his paper plate and sawed it lengthwise. As he concentrated, a pink tip appeared between his front teeth.

"What's that poem?" said Warren. "A loaf of bread, a salami, and thou beside me in the wilderness?" He wagged his thin—almost penciled—eyebrows at her. "I'm not a drinker, but gosh I wish we had more wine."

The girl under the tree leaned up on an elbow. Remarkable how her oval face, framed in fine curls, resembled Gram's. Trudy remembered visiting her once in the nursing home; they'd been looking through a box of old photographs. Gram picked one out.

Mama in her wedding dress. She held a tintype of a young woman in a high-collared white Victorian dress.

She told Trudy her mother had visited her the night before, sat on the edge of the bed and stroked her hair. *My poor Helenchen*, she'd said over and over.

Warren pushed himself onto his knees, then onto his feet.

"Water," he said.

Trudy watched him slowly cross the lawn, perspiration widening the black Y of his suspenders. Her gaze swung back to the young couple. Totally oblivious. He on his back, she beside him, tracing his red lips with a blade of grass. They could be Helen and Emil on a July afternoon in the first year of the century. Not even married.

Am I one of those creatures who mates for life? The question crossed her mind like one of those banners pulled by an airplane. Sixteen years she and Bert had spent together—and then had parted. Not angrily, traumatically, but—sadly. He had remarried. She hadn't. She wasn't unattractive, even now; but she didn't feel particularly like someone somebody would want. Her life was in order; she had a great job illustrating children's books. Her own apartment. She was cutting it.

Warren had been walking toward her for some time like a man in a telephoto lens crossing a blazing field. He looked pinkish, as though he were being broiled out there. His breasts jiggled in his T-shirt as he walked.

"Do you know how Staten Island got its name?" Trudy asked.

"Staten Island? No."

"A couple of Dutchmen were out in their boat in the bay on a foggy morning . . ." As Trudy repeated Gram Helen's story, she heard the lilt of the old woman's voice—the inflections, pauses, the half-flirtatious tone—as though Gram had lightly possessed her. "One of the Dutchmen pointed to a shape out in the fog, and asked the other: 'Iss dat an island?'"

Warren looked at her blankly.

"That's how it got its—'Iss dat an island'—Staten Island?"

"Ah." Warren cocked his head at her slyly. The heat released from him a bland permeating scent of body odor and aftershave, a smell Trudy associated with crowded subways. She regretted not having drunk more of the horrible wine—so Warren wouldn't have drunk most of it.

"You are a mystery," he pronounced. "A woman unknown. An iceberg, nine-tenths below the surface."

"I'm not exactly feeling like an iceberg."

Warren grinned not taking his eyes off her. "The past. It wraps around us like a bathrobe. As though that's what's real, while this—why did you happen to be downstairs in Rare Books? Like you'd stepped out of that edition of *Wuthering Heights*. An accident? Fate?"

Abruptly he was leaning forward, earnest, holding something out to her in the palm of his hand: a lump of dull silver: "Antietam. Bloody Lane. September 17, 1862. I was there." Warren's eyes glowed like blue lightbulbs.

Then Trudy recalled: at the Strand, Warren had been looking for General Grant's *Memoirs*.

He was turning the thing in his fingers: "A Minie ball—a bullet—that was actually fired during the fight. It's lopsided. It hit someone, went right through—*a hundred and twenty-nine years ago*."

He handed the slug to Trudy. Heavy and smooth, the top had been flattened and squashed to the side; two raised grooves encircled the base. The thing was hot from Warren's hand. She gave it back.

"I had it analyzed at the police lab—one of my customers is a lieutenant—and it definitely went through a body to look that way."

"You found it?"

Warren blinked, as though trying to recall who Trudy was. "The whole busload of us was standing in the Sunken Road—*Bloody Lane* after the fight—and the guide was describing how the Yankees were about to come charging over the hill right in front of us. She was Southern, and we were standing in the rebel position, where they would have been with their rifles resting on the bank in front of us. The first thing we'd see, she said, was the gold eagle on top of the Yankee flagstaff, then the Stars and Stripes, and then the screaming horde of blue. All at once I'm feeling—I don't know—I back up, I can feel the weight of a musket in my arms, I have on some kind of slouch hat, no shoes—I'm *there*! I stumble, drop against the opposite bank. Everyone was staring at me. I had shouted, they said, thrown my arms up. The little reb tour guide thought she had a sunstroker on her hands. And when I sat up, I had this in my hand. It had gone right through me. I was killed at Antietam."

The sun pressed a heavy weight on her head and bare shoulders. A relief to be moving—alive—in this kind of heat that would kill you if you couldn't get out of it. It was a long way from their tree to the blockhouse of the public toilet. Trudy wanted to keep going, to the subway and home. But he had her phone number, and she didn't think they would change it on a Sunday.

She had met Warren on Thursday. What could she have been thinking? She'd woken up to rain and decided not to go to the studio. She spent a few hours looking at Hoppers in the Guggenheim, then came downtown to the Strand. She had felt vaguely excited all morning, as if something were going to happen. Downstairs in Rare Books, she ran her fingertips over old tooled leather bindings; she opened a volume of *Wuthering Heights*, let her eyes run over the words which on the heavy, yellowed page, seemed printed in Braille.

A man in a trench coat squeezed by in the narrow aisle and apologized. He noted the Bronte she held and explained the chemical restoration process it had undergone. Warren spoke in a soft, earnest tenor, inclining his pale face toward her. His eyes shone with enthusiasm; he seemed a gentle, bookish man. After a quarter hour's whispered chat, they shook hands goodbye—but suddenly he came hurrying back, inviting her on a picnic. He was flushed and breathless; her heart jumped a little and she'd said yes before she meant to. Riding the train back uptown, she lost the mental picture of Warren. Neither tall nor short—bulky. Not old or young-looking. He told her he was fifty-four—almost right away, as if to avoid a misunderstanding, and she had responded by telling him she was forty-seven. An awkward moment of honesty that had felt nice. Gray suit, plain red tie. Face not fat exactly—loose-fleshed—sandy hair, parted on the side. Pale blue eyes. The details didn't seem to add up.

Trudy squatted an inch over the toilet seat, holding her breath against the disinfectant.

Outside, the reek clung in her hair. She walked to the snack bar and ordered two coffees. On the esplanade, a short line of tourists waited for the Statue of Liberty boat. The bay barely moved under the gold-plate sun. A distant, mustard-colored ferry toiled toward Manhattan. Trudy wondered, as the man pressed the plastic lids onto the coffees, if she could ever accommodate herself to another man.

Warren lay on his side under the tree. Trudy could see he was watching the young lovers. They lolled like drunks, the boy's pompadour given way to several ridiculous horns.

Trudy kneeled on the blanket, settling the cups of coffee. Warren's chin indicated the couple, and he spoke slowly as though in her absence his tongue had thickened:

"Bet we could show them a thing or two. You don't get older, you just get better, right?"

"I just got black coffee," she said.

"Black's perfect." He tore a little triangle out of the plastic lid. "Black coffee's just like you."

She tugged her skirt down over her knees.

"A rare experience," he went on. "Pure, clear, wakes up the taste buds . . ." Warren's smile was almost to himself. "I wish we could put ourselves away—" He motioned with his chin again—"like them. Pure feeling, without history, without—I don't know. They feel, therefore they are."

He put an arm around her shoulder. Fatherly, coach-like. She sat motionless, staring straight ahead. He droned on, taken with his own voice, and she was lulled by the low pitch, his smell wrapping her like the humid, slightly rotten odor of the city. Sleepwalkers drifted on the distant promenade in the shadows of parasols.

She drew away from Warren.

He grinned. "I'm sorry, I didn't mean to—"

"Sometimes, people are just not—"

"I guess I'm not someone's idea of a dreamboat." His grin seemed frozen.

Trudy found herself doing what she didn't want to do: telling Warren about Bert so Warren wouldn't feel bad about himself. So he could blame the afternoon on someone who had left her and gotten on with his life. With another woman. But, really, Bert a professor, pushing a three-year-old in a—

"It was a nice picnic," she said. "Why don't we leave it at that."

"Yes, picnic. Are we surfeited?" He looked at her oddly. "Is that the word, *surfeited*?"

Had Bert "used her up," "cast her aside," "taken up with a younger woman"?

The afternoon was being subtracted from Trudy's life—she could feel it streaming out. How long since time had been *added*? Joy rained down pure and abundant? Even Thursday she had been aware of straining for the little of it, like a horse reaching for a dry apple. And Gram Helen? No trace of her remained, except a little bit in Trudy's memory. And Bert's. She had begun keeping her journal again, writing *something* in it each day. *I want you to know I was here.*

The one-man band was playing the Marine Hymn; the brass notes from his trumpet prodding the hot still air. Where was her Latino lover, the sequins of her green dancing dress? *Is this really me*? The one-man band had stayed on as though he had a foot in time's door.

"What do you want?" Trudy said low in her throat.

He spun her around as if she were a barstool and lay flat on her. It knocked the air out of her. His mouth was over hers and she felt his hand go up her skirt, fingers sliding under the elastic.

"*Warren*," she gasped, trying to struggle.

People on the distant promenade, if they noticed, would take them for lovers. The young couple were asleep. Trudy felt like she was being crushed into the ground. Above the fringe of dry grass she could see the red-handled pocketknife sticking in the coffee ring they hadn't eaten, its sugar icing melted translucent.

She stood beside the railing. The water made no sound against the pilings, stretched away oily and billowing. The sun felt like an ax in the top of her head. The ferry emerged from its stockade hooting into the East River. The flat wooden top of the railing was blistering. The tourists had been taken away; no one was on the esplanade.

As the ferry passed the Battery it launched a broadside of light from its starboard windows; Trudy shielded her eyes. She and Bert had taken Gram's ashes out on a cold April morning. As they passed the Statue, Bert had uncapped the canister, and Gram streamed out a gray tail of ash, heavier clinkers falling almost straight into the water.

Now there are two ladies in the harbor, he had said.

She had read that anything that occurs only once is meaningless: it disappears forever. Which almost means it never was. All the little acts we perform—the daily repetitions to assure us we really are here, that we do matter—are less than nothing—pitiful, so utterly are we doomed to extinction. Ma was gone, Pop alone taking a long time dying.

She thought of Warren stretched out under the tree. Maybe he had been killed in the Civil War. We live our essential lives, then linger on as ghosts.

It no longer seemed a question of what she wanted to do with herself. This life she had was no better or worse than anything else. It came down to accepting it. Everything. Her father could tell her.

THE YEAR'S LAST SNOW

He had dreamed of his father. All day he thought about him. Walter Staub had been dead over six years, and Bert had never laid eyes on him again since directive ordering him and Trudy to stay out of Jeanette's and his life. More than twenty years ago.

He heard the 4:40 bell for the Morristown crossing. A few snowflakes had begun to drop out of the sky. A big storm was coming. He felt it all day; people talking in lower registers, leaving early if they drove. There was a damp gunpowder smell. Something was coming.

The engine appeared around the bend like the head of a huge eel—straining forward eagerly at the sight of him, the lone waiter at Convent Station. He heard it cease accelerating, coast into the platform on a cushion of air that moved his briefcase. The conductor didn't bother swinging down. Bert climbed aboard feeling the brakes release and the train move ahead—as though it had plucked him from the ground in flight.

The car contained an old man in a dark overcoat and Stetson hat, and two teenagers. Bert took a seat, opened his paper but gazed out the window at a wood passing in the dying light.

He had hoped for a reconciliation with Dad and Jeanette. It seemed it would happen after all this time. Susan wanted it. Bert had called and spoken with him after the baby was born; Jeanette sent a yellow sweater she'd knitted. They made plans to get together in the spring, but Walter didn't make it.

By Brick Church Station people were getting on with snow in their hair. Bert watched it falling through the station lights, gathering like a layer of dust on the platform.

He turned to the sports section. In a few weeks it would be baseball season. The Mets, Gram's team. And then he remembered his father had played baseball at Cornell—one of those rarities, a batting pitcher like Babe Ruth. And Walter Staub's fastball and sinker had been good enough for an offer to join the Yankee farm team. Instead he took a job as a chemical engineer at American Cyanamid in Elizabeth New Jersey.

Bert wondered if Walter had ever weighed a glamorous baseball career—Coop playing Walt "Fireball" Staub in the movie—against the security of engineering. He tried to recall how his parents had met. He could see his mother's face—superimposed on the beige ceiling of the car—rosy and animated, telling him they'd met at a battery factory in Queens. Queens or Hoboken? Summer job for him during college, full-time for her. That first glance? What had he said to her, she said back? He recalled Gram and Poppy hadn't approved of Emma. Now he was the only one left with an uncertain memory of a story—of something that had happened that he might relate to his daughter—in an even more fractured—or fictional—once upon a time.

There were six inches of fallen snow as he turned onto Wooster Street from Prince. Fanelli's sign was a blur of red neon in the blizzard. Halfway down the block the Wooster Art Gallery blazed.

Despite the weather the opening was fairly well-attended. Bert wanted to go home but had promised Bill Shultz he'd drop by. Shultz taught art at the school, and the opening, a group show, was his first in Manhattan. Bert liked Bill—they often lunched together in the faculty dining room.

They had been talking when Bert noticed Vicky Marchand across the gallery studying a painting on the wall. Succulent Doctor Victoria Maria Marchand, authority on the sonnets of Shakespeare.

"She hasn't said a thing to me about my two pieces," muttered Shultz. "Not even a 'How Dickensian' or some such bullshit."

Bert laughed.

"Whoops, look who's here. Give my regards to Consuela." Shultz left Bert, going over to greet a portly man knocking snow from his shoulders.

Bert halted just behind Victoria Marchand. A subtle perfume engulfed him. He would like to have placed his hands on her narrow waist, felt their flare into her hips.

"How would you describe that?" he asked.

"I wouldn't begin," she said in her dry tuneless voice without turning to him.

He was briefly distracted by his conflicting attraction to and dislike of the woman. She was in her mid-forties, at that voluptuous point that would soon pass into cushions of flesh. But these were Victoria Marchand's vintage years. Like good wine, she had achieved—

She turned to regard him, resting a long red-tipped hand on her hip. "What are you grinning at like a banshee?"

"I am mere iron filings aligning in the magnetic force field of—"

She pursed her lips.

"I love the tension between us. When you give in—Hiroshima!"

"That isn't funny."

He was focused on the conquistador curve of her full lips painted black-red.

She turned again to the artwork: "It's a piece of derivative—I don't know—*merde*."

She wore a black suit that must have fit perfectly eight years ago, which contained her now like a girdle. She had good legs and wore stockings. He knew she wore stockings because he'd glimpsed stocking tops and a garter belt as they sat at their desks in the English office. High heels. She must have carried them through the storm in her purse, put them on in the ladies room.

"But of course," she was saying, "to play devil's advocate, you'd call it 'Innovative,' carrying forward the ideas of—Mondrian?"

"Well," he began a riposte, but she cut him off:

"Where does the truth lie, Albert? Where do we become responsible? We can say anything. But really, *where*?"

After a moment, he managed, "We're alive; it's snowing like a son of a bitch. Doesn't that suggest something beyond words?"

She turned on her high heel and walked away, ass moving voluptuously like a sultana in her tent . . .

A voice turned his head in the other direction. "I had a feeling I'd see you here tonight."

Trudy's hair was long again, worn the same as he remembered, in a single braid down the back. He was shocked by how her face had aged, lined and softened and come to resemble her mother's. It was a long time since he'd seen her down at the Battery, dancing—and then not close up.

He leaned in reflexively for a kiss—she turned her head and he landed on her cheek.

"Quelle surprise."

"Manuel Diaz—" She indicated the painting before which Bert still stood. "One of my students. What do you think?"

"Oh . . ." He looked at the painting. It was a blown-up black-and-white grid of a street map of Lower Manhattan over which cartoon figures—commuters?—had been crudely painted in different colors.

"It's got ideas," he ventured.

"I hate it," she said. "But he's an interesting kid, full of potential. He'd like what you said. 'Ideas'"

Trudy launched into a description of what Manuel Diaz was trying to do—how he was "evolving."

When she finished, Bert said, "You look great."

Gone were the jeans, replaced with a sort of loose pantsuit. She had gotten heavier, had become, he saw, middle-aged.

"It gave me a start when I first saw you," she said. "You look an awful lot like your dad. Except he never had a pot"—she poked him playfully in the stomach, and he jumped.

"It's these pants," he said. "They're kind of baggy—"

"You look like the proper professor," she continued in the same bantering way. "Beard, turtleneck, tweed jacket—with elbow patches—"

"I'm teaching—Creative Writing—a small college in New Jersey—" He found her familiarity exasperating.

"That's great, really," she said, relenting. "You always wanted to be a professor."

There was an awkward silence.

"God," she laughed. "When is the last time we saw each other? Scattering Gram's ashes?"

"I guess." He decided not to bring up the time at the Battery.

"I still remember what you said after you'd poured her ashes out. The ferry was passing the Statue—"

"Yeah, I remember."

Trudy caught the eye of a man and waved.

"I'm doing all right," she said. "I'm planning to open my own gallery."

"*Your* work?"

"Oh . . . well." She smiled. "You have to make money in this city. I'll come back to it. But, you know, I painted for the wrong reasons. Sometimes the worst thing you can do is praise someone. They want to please you then. It becomes a habit you don't even know you have. Remember the still lifes I did at the cabin?"

"The onion in the water glass."

"It's all right when a person has a talent that they're encouraged. But they have to work through it to move forward. How about you?"

"Me?" He was startled to have the light turned back on him. "I keep writing." He shrugged. "Stories published here and there. Literary magazines. I'm putting together a collection. Some stories from our time together. Fictions."

She didn't seem curious.

"Margaret's six now," he said. "My daughter—"

"I know."

There was a pause, and then Bert said, "If Cass had lived she'd be—"

"Twenty-six. In September."

There was a pause.

"I've lived half a dozen lives," said Trudy. "Sometimes they get mixed up."

"I know. I have this one now. Once I lived with you. Once I lived with my parents. No way to imagine how one life—"

"I really need to speak with someone," Trudy said, abruptly leaving him.

She joined a small refined-looking man in an Armani suit. He gazed up at Trudy as she talked, cocking his bald head—the living bust of a Roman Emperor. She leaned forward assertively—not a Trudy he had known—gesturing occasionally at Manuel Diaz's painting. A collector or an art dealer—she was pitching her protégé.

Then Victoria joined Trudy and the man. The two women were about the same size and age, but what a contrast. Trudy without make up, her style of dress loose, concealing, cowboy boots with salt stains. Victoria's tight dress, heels, silk blouse with breasts lifted high.

He came on her later at the bar.

"Victoria Maria Contraria. Or is it plain Doc Marchand—"

She kissed him. Held it rather a long moment before leaning back against the bar.

Bert noticed Bill Shultz giving him a look from across the room.

"So what do you think?" Victoria asked.

She was looped. She took a drink of her scotch, rattled the cubes.

"I'm not sure," said Bert. "About what?"

"I'm telling you what a woman doesn't say, that she wants something—that she understands nothing else is important—*as important.*" She gazed for a moment at the crowd which had thinned. "All window dressing, peacock feathers—fancy clothes, hips and jewelry, and money, oh, yes—Queensborough Bridge garlanded with pearls.

R'member *Great Gatsby*? Brilliant conversations, simulating parties—like somebody wrote it!" She looked at Bert. "Warm-ups for the main attraction. We are Pavlov's—Phenomes—a million years so you—" she poked a finger into his chest—"can recognize—" she modeled her hands over her own figure.

"Interesting," said Bert. "You might lower your—"

"Listen—" she took a drink—"I'll completely explain—curvy mate—ergo—curvy mate—" she laughed and Bert felt the spray on his cheek—"fecund. Fecunder?" She looked at him with uncertainty.

"Do you want to have a kid?" he asked, genuinely curious.

"You could give two crooked shits. You—*prototype*—demands immortality—Fuck and multiply, isn't that what the Bible says, Staubie? I'm not blaming you—your genes—spelled with a 'G'—oh God—"

She fled more or less in a straight line for the ladies' room.

He was putting on his overcoat when Trudy appeared at the clothes rack.

"I'm leaving too."

The snow was still falling thickly, big flakes in perfect stillness; nearly a foot had accumulated.

"We could share a cab," he said. "Except there aren't any."

"I rode my bike. I didn't listen to the weather report."

He waited while she unlocked her bicycle from a parking sign. The same maroon ten-speed she'd bought when they first lived together in the city. Beat-up looking but with a new seat.

They walked out to Houston Street then east. There was no traffic. It had not been plowed.

His ears were warm, he could feel the flakes hitting them and melting.

He asked how her folks were. Her mother was dead, and Pop was living in a boardinghouse in Troy. On River Street—a block from where he'd been born ninety-one years ago.

She scooped snow and packed a snowball, threw it at a parked car, dimpling the marshmallow roof. "He still owns the Cadillac. That big snowstorm last year? My brother and niece hiked down to the boardinghouse to check on him. He talked them into going for a ride. He drove, following his old truck route to North Adams. They were almost clipped by a snowplow. Coming into Eagle Mills, Pop started acting—Buddy thought he was having a heart attack. They went off the road into a field. There was so much snow it was like hitting a featherbed."

A big SUV went slowly by.

They crossed Broadway and then the short block to Lafayette. The Puck Building loomed like a fort on the corner. They walked in the street, following the fresh tire tracks. It was coming down so thickly, obliterating everything, they could have been in the country. It seemed to Bert no time had passed at all: he could reach out and touch Trudy's shoulder, and she would turn a face to him smooth with their lives yet to come. It seemed to him they could as well have gone on together. What was the point of the struggle, pain, blindness—change? So much fuss. As though there were some way to advance, to improve things.

"I'm glad we ran into each other," he said.

She glanced at him, snowflakes caught in her long lashes, smiled.

At the Bowery, Trudy turned south. He watched her, head down pushing her bicycle into the whiteness until she vanished.

At Second Avenue he turned north. Trudged through the deep snow.

He sips a glass of scotch in the kitchen, gazing through the back window at the snow falling, heaping along the bare branches of the ailanthus tree, on the fire escape railing, the rims of empty flowerpots.

He takes out his journal.

SNOWSTORM

It's snowing heavy, burying everything. Maybe that makes me think of her. She stayed at the boardinghouse in Eagle Mills, worked at the factory there. Fingertips always red and tender. Did she run a lathe? That doesn't sound right. This is in the twenties. You could have a meal at the boardinghouse and they served drink. I would stop on the run back from North Adams. Older than me, didn't ask a thing. I didn't give her up for nine years. She gave me up.

Radio says we'll get two feet. Travelers' warnings.

I put my galoshes on, tuck the cuffs into the tops, buckle them. I eat out, can't be bothered with the hot plate and there's no refrigerator. But the room suits me. Since Grace went into the hospital what do I need a house for?

The truck—was it the Maxwell?—Ran out of gas on the flats this side of Eagle Mills. Me and my helper, Tom, pushed her all the way into Troy. Dirt road in those days, we kept the gas headlamps lit—they were for being seen, not seeing. That was a long push but it was spring and we had something along to drink, and Tom—Irish, good voice—sang about love and losing your true love. There was no one but us on the road, a sickle moon, mist on the harrowed fields. The hills run down to Troy, that's how we did it—jumping on the running boards downhill, jumping off and pushing up the next crest. Peepers were calling in the ditches. I kept thinking how she and I had been together in the last hour.

Snow and more snow. You could almost step out the window and walk on air.

I look at the side of the next building. The bricks are worn, like red sponges stuck in a wall. It used to be the warehouse for the Mount Ida Paper Company. I drove for them forty-odd years, delivered thousand-pound rolls of paper to North Adams, Pittsfield, Great Barrington, hauled back barrels of pigments and acids, bundles of rags. The city now uses part of the building to store snowplow equipment. They're coming and going over there this morning.

I lock my door and walk down the hall. A dog whines. The old woman says no pets. When my foot hits the first floor, her door opens. Her red face sticks out like a turkey in a shooting gallery. I don't give her the time of day. I've paid my hundred and twenty dollars on the first of the month for two and a half years. She has nothing to complain of.

Nearly a foot down but the walking is easy, the snow light and dry.

I bought an Indian on poker winnings and kept it in a shed behind the boardinghouse. We flew the country roads at night. We didn't stop at gin mills or drive into Troy for fear of being seen. The places we stopped weren't on the state map. Then our luck ran out. The ambulance came from Troy and it got in the paper. We hit ice, the back wheel kicked under—she got thrown and the bike rode my leg fifty feet. I was skinned hip to ankle. Her back broke. I would visit her in Saint Mike's—damned if I would quit on her because the fun was over. Grace didn't ever say one word, but she could poison. The back healed but she couldn't hardly bend. She left after a year of recovering—somewhere up in Michigan.

Cars are crawling. It's not hard seeing them as horse-drawn sleighs. I'd almost get the Caddy out. She's made for snow with that weight. I might do it except for this damn vision. If something happened they would have my license, and where would I be?

I never lost a day's driving to snow.

Mooney's. I take my stool at the counter. The short-order cook is new and I have to order breakfast. The eggs aren't hard-cooked. I won't eat them loose, same as I won't eat a fish with the head on.

"Where's Ralph?" I ask him.

"Who is Ralph?"

"The regular guy."

"I don't know. I'm new on the job."

He goes down to the end of the counter to the cigarette he left burning.

I left Cherry Street because I had to. Grace's stay in the hospital wiped out our savings and took the house. Grace can't appreciate it. Her brain's gone. I visit her about every other day, nothing better to do. But I won't take the car out today. It's safe in the garage.

"Hey, pal, didn't you forget something?"

I would sooner put my fist in his face as tip him.

I make a loop along the base of Prospect Hill, through the mall downtown, and back River to the boardinghouse. The Russian hat Buddy gave me makes me sweat and I stuff it in my coat pocket. I never was a hat man.

Buddy had a job last winter at the state office buildings in Albany. I went out a couple of times and watched him take care of the snow. He had a Ford pickup with a plow and bags of sand in back. For the walks he used a big walk-behind blower. He quit that job. I don't understand him. It was good work.

A station wagon is stuck. Dumb cluck sits there spinning the wheels. I knock on the steamed-up glass—it's a girl. "Rock it," I say, "back and forth." I get behind and push. All she knows is Drive. Spinning and spitting packed snow, she gets clear and beeps.

It is deepening, the plows can't keep up. What if it never stopped?

She took the train from Albany. I saw her off—maybe should have gone with her. Things would be different, that's for sure. Because nothing was different after. Grace, house, kids. Michigan was the end of the earth. She didn't write. One vacation, the kids weren't grown, we drove through Michigan. We were going to California but we went by way of Michigan. I was restless on the way through, thought I might see her. But she was a cripple and older than me, said she was going to an aunt out there. Go to New York, I said. But she was leaving me.

"Your son is up there," the old lady stretches her neck out. "I let him in."

Country music spills into the hall. Buddy is standing in his peacoat staring out the window at the bricks. Mary Grace is reading a book in the chair, feet pulled up under her, glasses on. The only one of our family in line when God passed out brains.

"Hey, Pop," says Buddy. "C'mon in and joint the party."

I squeeze Mary Grace's neck and she pulls away with a face. She doesn't stop reading.

"Some snow, huh?" grins Buddy.

"What are you doing here?"

"They canceled school," says Mary Grace.

"In my day we'd tie pot lids on our feet."

She just gives me that look.

I take my coat off and shake it.

"It's a day to goof off," says Buddy. "We don't get snow like this but once a winter—once every five."

There's a puddle under his feet like the snowman came inside.

"I guess they closed the restaurant and gave you the day off with pay?"

"Naw, I called in sick."

"Daddy made us walk all the way here," says Mary Grace. "He said we had to rescue you."

"What's so great in the book?" I ask.

"It's *Heidi.*"

"Hi-dee hi hi ho!" Buddy imitates Cab Calloway. "Thought we'd see if you needed anything, Pop. Saint Bernards charging through the blizzard."

Buddy's ten-year-old is more adult than him. Sits there like an old lady—ain't even bled yet. Granny Grace. How did Buddy get that one? She's all right, though. She knows her own mind. She'll have nothing to do with him when she has a say.

Buddy takes a box off the windowsill: "We didn't bring a barrel of schnapps, but Stephie sent along a little present."

"It's candy Momma didn't want," says Mary Grace.

Buddy sets the box on top of the TV. He tips back and forth like he did when he was a kid wanting to go outside.

I go down the hall to the bathroom. It has an old-fashioned tub with iron claws set onto balls for feet. Glass balls. I sit on the can.

Marian . . . I don't remember the last name.

Old man Kroeder bangs on the bathroom door.

"Occupied!"

She never forgot my birthday, December twenty-second. She felt sorry for me being born so near Christmas. "Bet you never had much of a birthday," she'd say. I didn't. Irish—McGarrety, maybe. They would let her use the boardinghouse stove to bake the cake. My birthday only fell a couple times on the North Adams run but I always had a cake. She didn't want to stop and lay together. "Take us to the moon, Eddie," she said. "What if we threw the clutch up there?" I kidded. "Then we'd have to stay, wouldn't we," she said. "Be moon people."

Buddy is sitting on the bed with the box open, eating candy. "Trudy called last week," he says.

"Aunt Trudy is living with a man," Mary Grace snaps her book shut, interested for once.

"Married?"

Buddy shakes his head. "Na, they don't get married these days. I told her, watch out. There's sons of bitches in New York City. I told her, she has any trouble, give baby brother a call. I'll straighten him out."

"You and who else?"

"Me and you!"

I have to laugh at that.

"Trudy sounded good, Pop. Things are starting to look up for her."

"When's she been up here?" I say.

"You didn't exactly make things pleasant for her when she was up Christmas. She wanted you to move outa this dump."

"Oh, yeah? Maybe in with her and her boyfriend? I could wash their dirty underwear."

"Anyway, she says hello—"

"Hello!" I shout, "HELLO!"

Mary Grace looks at me.

Buddy moves a dust bunny with the toe of his boot.

I go to the window. The snow has melted, staining the bricks. I get my retirement from the mill. Social Security. We weren't millionaires but we lived okay. Grace could cook a pot roast—and after that we'd go in the parlor and watch TV. Where am I now? What is this—dump? Like I stepped out for a beer and everything changed. Not a trace of the boardinghouse anymore, or the factory. It's just inside this head. She's long gone, and I'll be too, and those nights I stopped for a warm dinner and then upstairs. That little room so damn cold and the patchwork quilt she never let us lay under but had to fold and set on the chair. What did she tell me, what things? She wasn't a talker for a mick. Who was I to her? Eddie? I was the only one.

"How's about taking a ride Sunday?" asks Buddy. "The snow'll be cleared. We could take the Caddy up the Thruway to Saratoga."

"What's in Saratoga?" Mary Grace wants to know.

"I don't know," says Buddy. "Something. How about it, Pop?"

Old man Kroeder in his pajamas stops in the open door. Then he shuffles on, down the hall with a sound like sandpapering.

"Let's get out now," I say.

Buddy looks at me.

"Oh, let's go to the Latham Shopping Mall," cries Mary Grace.

"There's a hell of a lot of snow down, Pop," says Buddy. "And it ain't quitting."

I get my coat on, it's wet from earlier.

"Please, Daddy, can we?" Mary Grace is pulling at Buddy's coat.

"I don't know. Your mother—"

"She said we don't have to be back for lunch. We can eat at Rolly's in the mall!"

Buddy pushes on the bottom of the garage door and pivots it down shut, gets into the passenger seat. Mary Grace has the whole back to herself. The engine's warmed up so I kick the pedal and she idles down. Wish we still had the manual choke. I back out using the rear view.

Snow is hitting the long-polished hood like it's a surface of ice. This car is practically new. Aunt Margarite sold it to me when she went into the home. She and Uncle Arthur always owned Cadillacs. She'd put twenty-eight thousand miles on in twenty years, and the car never slept a night outside its heated stall. Treated better than my old man's horses.

"You're going the wrong way, Grandpa," calls Mary Grace. "Turn left—"

I swing right, up the hill, east.

"Where are we going?" She whines. "On some boring ride to nowhere?"

"Mind if I turn on the radio?" asks Buddy.

I send the electric aerial up.

He gets the country station he had in my room.

I catch Mary Grace looking at me in the rear view.

"Where are we going, Grandpa?"

I grin: "The moon."

She won't be kidded. She puts her feet up on the seat, sitting back against the door, and opens her book.

"Could be July," says Buddy, "way this baby sticks to the hill. You can't beat a Caddy."

We pass the old Farnum Steamer and Stewart's Ice Cream. No one's out, not even kids specking. We go up the hill past the cemetery, past where Margarite used to live, and pretty soon we're in country.

Buddy sings along with some woman who is leaving her husband for a disk jockey.

It's like being on water, cutting along. As white in the air as it is on the ground. No need for wipers, the snow is dry. I could let go of the wheel and the car would drive itself over this road.

"This the road to Uncle Zak's?" asks Buddy.

"Does it look like it?"

"It's out this way, ain't it?"

"Poestenkill," I say. "This ain't the road to Poestenkill."

Quiet, not even a purr of snow up against the bottom. We could be a horse-drawn sled. Three hundred and fifty horses.

Mary Grace has fallen asleep with her mouth open like her grandmother.

"HOLY HELL!" yells Buddy.

The snowplow is almost on us, turret light going and snow whipping around the cab—taking his half out of the middle. I cut the wheel, taking us onto the shoulder, not even breaking traction—catch the plowman's passing grin. Probably a thermos of coffee up there beside him and a sandwich. Those fellas plow around the clock. I wouldn't mind that, long steady hours peeling snow, keeping the steel just off the berm, watching for culvert poles.

"Jesus," swears Buddy. "That was a close one."

A miss is as good as a mile.

"Hadn't you better slow down, Pop?"

Mary Grace woke up with Bud's yell and now wants to get in front with us. Buddy helps her over the seat.

We're running with one set of tires on the cleared surface, one in the snow. I can feel that deep side holding us on the curves. The old dirt road there under the macadam.

"We ought to turn around when we find a spot," says Buddy. "We're getting out pretty far."

"You gonna miss a wedding or something?" I ask. "We got a full tank of gas and the car's going swell."

"I don't care if we ever stop." Mary Grace switches the channel to rock and roll.

"The car needs some highway miles," I say. "Smooth out the valves. It don't get out much since Ma went in the hospital."

"But Grandpa, Grandma is . . ."

Buddy twists in his seat trying to make out a sign.

"We're going to North Adams," I say.

"North Adams? That's over the mountains."

"What's in North Adams?" asks Mary Grace.

"MacDonald's." I grin at Buddy.

A second plow goes by, chains ringing. He is farther over, plowing in tandem with the first. They ought to be closer together.

It's all the same and all changed. This old road, the same one. Something stopped back then. I can just think about it over and over—moon on the new fields, the peepers, the headlamps flickering. I turn to Tom—Jesus, that skull-like face lost in its singing—

"Eagle Mills!" announces Buddy.

But I have already felt the car drop, beginning the long curve down into the hollow, the mill set back by the pond and the boarding-house beside the road.

CHEZ JULES

Sunday afternoon. A man and woman eating a late lunch in the dining room, another man drinking at the bar. The waitress is filling saltshakers. We take a front table next to the window. You and I sit against the wall while Margaret has the whole bench seat opposite. A day in early spring.

There must have been a party: colored balloons drift around. Jazz coming quietly out of speakers. Between two mirrors that take up most of the back wall, a framed poster of *Port du Désir* with Jean Gabin. The waitress, a narrow, razor-cut blonde, French as the Eiffel Tower, appears oblivious to us. The bartender is talking to the man drinking.

You say, "Maybe if we left, they'd notice us?"

Margaret has been playing with the balloons: she'll capture them by their ribbon ties, and they'll escape bobbing up against the ceiling or gliding under a table. She is stretching for one that clings near the top of a curtain when the waitress comes over.

We order glasses of red wine and a Shirley Temple.

Margaret holds balloons to her head like Carman Miranda and sways to the music. Static electricity makes her fine hair rise, clinging to the balloons. The bartender, a young skinny guy with a vest and an earring, leans against the back counter of the bar and watches her.

The wine is good—"From an area just outside Bordeaux—as good as Bordeaux," the waitress informs us in her French accent. "Not as expensive."

Two men with a woman come in and stop at the bar. The bartender pours white wine for them without their asking.

There's an old lady at a window in the apartment building across the street. She leans out on her hands for a look, then sits in a chair so she can see down into the street.

We finish our wine and order more.

The balloons seem alive trailing along the floor after someone who passes. What we thought at first was coldness in the waitress is Gallic reserve. That matter-of-fact frankness like Gabin's: faint smile, world weary eyes, uninflected voice.

The near-Bordeaux tastes fine—earthy, almost like food. We should have ordered a bottle.

The old lady stands up to stretch, a real arms-over-the-head stretch, then sits again to lean on her elbow. I point her out and you rest your arm on my shoulder, looking up.

"Doesn't she remind you of the Old Lady in *Babar*?" I ask.

"Yes!" you say, and for a moment we are both absurdly happy.

The old lady may have seen Auden come and go forty years ago; he'd lived a few doors down on our side of the street. She may have been in her thirties, in the middle of life instead of the end. She probably wouldn't have had time to spend idling at a window.

Margaret is flirting with the bartender; he offers her a green balloon that has drifted up among his bottles.

"Can you say merci?" you call to her.

She tucks her chin down shyly and comes back to us.

We sip our wine and talk. I glance up now and then and see the old lady. Sometimes she moves ever so slightly as though to show she is alive. I ask what you think her sense of time is like. You answer that her time is full and goes from one thing to another, as you did when you were a little boy. I realize you think I'd asked about Margaret.

When we order wine again we ask for the cheese plate too. We're getting a little tight and it feels fine. We're hungry and don't want to leave. Time is moving along somewhere without us.

On the plate are wedges of four different cheeses, a bleu Auvergne and a Brie and a Port Salut and one more. They are all delicious and different and come with a bunch of red grapes in the middle and slices of apple. Served with a basket of sliced baguette.

"So much for the diet," you say, happily eating another piece of cheese.

High in the blue sky above the old lady's building a great cliff of cloud is passing, a 747 like a toy plane cuts across—for an instant they're all there, held in my glance: old woman, cloud, jet. And you and Margaret and your lives at this moment. Louis Armstrong singing, Gabin stares from his poster, a pink balloon drifts, the bartender leans in to say something to the waitress.

"We could be in Paris," you say. "It'll be strange when we step outside and find ourselves on Saint Marks."

The waitress tells Margaret she can take home all the balloons she wants. She begins collecting them, tying the ribbon strings together.

A tired-looking man comes up from the back of the café pulling an amplifier on a suitcase wheeler. The bartender pours him a red wine. He has a long French face, pointed nose and sad eyes. A young woman who has been sitting at a table in the dining room comes over to him. Stands there expectantly.

"You don't know me, do you?" she says, not at all surprised or disappointed. She tells him that she has flown in from the west coast on two hours sleep. Apparently she has heard him play somewhere.

"You look so tired," she says, touching his arm.

He nods and smiles a little wearily.

As she returns to her table, I notice she has a limp. Her right foot is turned in and she limps.

An outdoor stairway angles down to the street from the building above. An old lady comes slowly down; she uses a cane, the other liver-spotted hand gripping the iron railing. She descends one step at a time. The old lady at the window watches her. I wonder if she knows her. If she sees her as someone like herself, ancient. Or if she observes without much thought, noting how the other shifts from one leg to the other slowly rocking down the stairs.

"I'm glad you suggested stopping in," you say taking my hand. "It's nice being impulsive. We aren't so much anymore."

I kiss your hand, aware of Gabin's gaze.

"I love it," you say. "It's around us all the time and we hardly know it."

We finish our wine and leave. Margaret walks ahead bouncing her colored bouquet under the trees.

EPILOGUE

JOURNAL 2018

9 October

Over the past weekend Margaret and I went to Vermont and climbed Camel's Hump, her gift to me for my eightieth. Well, we nearly reached the top. Fifty years ago Trudy and I had just been settling into the cabin.

We flew from Kennedy to Burlington on Saturday. Rented a car and drove to Waterbury. Since it was early afternoon, we crossed the bridge over the Winooski and drove the river road back to the old neighborhood. Wayne and Norbert's houses looked the same, but the barn had been converted to apartments. The field, across the tracks below the house, had been mowed, but other patches Farmer Martin had hayed were grown up to brush.

Across the overpass where our brook (Ripley) came out into the river, I wondered if the Duchess apple tree was still there giving its bounty every other year. Up the Hill Road, past Granny Beston's old red farmhouse—yellow now, and with a new wrap-around porch. She had passed years ago. The Kneelands' house, always unpainted and ramshackle, was empty and looked ready to collapse into the road. John's house, next to our garden, had a new name on the mailbox. Where the garden had been, above the cabin, was still garden, marked by dry cornstalks. And our one-room cabin had grown a second story, visible from the road.

Margaret drove us up to Old Farm Road, where Trudy and I had often followed it looping back to the cabin. The deer camps, Antlers and The Shamrock were there exactly as I remembered, but there were many new year-round houses, and Old Farm Road no longer went all the way through. The little cemetery was there, still cared for, Amelia and Ophelia, and the rest, no older.

As we drove back down past the Kneelands' place, I wondered what had become of them: Ma Kneeland whose head, bent down from arthritis, grinning and toothless, looked up slyly at me with her secrets. Homer, who'd gone with us to the Wind Harp, was he still alive somewhere. The chickens always running around out back. The hound dog, chained under the porch.

"Gone Fishing to the Falls," or "Down Grandpa Jack's Rock," or "The Butternut Tree," signs that Granny clothes-pinned to the light-pull in the kitchen. Granny sitting in her collapsible beach chair on the sand bar by the falls, fishing pole propped on a Y stick stuck in the sand. Straw hat. She didn't go there to catch fish so much as see that big blue heron again, listen to the river.

Starting off early, Trudy and I would climb the Hump and get back to the cabin late afternoon. My daughter and I spent seven hours climbing to reach the place just before the steep bare-rock ascent to the summit. It was late and I was tired, so we headed down the Alpine Trail. Darkness caught us, and we stumbled out to the parking lot after nine and a half hours. Chilled through, grateful to be in the car with the heater going full blast.

Next morning, we stopped on the dirt road across from Catherine's house. Right around the corner from Gran's place. It looked empty, stark. Catherine had taken her mother in, cared for her to the end. Susan and I had stopped and brought baby Margaret up to the house. Gran lay in bed, not the "high yellow bed" of yore. With Margaret awake on the spread covering her legs, Gran had smiled, "My what a pretty boy."

Clear that no one lived at Catherine's, I didn't go up and knock. We drove on to Burlington.

If We'd Stayed

The cabin where we lived
I passed it toward evening
And remembered our life together
Fifty years ago
It had been everything, everything there was
And I saw us clearly, remembered
As it had been
And thought if we'd stayed
We'd be there still
The cabin was there
(Oh, a second story added)
But still the brook ran below
The road went up the mountain
And if I knocked on the door
You would answer, an old woman
And over your shoulder I'd be
Putting a chunk of wood into the iron stove

Acknowledgments

Sincerest thanks to:

Jon Lavieri—always a poet's eye who believed in this book.

Josh Mackie—for your superb feedback, friend, fellow writer, and thanks for the title.

Stephen Yaffe—for your accurate merciless critiques—you didn't let me get away with a thing!—and for your friendship.

Carol Burbank—smart, gentle editor who helped me see the stories as a novel.

John Duffield—Montana Renaissance man: sculptor, poet, photographer, fiddler, conservationist, friend.

MaryKate Harris—dear friend through thick and thin, moral support, love and thanks.

Carter Hawkins—editor with a fine eye and patience of Job—who believed in this book from the get-go and helped birth it—couldn't have done it without you.

Joseph "Onion Man" Sweigart—such attention to detail. Thank you for your practical and useful suggestions and your friendship.

Leo Connellan—poet whose work has shown me that less is more. Thank you for your help, advice, and the example of your work.

Andy Epstein—your wise, useful opinions, your puns, all helped launch this boat.

Kathryn Alma Ploetz—amazing woman, daughter, helper, moral support, organizer, friend—cannot thank you enough. Love you, Pop.

Reed Talada—amazing son-in-law, thank you for your support and advice throughout the process of making this book a book—love and gratitude.